MURDER

ON

CUE

Copyright © Michael Ashley 2024

All rights reserved.
No part of this publication may be reproduced,
Stored or transmitted in any form by any means, electronic,
Mechanical, photocopying or otherwise, without the
prior written permission of the author.

The right of Michael Ashley to be identified as Author of this
work has been asserted by him in accordance with the
Copyright, Designs and Patents Act, 1988

This is a work of fiction. Names, places, events and incidents are
either the product of the author's imagination or used fictitiously.
Any resemblance to actual persons, living or dead, or actual
events is purely coincidental.

MICHAEL ASHLEY

MURDER

ON

CUE

Murder most foul, as in the best it is;

But this most foul, strange, and unnatural.

**William Shakespeare
From 'Hamlet', Act I, Scene 5**

To all my family, for waiting so long for the muse to manifest itself and being so supportive during that time.

WILLIAM SHAKESPEARE'S

HAMLET

PERFORMED BY THE PIKESMERE PLAYERS AT PIKESMERE TOWN HALL

DRAMATIS PERSONAE

HAMLET	Roger Heart
CLAUDIUS	Mike Brown
GERTRUDE	Lorraine Davies
POLONIUS	Derek King
OPHELIA	Angie King
LAERTES	Andrew Cross
FORTINBRAS	Steve Grey
HORATIO	Mark Prince
ROSENCRANTZ	George Mansfield
GUILDENSTERN	Arthur Mansfield

Other parts played by society members

STAGE MANAGER Stewart Manning

PRODUCER Charles Blackwater

PROLOGUE

Admit me Chorus to this history

The knife felt strangely at home in my hand. Although my palm was slightly moist, my heartbeat was strong, regular and calm, even though the sense of hate seems all pervasive; within a few minutes, I will feel more content than I have felt for a long time. All that anger, all that resentment, all that hate will dissolve in the instant of her demise. This act is to be on her head. She was the one that had said no; she was the one who had the audacity to spurn the proposal she had been offered.

The ground is still water-logged from the rain earlier this afternoon, but the south-westerly breeze is now warm and comforting and a new moon shines through a clearing, spring sky. The door is only on the latch.

Unlocked!

Of course, it is! She never locks up until bedtime. There is no need is there, not round here? She'll be sat in the kitchen, at the large oak table, a glass of red wine near her right hand and a slushy paperback held in her left. She won't hear the soft click of the latch, nor the carefully placed footfalls along the hallway; her killer-to-be, me, knows that the latest news reports will be blaring out from the small, flatscreen TV strategically placed in the corner of the kitchen, so that the picture can be seen from anywhere in the room. The kitchen will be immaculately tidy. She always keeps it spotless. The large, green range will shine in the glow of the peach, soft-glow bulb that hangs low over the rustic table and chairs.

My palms are a little clammier now as the door handle turns.

There is the news programme; ironically, a report on a double murder in Swansea.
There is the red wine on the table.
The chair, however, is empty.
Where is she?
For the first time since the plan had formed, there is an awareness of a rush of panic creeping into my brain. Hairs stand up on the back of my neck and at the base of the spine.
The picture of how the deed was to be done was all important. It is only three paces from the door to the chair and the knife would have been through the back and into the ribcage before she'd even had time to turn around. Hardly any strength needed at all.
But now?
Where is she?
Eyes that had been cool and collected, brief moments before, now frantically scan the kitchen for anything that might provide a clue to her whereabouts. And then, I hear it: the toilet flush and footsteps crossing the laundry room floor, coming ever closer to the door at the far side of the kitchen.
So, there it is. No longer any chance of a swift and unseen attack. The door opens and she enters.
For a brief moment, she doesn't register that there is anyone else in the room. Her eyes go first to the television screen and then to the half-drunk glass of red on the table. Only my slight movement on the far side of the room enlightens her to the fact that she is not alone.
'What the hell...', is the only thing she has time to say before the thick, serrated blade cuts through the thin material of her dress and enters her torso.
The second and third stabs seem to happen in slow motion and by the time the woman eventually falls to the floor, her eyes staring unseeingly, the calmness with which I had

entered the house has returned.
There is less blood than the gorier horror films would have one expect and only a small, red pool is beginning to form under the body. The knife that had dealt such a terrifying end to her life is, almost casually, cleaned and wiped under the hot, sink tap and then left on the work surface next to the microwave. There is no point in trying to hide it. Forensics will find nothing to help with police enquiries. Indeed, nothing that has occurred in the last five minutes will give the detectives any help in their search for the truth. Another unsolved case. Another crime statistic. I feel at peace once more as I leave the cottage. I feel vindicated in my actions! I feel, how can I describe it? Yes, elated!

ACT I

All the world's a stage,
And all the men and women merely players

CHAPTER 1

'For the love of everything that is sacred, could we please have a bit of quiet in here? Do I have to remind you all that we are on stage in just a few weeks and we haven't even begun to rehearse Act Five?'
'Keep your hair on Charlie, boy. It'll be alright on the night; it always is!'
'Yes, Stew, but just about managing to get through a Ray Cooney farce is not quite the Bard and a bit less hammering from you would be helpful.'
'Ok. But don't blame me when your precious set collapses on opening night.'
'I'm sure it will be as epic as it always is. Now, where are Angie and Roger? I need to do a bit more of Act Three, Scene One.'
'They're outside vaping, I think. Shall I go and call them?'
'If you would, Lorraine dear. But don't wander off. I'll need you in a few minutes to do one of your scenes with Angie.'
'Righto!'
'Charles, any chance you could get the heating put on for the next rehearsal? It's freezing in here again!'
'Yes, Mike, I know. I did ask when I hired the hall, but I'll try again. Not as if I've got anything better to do with my time. Just keep your dog collar on for now!'
'No need to be quite so rude, I'm sure! I think we're all a little chilly. It's not just me.'
'Sorry! Ah, the star-crossed lovers return! If you could manage to stay in the hall for the duration of the rehearsal

next time, it would be appreciated.'
'Here, here.'
'Shut up, dad!'
'Now, Angie, no need to be rude to your father, is there? And Derek, if you could leave the family squabbles at home, that would be much appreciated. So, now that we are all gathered together, could we please have another big push on learning lines? Shakespeare is not easy to learn and ad-libbing like Widow Twankey will not be tolerated; and, yes, I am talking to you, Mike. Now, can we please get on before, what is left of my hair, falls out?'

CHAPTER 2

Carol Wainwright laid her head back onto the pillow and tried hard to remember the evening before. Rays of speckled sunlight shone through the crack between the curtains and landed delicately on the cotton sheet that covered her and Harry Bailey. Both of them were naked and, as she pulled the sheet up about her body, the innocent swelling of her breasts became apparent. For some reason she blushed as she pushed her fingers through her dark hair and tried to untangle the knots left by sleep.

The prosecco had been marvellous; that at least she could remember. Quite a luxury, considering it wasn't even Christmas, or New Year. Memories began to manifest themselves. There was the surreal, yet sensual, Spanish film that they had watched, part of a season of modern, foreign 'classics' just landed on Netflix: Harry had set himself not to enjoy it, but she'd persuaded him that he would.

He had, once the voluptuous, supporting actress had divested herself of her clothes and cavorted along the sun-drenched beach. Unfortunately, at the entrance of the handsome leading man, her own memory began to fade, as the second bottle of prosecco had taken effect, along with the soporific expectancy of a week's holiday away with the man she loved. Harry had carried her to bed where sleep had fully taken her over. She slept, perchance she dreamt.

'What are you thinking about Caz?'

Harry had woken up and placed his hand on her arm.

'Nothing, really,' she murmured, turning over to look at him.

'You're not on holiday yet you know? You'd better get up. You've still got a day plodding the beat.'

'Sorry to disappoint you, love, but I haven't plodded anywhere for quite a while'.

The rebuke for his tardiness was, however, grudgingly accepted and Harry Bailey stood up, pulled a dressing gown over his well-defined, reasonably muscular torso and he headed for the bathroom. Not quite a bronzed Greek god, Carol thought; the sun rarely shone enough in Manchester for that, but certainly divine enough for her. He was, by any reckoning, in pretty good shape. His thirty-eight years didn't really appear to have taken their toll and his swept back, blonde hair gave him the appearance of a playboy, rather than a detective chief inspector of his majesty's constabulary.

'I'll get some strong, black coffee in a minute,' Harry shouted from the shower, 'then I'll get off.'

'I think I need a cup,' she replied, 'I've still got the day from hell, with two hours of year ten and a bottom year eleven group last thing this afternoon.'

'Give me a bit of GBH and a couple of murderers any day. I've met some of your year elevens, in pursuit of my duties, and I wouldn't like to have to teach them Shakespeare on a

Friday afternoon.'

'You couldn't teach them Shakespeare any afternoon, my darling'.

'You're right there,' Harry replied, hanging up his towel and re-entering the bedroom, 'but, then, I really wouldn't want to!'

Harry left their apartment at eight-fifty, forty minutes after Carol, despite being in the shower first, leaving himself ten minutes to travel to work and get into "the office". In actual fact, he arrived at nine minutes past ten. The greetings of derisory comments from his section were met with his usual, low-key responses.

'Alright, shut up, you lot. I'm late. I know I'm late. But I am the best damned detective in this room! And, I'm off on holiday today, so you'd better get used to not having my happy, smiling face around for a week. So, tell me what we've got on the Chesterwell case and I'll try and solve it before tea-time.

The day, however, did not see a breakthrough in the Chesterwell robbery or, indeed, in any of the other six, live cases that were sat in Harry's in-tray. By half seven, however, he was sat in a seat of an Arriva rail carriage carrying him and Carol Wainwright to Shrewsbury. Owing to Dr. Beeching, later cutbacks and cash limits, this was the nearest station to their destination, a small, Shropshire market town called Pikesmere, where the couple meant to spend a week of peace and relaxation away from their respective pressures and duties.

'How were Year Eleven?' Harry asked, as they passed through the Cheshire countryside.

'When troubles come, they come not single spies, but in battalions.

'Come again?'

'Two fights, two teenage pregnancies and not a single piece

of homework in sight.'

'You could have said so in the first place.'

'I thought I had,' she smiled and turned back to looking out the window.

'Want to hear about my day?' Harry ventured.

'No,' Carol grinned, 'we're on holiday and I don't want to hear about work for the next seven days.'

And that was that.

CHAPTER 3

They stayed in Shrewsbury overnight, at a rather run-down hotel that had looked a lot smarter and more modern on the website, and sounded better in the 'TripAdvisor' reviews; they opted, therefore, for bed and breakfast, especially after taking a peek at the back of the kitchens. The evening was spent exploring the dubious pleasures of Shropshire's county town and taking in an Indian where the 'all-you-can-eat' banquet, at fifteen pounds a head, certainly managed to satiate both of their appetites. Over coffee, at the end of the meal, Harry reflected upon just how lucky he had been to find Carol Wainwright, or Caz as he preferred to think of her. She was a stunningly beautiful woman. This was not just Harry's opinion, but was universally acknowledged by all who met either her, or Harry. Many of his male colleagues, and a few of his female ones, had expressed their appreciation of her physical charms, but that beauty was certainly not just skin deep. She was, Harry mused, the wittiest and most intelligent person, male or female, he had ever known, including the family he had left behind, at the age of seventeen, in Devon. None of his teenage passions, nor the three incredibly intense, yet latterly meaningless,

relationships at university, had come anywhere close to what he felt for the woman sat opposite him now. She was five years his junior and yet always seemed to be the more mature and sensible in the partnership.
Yes, he thought, partnership. That's what they had.
'Snap out of it. Don't think I'm paying for this. You're the one who got the holiday money out today!'
'Oh, yea,' said Harry, getting up and making his way to the bar at the far end of the restaurant. Surreptitiously, he extracted his Visa card from his wallet and handed it over to the waiter, apologising for the absence of cash and wondering which ATM he could get to before morning, without letting Carol know that the one and only thing she had appointed as 'his job', had been forgotten. She had been worried that, despite the inexorable rise in cashless sales, in a country town, like the one they were to stay at, there would probably be shops that preferred cash.
A moment later, he was back at the table and, in a typically old-fashioned, yet understated, manner, he held Carol's coat for her to put on and they made their way out of the restaurant and headed back to their hotel, pausing only once, at the bank, where Carol suggested that Harry draw out some cash and not forget his 'chores' so readily in future.
'How did you know?' he asked, as they continued up the incline towards their hotel. 'Did you see the card at the restaurant?'
'No, just the look on your face when I told you to pay.'
'You should be a detective.'
'Too easy. Wouldn't stimulate me like Year Eleven on a Friday afternoon.'
'Penalty points to you. No discussing work remember.'
'Touché.'
They both laughed, linked arms, and returned to the less

than pristine surroundings of their twin-bedded room, no ordinary doubles being available, even though the reservation had confirmed the status of the latter several weeks earlier.

****

The next morning was bright and warm, as Carol and Harry found themselves being shaken about on the service bus that was carrying them from Shrewsbury bus station to Pikesmere. The winding roads were reasonably quiet, but a slow-moving tractor and the late arrival of the bus at the depot in Shrewsbury, meant that their own arrival at their destination was over twenty-five minutes later than the timetable had promised. Indeed, the large, ornate clock, which looked down on the town square, from a large, Victorian edifice, was just striking eleven, as they stepped off the bus and took in their new surroundings.
'Bit different from Manchester,' Carol remarked.
'Only in size and on the surface,' Harry mused. 'From my experience, people are pretty much the same, wherever you find yourself. A lot of them are decent and good and a few of them are rotten. If you've got more folk, then you've just got more bad 'uns.'
'And on that happy thought, let's find our hotel; I hope it's a bit better than last night's effort,' retorted Caz.
'Let's hope it's a proper double room,' Harry grinned.
'Tiger,' growled Carol and they started to walk across the square and towards what would have been a village green if Pikesmere had been classed as a village. A grand, five-hundred-year-old oak stood in the centre of a grassy verge and, to one end, a set of wooden stocks had been left standing, partly as a tourist attraction, partly as a reminder, by the town's councillors, that criminals would be dealt with swiftly and effectively in their town.

The two of them strolled across The Green towards the largest building in their line of vision: an old, Regency edifice, built centuries before by a local landowner who wanted a country retreat, but which now served as a retreat for others who were in search of rest and relaxation: those such as Carol and Harry.
'This is it, 'The Golden Pheasant Hotel',' said Harry.
'Looks alright, doesn't it?' replied Carol.
From the front, the building could be seen to be three storeys high, each of the second and third floor windows being of a bow design. All had lace curtains and the glass of those same windows, was spotless.
'Not quite Manchester,' Harry observed ruefully and jokingly, to repeat Carol's opening gambit as they arrived.
'No, thankfully,' said Carol and she pushed open the heavy oak door and walked into the lobby. Harry dropped the suitcases by the desk and rang the brass bell set into the teak veneer to his right. A smiling, young receptionist immediately appeared from the inner office and dealt with the signing in paperwork. Harry breathed a somewhat overly excited sigh of relief when confirmation of a double room was made. He turned to find Carol reading a home-produced poster advertising the town's amateur dramatic production: Shakespeare's 'Hamlet'. Carol, as an English graduate and teacher was showing great interest in the idea of possibly the Bard's greatest play being performed by a local, amateur group and, as Harry walked over, she was already formulating reasons why they should try to attend. Harry took one glance at the poster and said, 'No way, Caz. Before you say a word, you are not getting me, on my holidays I hasten to remind you, to anything written by Bill Shakespeare. I can't abide them!'
'Bet you've never been to one. I've certainly not seen any with you.'

'That's because you always go with your students and never invite me.'
'Rubbish! I wanted you to come to 'Macbeth' last month and you gave me some lame excuse for not being able to get.'
'Some lame excuse? A double murder I think you'll find it was.'
'Very opportune, I'm sure.'
'Oh yes. That's right. I always arrange for a juicy murder to occur, just so I don't have to watch a load of blokes in kilts dancing round a cauldron.'
'Seems to me you know more about Shakespeare than you let on. Certainly more than some of my pupils that have been studying the play for a term.'
'Just basic knowledge I assure you and it still doesn't make me want to spend my evening watching, what is it? Oh, 'Hamlet'.'
The receptionist who, until this point, had not interfered in this altercation, shouted across the lobby.
'I'm sure our production will be different to anything you'll have seen before. They always are.'
'Isn't 'Hamlet' a bit heavy for a small town like this?' Carol asked, walking over to the checking-in desk.
'Yes, probably is,' replied the receptionist, whose name badge, Harry now noticed, was Isobel, 'but they've got a relatively new producer and he wanted to try it. He'll soon learn that the only thing that sells tickets in Pikesmere is the annual pantomime. Stew did try to warn him, but he took no notice. Until he does, he'll carry on thinking he's bringing 'the arts' to us poor, uneducated yokels.'
Carol smiled at the grammatically incorrect irony of the comments, but smiled even more when Harry surprisingly said, 'Alright, we'll go and buy some tickets tomorrow.'
Unbeknownst to Carol, Harry had already noticed that tomorrow was actually first night and his hope was that all

the tickets would be sold out by now. This subtle piece of detective thinking, however, was kept to himself as they made their way upstairs.

'I think you've earned a treat this afternoon, lover boy,' she whispered, once they were out of Isobel's earshot.

'Good job that double bed was confirmed then, wasn't it,' he grinned and they entered their room like newlyweds.

CHAPTER 4

The new day saw a light drizzle falling outside the bedroom window. Always a good start to an English holiday, thought Harry, as he shuffled his way, still half asleep, across to the 'tea and coffee making facilities' that were the obligatory requirement of any English hotel room. As so often happens, however, in the English spring, the clouds soon blew over and by the time Carol and Harry had devoured their 'full English' breakfast, the day was pleasant and balmy.

They walked out of the hotel into brilliant sunshine, which made them both squint for several seconds, until their eyes adjusted and they could once again focus on the delights of Pikesmere's 'village' green. It really felt, thought Carol, as if they had stepped back in time. Not too far, just half a century or so, maybe the 1950s or early Sixties. Not that Carol could remember either of these time periods. Her points of reference were television dramas set at that time and these, of course, by their very nature, were idealised and unreal. Even so, she expected, at any minute, that a 'butcher's boy' would come cycling past on an old bicycle with a wicker basket attached to the front, or that a horse drawn milk cart would make its way around the green. Neither, however, made their appearance!

They made their way past the old stocks and towards a conglomeration of shops situated down one of the three small side streets that led off from the main road that ran alongside the green. The first shop was a small, family run chemists that also seemed to have just emerged from the set of a 'Miss Marple' drama. Suntan lotions and multi-vitamin supplements sat cosily besides greying bandages and surgical stockings. As Harry walked past the door, an elderly gentleman pushed the heavy glass door open and a familiar smell of soap, perfumes and disinfectant assailed his nostrils.

'I'm just going to pop in here,' Caz said, making to enter the shop, one of two chemists in this one street that seemingly competed for the bulk of daily prescriptions in the town.

'Are you after something in particular?'

'Just where the Town Hall is,' replied Carol. 'Do you want to get a paper?'

'Definitely not. I'm on holiday. I don't want to know anything about the real world for the next seven days.'

'Right, well I'll just get some mints and do a bit of questioning.'

Harry remained on the pavement letting his investigative eyes wander along the rest of the street. On the other side stood a small garage which no longer sold petrol, although the old pumps still stood idly to attention on the roadside, now simply a talking-point. Harry's eyes were drawn into the near-dark interior, however, where a young mechanic was struggling to get under a beautifully kept Bentley. There's wealth around here somewhere, thought Harry, but then there always is beneath the surface of rural towns like this. Not the flash, new wealth of the criminal classes, either, accumulated from gambling, vice, or ever more sordid ventures; no, this would be wealth handed down through the generations. His eyes continued to wander up the street towards a butchers, a clothes shop and, at the far end, almost out of sight on the corner, a garden centre and DIY store with a brashly painted and totally out of place sign above its entrance. It was difficult, at this distance, to discern any of the lettering, even though its gaudiness should have made it visible for miles, but Harry thought he could make out the word 'Manning' prominently displayed at its centre.

'God, that took forever.' Carol had finally bought her mints and returned to Harry's side.

'I cannot believe how slow everything is round here. There was only one other person in the queue, but it took them forever to serve him. Two of them on the till and it still took a lifetime. Still, I do know all about this old chap's ailments which began at his toes and worked up. I think they must be identical twins. Behind the till, I mean, not his toes! Anyway, this play, at the Town Hall: apparently, it's back onto The Green and down a road to the left.'

'Nice piece of metal over there,' Harry said, pointing to the Bentley in the garage, but Carol was now on a mission to get her tickets and was already twenty paces in front of Harry, making her way back to where they had first ventured out.

The street that Carol had been told about was even narrower than the previous one and was lined by Georgian town houses on its one side and modest Victorian terraced properties on the other, each of the doors on the latter having been brightly painted in a different colour and each window having a distinctive flower box painted in a matching colour. The total effect, although rather pretentious, was, Carol had to admit, quite charming. As they approached the end of the terrace, they passed a large, white, Victorian building which, the sign by the door proclaimed to be, the town's library and then the road opened out onto grassy slopes and atop one of these slopes sat, what Harry could only describe as, the most hideous of modern monstrosities: Pikesmere Town Hall.

Built in the local government expansion of the 1970s, the red brick and prefabricated concrete structure would have been obscene even in the more run-down parts of Manchester; but here, amid the Georgian frontages and window-boxed terraces, it stood out as a disaster of almost biblical proportions.

It was not, by any standards, a huge building, but it was certainly plenty large enough to cater for the needs of the population of Pikesmere, who, it seemed, used it for bingo evenings, whist drives, quizzes, town and rural parish council meetings and, of course, dramatic productions. All this became known to Harry, not through his considerable investigative powers of deduction, but from the list of forthcoming events posted in a small, glass covered noticeboard situated by the entrance. Next to this was yet another poster for 'Hamlet'. Carol, however, was still several steps ahead of Harry and was attempting to gain access to the hall, but all attempts were thwarted by the fact that the doors seemed to still be locked.

'Oh, great,' said Carol, 'I'm sure you've paid somebody to make getting tickets difficult'.

'As if,' murmured Harry, but he considered the idea to be an extremely sound one. Just then, he noticed, at the bottom of the 'Hamlet' poster, a small line of print which read, 'Tickets available from Lorraine's Lingerie'. He wondered whether to keep this valuable piece of information to himself, but knew that this would not endear him to Carol for the duration of the holidays. Indeed, the sharing of this information could only gain him Brownie points!

'I reckon we should try Lorraine's Lingerie shop for tickets.'
'Why?'
He pointed Carol in the direction of the poster and after a momentary pause for reading, the hunt was on again.
It took the two of them ten minutes and another couple of mints to get them outside the small dress shop which read "Lorraine's Lingerie and Linen". A small poster in the door window, again hand-drawn, advertised the fact that tickets for that night's production of 'Hamlet' were still available inside.
'Great,' said Carol, 'I told you they wouldn't sell out. Come on, let's see what they've got.'
Harry did not give vent to his disappointment, but merely replied in the affirmative and they entered the shop.
From Harry's vantage point next to several rolls of coloured satins, he could see the shop was on two levels, joined by a small set of steps, bordered on either side by ornate iron work. The bottom part of the shop contained material, while the upper level was for dresses and lingerie. A small office stood at the far end of the upper level and it was from here that the owner of the shop emerged.
Lorraine Davies was in her late forties and it became clear to Harry, as she got closer to them, that she was, what a more unpleasant person might describe as, 'mutton dressed as lamb'. The heavily made-up face did little to hide the crows-feet adjacent to her eyes; eyes, Harry thought, that had seen more than their fair share of troubles. The low cut, short dress seemed to cling obscenely to her curves, both those parts of her body that should be curved and those that should not, and the entire effect was one of repulsion rather than provocation. Harry had seen it more times than he cared to think of, whilst frequenting the seedier quarters of the city he now called home, but he had not wanted to be faced with it in this rural backwater of Shropshire: husband

abandoned her years before, probably for a younger woman; she, now, trying to be that younger woman for another man. A pitiful game that was played out so often and in so many tragic circumstances. Harry's musings, however, were cut short as Lorraine asked,

'Can I help you? Is it a dress, or material that you're after?'

'Neither!' Carol replied. 'We wondered if you had any tickets left for 'Hamlet' tonight. We only arrived in town yesterday, but we're hoping we're not too late.'

'Don't include me in this royal 'we',' thought Harry.

'I'm afraid,' Lorraine started and Harry's eyes lit up, 'that the tickets aren't selling very well and we have plenty left for tonight, or any other night for that matter.'

Harry's face returned to its rather stern frown.

'If you'll just step into my office, I'll show you the seating arrangements.'

They followed her up the small, carpeted steps and through the rows of underwear, towards the office. Harry stopped, just once, to examine a rather trashy looking rail of bras and knickers, but one glare from Carol told him this would not be a suitable birthday present for her. 'I was rather thinking of it for my birthday', he thought, as they entered the cramped and untidy office. Once inside, Lorraine opened the top draw of her old, wooden desk and took out four seating plans, joined together with a garish pink paperclip.

'It looks as if I can offer you two seats on the centre aisle in Row D, or an outside set in Row C.'

'I think we'll go for the centre please,' Carol answered. 'How much are the tickets?'

'Oh, you don't buy them here. We're only the advertising agency.'

'Where do we buy the tickets then?' Carol asked, somewhat tersely.

'At the Town Hall, off the producer. What time is it?' The

question was obviously rhetorical as she looked at her phone and continued, 'He should be there by now, although he isn't a very good timekeeper. Do you know, we've been known to be standing around at rehearsals for over three quarters of an hour before he's turned up to start. And he never even says sorry?'

Caz could sense that Harry's patience was beginning to wear thin. It wasn't that he actually said or did anything, but his stance and breathing altered just enough for Carol to be aware that a volcanic eruption was only moments away. Cutting Lorraine off in full flow, Carol said, 'Do we just tell him which seats we want then?'

'Oh, silly me,' Lorraine replied, not in the least bit concerned that she had been interrupted, 'you need one of these little notes.'

She tore out of a small, blue receipt book, a single page and wrote 'D5 & D6' on it. She began to hand it to Carol and then shook her head vigorously, withdrew her hand, and wrote '£8-50 each' next to the seat numbers. Satisfied that she had, at last, written as much detail as was necessary, she handed it over again.

'Do you know where the Town Hall is?' she ventured.

'Oh yes,' Harry replied, before Carol had time, 'we're beginning to get to know Pikesmere Town Hall quite intimately.'

'That's the ticket,' said Lorraine, obviously unaware of the implied irony of Harry's reply, or her unintended pun, 'just hand this over to Charlie and you're all done.'

'Charlie? That the producer?' Carol asked. It seemed obvious from Lorraine's previous comments that it was, but she just didn't want to leave on Harry's sarcastic remark.

'That's right. Charles Blackwater,' Lorraine affirmed and the emphasis she put on the now, more formal, nomenclature of Charles, indicated that this was how he liked to be known,

rather than by any shortened or, friendlier, possibilities.
'Producer, director, publicist, designer and all-round egotistical clever dick.'
'Can't wait to meet him,' said Harry, as he stalked towards the shop door with Carol shouting her thanks to Lorraine for all her help, whilst being whisked away by her less than patient partner. Once down the steps, however, Harry's groans were cut short by the opening of the shop door and the entrance of two males, engrossed in a heated argument. The first to enter was a tall, somewhat stout gentleman dressed in a heavy overcoat, worn, Harry thought, rather foolishly, considering the day's rising temperature. The beard he sported was well trimmed, with a moustache reminiscent of a squadron leader Harry had once arrested on fraud charges. His adversary in the argument was a young man of about eighteen or nineteen. Like Harry, his hair was blonde and swept back, but was rather longer and looked as if it was in need of washing. The older man's voice was the first to be distinguishable.
'You young lads are all the same nowadays. Love them and leave them, that's your motto. It wouldn't have happened in my day. No sir, we knew our responsibilities then. Self-discipline, that's what the younger generation needs to be taught. So, listen to me, sunny Jim, and listen good. If I see you with my daughter again, anywhere outside of the play, then I'll personally take my stick to you. She's only seventeen and still my responsibility. Got that?'
Harry and Carol felt rather trapped. The argument was obviously a personal one, but it was blocking the doorway and thus their escape route. The two men were so engrossed, that any move to push through them would have seemed ruder than what they were now doing: eavesdropping and voyeuristically watching the whole aggressive exchange.

The young man had begun his counterargument.

'I love your daughter, Mr. King, and I do not intend to love her and leave her. I intend to marry her once I can find a decent job and support her. And, if you think she is still your responsibility, I suggest you talk to Angie and see who she wants to look after her.'

Carol could see the same opening lines forming in the older man's mouth. She'd been to too many parent consultation evenings not to recognise the characteristics of the man referred to as King.

'You young lads are all the same. "When you get a job. When you can support her." You'd have no trouble finding employment if there was still National Service. Learn a proper trade like I had to!'

'I am a pacifist as you well know, Mr. King, I would never join the army, or do National Service. I want to help mankind, not see it destroyed by warmongers such as yourself.'

Lorraine Davies had joined Harry and Carol at the steps and in a clandestine, yet gossipy, voice was saying, 'The older man is Derek King; he's our Polonius. Moved to Pikesmere soon after I came here. The nice young gentleman,' Harry noticed the change in the tone of her voice, 'is Roger Heart; our Hamlet. He's going out with Derek's daughter, Angie, who happens to be his girlfriend in the play.'

'She's playing Ophelia, then?' Carol stated, as much for Harry's benefit as for Lorraine's.

'That's right. We all try and help Roger and Angie by covering for their assignations, but Derek always seems to find out and starts on about his early career in the army and 'the young ones today.' Under normal circumstances, we might have felt sorry for Derek, but he's such an obnoxious sod.'

'I notice you say 'our' Hamlet and Polonius. Are you in the

play as well?' asked Harry.

'Oh, yes, I play Gertrude, Hamlet's mother.'

'Is there anyone in Pikesmere who isn't in this play?' Carol asked, half-joking.

'Not many,' was Lorraine's reply, 'and that's why we're not very full. Apart from a few elderly relatives who come to see their offspring perform, anyone who's interested in theatre is in the society, so we don't get very big audiences at all. But that's not why you do it you know. It's the fun of the rehearsals, the camaraderie, and the achievement of getting something on stage, not the material gain or anything!'

By this time, the argument at the door had got so heated that even the gossip loving Lorraine could not allow it to embarrass her customers further. She made her way past Harry and Carol and, rather expertly, Harry thought, separated the sparring partners, whilst at the same time whisking both of them up the little steps and away to the back office where, presumably, their altercation could continue under the expert supervision of Lorraine Davies. As she passed Carol, she mumbled something about not forgetting the Town Hall and then she was gone, into the furthest recesses of the frilly knickers.

CHAPTER 5

Harry and Carol once again made their way, through the now 'bustling' streets of Pikesmere, to the Town Hall. The second appearance of this oddly, out-of-place building made it no less pleasant a sight, but at least, this time, the main doors stood ajar and the two of them were able to enter. The detective in Harry always meant that he could never just go into a new building; he had to always examine it, as if it were a murder scene. Whilst Carol looked for the producer of the now, even more hated Shakespearean extravaganza, Harry noted the reasonably large hall to his right, with the plush, red, velvet curtains separating a seating area from what he presumed to be the stage. Ahead of him was another door leading off to what appeared to be another, smaller space, perhaps for meetings and such like and to his left were toilets and an old telephone booth, a remnant from a now bygone age.

Caz, by now, had heard a voice emanating from the smaller hall and both of them made their way in that direction. Set into the left wall of the room was another door to what appeared to be a tiny office. The door was slightly open and it was from here that the voice was coming. Harry wondered whether they should wait for whoever it was that was having the conversation to finish, but Carol, impetuous as ever, and now getting almost as frustrated as Harry about this whole experience, knocked and was called in.

They found that the voice belonged to a rather robust looking character sitting behind a desk, talking on his mobile. His black jacket had been taken off and lay on one end of the desk, allowing the man to roll up his sleeves and show an old-fashioned pair of braces. At his neck was a gaudy puce and yellow bowtie which gave the man an altogether rather elegant, yet overtly, self-knowingly smart, appearance. His voice had no trace of an accent and seemed almost out of place with the rest of the town. Papers lay scattered across the rest of the desk and an old portrait of Churchill hung on the wall above and behind his head. The bookcase to the left contained play-scripts and several old posters could be made out, rolled up and forced onto the lower shelf. The office had, obviously, been given over entirely to the Dramatic Society of the town and, more importantly perhaps, to this man. His conversation on the mobile was just winding up, as Harry and Carol entered.

'I beg your pardon for swearing reverend, but this cannot continue. If we don't do something about Derek's obsession with Roger, we're never going to get this play on. Now you're the local, busy-bodying social worker, as well as vicar, round these parts, can't you have a word with him?' There was a pause whilst the other person, the local vicar by all accounts, said his piece and then the producer concluded.

'Well, do your best anyway. I'll get back to you later. Thanks, Mike. I'm seeing Stew later about a couple of things, so I'll see if he's got any bright ideas. Please don't let the society down on this one!'

He replaced the phone and looked up at the couple stood opposite him.

'What can I do for you two? Don't tell me, you want to book a hundred seats for a party from Shrewsbury?' A smile crossed his rosy-cheeked face.

'Sorry, we can't oblige on that score,' said Carol, 'just two tickets please. We were sent from Lorraine's with this slip of paper.' She handed over the now rather crumpled paper.

'Thanks. I'm Charles by the way, Charles Blackwater.' He held out a hand, for shaking, not to Carol, but to Harry, who, so far, had not even entered into the conversation. Sexist pig thought Carol, but she thought better of it as Charles took her own hand and kissed it with a Cavalier flair that implied that this was his usual greeting for ladies, particularly attractive ones.

'I'm the producer of this little fiasco. I'm sure we can find you some seats. Now, let's have a look where Lorraine has put you.'

He perused the slip of paper and then threw it into the already overflowing waste basket. 'This system of purchase was not particularly environmentally friendly,' thought Carol. 'Right, Row D it is then.'

He rummaged through the huge pile of papers on the desk until he found a set of handwritten, blue tickets secured by an old rubber band which looked as if it might give up the fight to hold them together at any instant. He sorted through them and said, 'There we are, five and six. I hope you enjoy the performance and thank you so much for supporting us.'

Carol took the tickets and led Harry out the door, closing it behind them.

'So, we're going to see 'Hamlet' after all,' Carol said.

'Hm, seems so,' replied Harry as they vacated the small hall and made their way through the vestibule to the main entrance. 'Got any more mints?'

Harry undid the cellophane wrapping and, without a second thought, threw it to the ground. They had only walked a couple of steps when Harry felt a large hand on his left shoulder. His body immediately tensed in its trained way, but the voice that accompanied the hand was not what he had expected.

'Do yow realise, sir, that Oy could 'ave yow fined a considerable amount of money for that, sir.'

The repetition of 'sir' made the whole sentence seem rather comical to both Harry and Carol, but they hid their smirks as they turned and found the anonymous voice belonged to an old, yet burly, uniformed sergeant of the local constabulary.

He looked, to Carol, to be in his late fifties and certainly nearing retirement age. He was also, obviously, a stickler for the letter of the law.

'Do you realise,' Harry replied in the same officious tone, 'that you are addressing a detective chief inspector of police?'

'Harry,' Carol said, 'don't make a scene. He's in the right!'

'I should listen to your wife, sir,' the policeman continued, unaware of the incorrect assumption that he had made. 'If you're a policeman yowself and, of course, without further verification, I only have your word for that...'

'Do you want to see my warrant card.?'

'That won't be necessary, sir.'

Good, thought Harry, because I've left the damned thing at the hotel.

'If, then, yow are a policeman, sir,' That 'sir' was beginning to be infuriating, 'then that's all the more reason for yow to obey the law. They might allow littering where yow come from, but I don't like it on my patch. Now, in the spirit of mutual respect, sir, would yow like to pick it up and place it in the litter bin positioned over there?'

Harry, after the morning he'd had, was going to continue the argument, but Carol, seeing the futility of it all, picked up the cellophane and dropped it in the bin attached to the wall of the town hall.

'Thank yow very much, madam,' the sergeant said and wandered off, hands behind his back, like, Carol thought, some gross parody of the chorus in 'The Pirates of Penzance'.

'Come on 'husband',' she said mockingly, 'you can't win them all.'

They walked back, hand in hand, to the hotel for lunch, with Harry trying to work out just which, if any, of the many and varied incidents that had taken place that morning, he had won. Certainly not the fact that they were now going to be subjected to several, tortuous hours of amateur Shakespeare, later that day. Still, he thought, better than work.

CHAPTER 6

'Come on Harry. For heaven's sake, cheer up. You'd think we were going to a funeral instead of a play. You can't hate Shakespeare that much.'
Carol had watched Harry become more and more sullen as they had eaten their early hotel dinner of reasonably good home-made tomato soup and roast loin of pork with various '*seasonable* vegetables'. Conversation had been sparse and had mainly revolved around the afternoon walk that they had both taken around the more charming parts of Pikesmere. Towards one end of the town was a fairly large lake, or mere as it was referred to in North Shropshire, due to the fact that the expanse of water was fed, not by a stream or river, but by underground springs. After the frustrations of the morning, Harry had particularly enjoyed walking hand in hand with Carol through the beautifully landscaped gardens that surrounded the water's edge of the mere and taking in the sheer calm and tranquillity of the scene. On returning to the hotel, they had checked that it would be alright to eat early so that they could get to the Town Hall for the show. Isobel seemed to be a fairly permanent feature behind reception and had now asked Harry to call her Izzy if he so chose. He did not, yet, which was as much a matter of propriety, as it was to keep Carol's jealous streak contained. Although Harry had dealt with some of the most horrific and brutal crimes that human

beings could inflict on each other, he tried, in his private life at least, to be almost old-fashioned in his behaviour, believing, however incorrect he may or may not be, that the evils he saw elsewhere could be kept out of his homelife by pretending he belonged to a more chivalrous age of gentlemanly conduct.

Isobel had confirmed that an early dinner was possible and both Harry and Carol had retired to their room for a relaxing bath and to dress for the evening's 'entertainment'. It had only been after they had sat down for their food, that Harry's demeanour had seemed to alter. Carol hadn't noticed it at first, but after her third or fourth attempt at explaining the play of 'Hamlet' had failed to get any response, she realised that something was worrying her partner.

'It's not the play, I promise,' Harry replied to her question. 'I honestly don't know what's up with me. Perhaps it was our run in with 'Constable Bumble' earlier on. Or perhaps I'm just tired.'

'That constable was only doing his job and you know it. There's something else and you're starting to make me nervous. You haven't brought me away to tell me you're fed up with us and want to call it quits, have you?'

'Don't be daft. I'd never do that.' Harry paused just long enough for effect. 'Who'd sort my socks out for me if I did that?'

Carol kicked him under the table and hoped that the moment had passed and that Harry could at least, partially, enjoy the evening ahead.

'Well,' Carol continued, 'I'm sure 'Hamlet' will prove to be a surprise. There's lots of murders you know. You should enjoy that.'

'Great, a busman's holiday. Listen, you'd better tell me a bit about it, or all that 'theeing' and 'thouing' is going to go right over my head.'

'I've been trying to do that for the last half an hour,' Carol said in desperation.
'Sorry. I wasn't being a very good listener. Try again and I'll try and be a better student. Wouldn't want you to put me in detention, or anything would I?'
Just at that point, their plates were taken away and sweet menus left for perusal. They both decided not to rush a sweet, but to settle for coffee and then get off to the play.
'The play is all set in Denmark,' Carol started once again. 'Hamlet, who is the prince, finds out his father was killed by his uncle Claudius and...'
'Wait a minute. How does he find out?'
'O, I should have said. A ghost tells him.'
'A ghost? Of course, I should have guessed. This is Shakespeare, isn't it? It couldn't just be a friend; it had to be some supernatural visitation. I'm always getting ghosts turning up to help with my enquiries!'
'They were very popular when the play was written and it was all part of the plot because Hamlet doesn't know whether to believe it, or not, in case it's an evil spirit come to tempt him to Hell!'
'Uhm. I think that's as much as I can cope with.'
'No, there's much more to get into.'
'I'm sure.'
'His uncle has married his mother, Gertrude.'
Harry interjected, 'Lorraine with the lingerie.'
'So it would seem. Anyway, most of the play is about Hamlet's hesitation in revenging his father's murder.'
'Because he's not sure about the ghost?' Harry said quite pleased with the way he'd taken it in so far.
'Good boy. You get a merit mark for later on.'
Harry smiled to himself. He couldn't wait for later on when all this would be over.
Carol, however, was now on a roll and was treating Harry to

her best A-Level introductory lesson. 'Along the way, pretty much all the main characters die, the first one being Polonius.'

'Oh, trust them to get rid of that King chap first. I expect it's because they don't like the way he treats his daughter.'

'I doubt the whole of the play revolves around private problems, Harry. You'd see intrigue anywhere.'

The coffees finished, they pulled on their coats and walked, at a fairly brisk pace, to the Town Hall. The air was becoming chill, due to a cool easterly wind that had blown up, and once or twice Harry thought he could feel the beginning drops of a spring shower. As they reached the hall, Carol was pleased to see that there were none of the city queues that she had come to expect at the theatre, just one elderly lady trying to climb the steps to the door.

'Can I help you?' Harry asked, quickening his pace to get beside the lady.

'No thank you, young man,' came the terse response, 'I'm not an invalid yet.'

Carol smiled and, as Harry dropped back to her side, whispered, 'independent lot round here, aren't they?'

The two of them were shown courteously to their seats by a young girl dressed awkwardly, Carol thought, in a long, black, velvet, evening gown. Carol moved into seat 5 so as to give Harry the aisle seat, in order that he could stretch his long legs during what, she hadn't told Harry, might be a three-hour show. As he sat down, he recognised the back of the head of the elderly lady that he had tried to help a few moments earlier, sat in the seat directly in front of him. The space between the rows of chairs was quite tight and as Harry went to cross his legs and get comfortable, he managed to kick the seat in front and again elicit a rebuke from the lady he was fast learning to be very afraid of.

Carol, during Harry's problems, had begun to look around

the small hall that should now, she thought, technically be considered to be an auditorium.
'They must have sold a few more tickets during the day.'
'Why's that?' Harry asked, not having had chance to really take in his surroundings.
'There're quite a few people in the seats behind us. The plans this morning showed them as empty.'
'Very clever, Miss Holmes.'
'Elementary, my dear Watson!'
Just at that moment, the house lights dimmed and the first chords of the National Anthem were played on what sounded like an antique, out of tune, piano. As the audience rose, Harry was careful not to again annoy his 'fan' in front and, as they all sat down, the plush, red curtains before them opened and the spotlights blazed into life.

CHAPTER 7

The stage was fairly deep, but obviously a moveable feature that disappeared when productions were over. It seemed to be constructed in sections and, as a couple of performers entered, parts of it creaked where joints had not been tightened sufficiently. The scene was, Carol informed Harry in a whisper, the battlements of a castle in Denmark. What was made to look like a small fire, blazed stage right - an obvious fire risk Harry chuckled to himself, knowing full well that it was only made to look like a real fire - and a wooden cut-out of a truncated wall stood precariously at the back. As the actors creaked their way around the stage, the 'wall' wobbled and what should, apparently, have been an atmospheric opening, began to turn into farce, with the

audience suppressing their laughter and the actors carrying on regardless.
'Who's there?'
'Nay, answer me. Stand, and unfold yourself.'
'Long live the king!'
Harry's face was expressionless. 'I'll never stick this,' he thought and looked across to Carol who was lapping up every unintelligible word. He tried to sink a little into his seat in order that a quick doze might be forthcoming, but the leg room allowed for little comfort and the fear of annoying the 'old lady from Hell' in front, meant Harry endured the whole of the first two acts until, eventually, the houselights went up and it was the interval.
'What do you think?' Carol asked, obviously having enjoyed the whole of the last one and a half hours of agony.
Harry thought about telling her the truth, but then decided that discretion was the better part of valour and opted for a simple, 'It's okay, isn't it?'
'It's more than okay. I reckon, for an amateur group, the acting is pretty good. There's a hell of a lot of lines to be learnt and most of the cast are saying them with meaning. I think Hamlet is terrific. He should try and go professional.'
'I bet Mr King thinks so too. Get him out of his daughter's life!'
'I like her as well. I mean Ophelia. She's really giving a sense of vulnerability and yet inner strength to the...'
'Thank you, Miss, can I stretch my legs now, or should I wait for class to be dismissed?'
'Sorry, was I lecturing?'
'Just a little'. Harry stood up and began to get some feeling back into his lower vertebrae, but the ecstasy was short lived as Carol pulled him back into his seat and handed him a set of raffle tickets. Two quite elderly ladies had appeared, almost like the ghost of Old Hamlet, at the front of the

curtains and were clutching an assortment of horrendous prizes, ranging, Harry thought, from last Christmas' unwanted toiletries to a hideously home-knitted soft toy. An old bucket filled with raffle tickets was ceremoniously handed along the front row of punters and various unfortunates were forced to choose which of the undesirable prizes they least disliked. Harry's relief was immense when he and Carol failed to win a single item. As the old ladies wandered off into what looked like a small kitchen to the side of the main hall, Harry again stood to stretch, but the houselights had already started to go down and he was again pulled back into his seat.

'But I need a..'

'Shh', came a response from in front of him and the look on Carol's face told him to keep both still and quiet.

Act Three was in full flight,

'To be or not to be, that is the question.'

The famous line reverberated around the small hall and Harry began to see what Carol meant by Roger Heart's performance skills. The lad was good. Amidst his admiration, Harry's thoughts were also flooded with painful memories of an unlearnt soliloquy set for homework twenty odd years earlier. Painful because the lunchtime detention set as punishment for it not having been done, meant Harry had missed seeing Susan Hargreaves by the science block and his supposed best friend James had asked her out. She was one of the best-looking girls in their year and Harry had missed out.

'I hate "Hamlet",' he thought, as his mind returned to the stage.

By the end of the next scene, Harry could stand the boredom no longer. He stood up, signalling to Carol that he was going to the toilet and made his way down the aisle and out the back of the hall. As he entered the foyer, he found all the minor actors playing cards at a table near the entrance, their parts obviously being such that their presence backstage was unnecessary for the next few scenes. Small amounts of cash seemed to be changing hands and Harry was sorely tempted to ask whether he could join them, rather than return to the purgatory of the auditorium. The actors, however, didn't even look up as he walked past, merely moving their chairs to allow him access. As he entered the toilets and took up a stance at one of the urinals, he thought he heard a groan coming from one of the nearby stalls, but felt it was not his place to investigate the noise further. He was, after all, on holiday.

He was just about to return to his seat, when he heard heated words coming from the producer's office where they had bought their tickets, what seemed like an eternity ago. Harry had learnt over the years that ignoring emotional situations often led to more serious problems, so he wandered over and pushed the door open slightly.

The actor playing the character that he thought might be playing Fortinbras was holding King's daughter, Ophelia, for want of her real name, in rather too passionate an embrace for it to be part of their rehearsal process. Harry tried to take the situation in as quickly as he could. To intervene or not to intervene was often the most difficult question that a policeman had to think about. Fortinbras, or Steve Grey as Harry later found out his real name to be, was clutching the girl by her shoulders and she, in turn, was pummelling his chest and shouting abuse at him. The situation did not seem to be one that Harry could easily ignore, so he pushed the door open further and walked in.

'I don't think the young lady likes what you're doing,' he said, somewhat self-consciously, 'so why don't you just let her go like a good chap?'

'Why don't you just butt out of something that's none of your

business? Who asked you to interfere?'
Despite the show of bravado, Steve, Harry noticed, had, at least, let go of the girl. She pushed her way past the desk and looked, momentarily, into Harry's eyes whilst seemingly thanking him for his timely intervention. He knew the look in the eyes. It wasn't a look of fear, or gratitude, or even relief, though. It was the look of someone who wasn't truly aware of what was happening around them. It was the look of someone under the influence of either drink, or drugs; and, if Harry had to place a bet, he'd go for the latter.
Putting that little piece of evidence into a mental compartment for later, Harry's mind re-focussed on the present situation. Steve Grey had taken a step forward and was now eyeballing Harry in as aggressive a posturing as was possible for someone dressed in Elizabethan armour.
'If I see a lady in distress, I make it my business to interfere. Now, why don't you get back to the play before I show you my warrant card and you become even more embarrassed than you are right now?'
Harry missed the expletive, as Steve Grey pushed past him and left Harry standing in the now empty office.
By the time he came out into the foyer, Grey was nowhere to be seen, so he returned to his seat and a rather annoyed Carol, just in time to see the latter moments of scene three. The lights dimmed and then came up on Scene Four, the queen's bedroom: a large piece of what looked, to Harry, like carpet, hung to the back left of the stage and Derek King, who had delivered a couple of lacklustre lines, crossed the stage and hid behind it, almost pulling the rather flimsy pieces of string holding the carpet, away from the set and again causing mirth in the audience.
Harry closed his eyes and again wondered whether a short snooze was possible, but a sharp nudge in the ribs from Carol, forced his eyes back open.

'Don't laugh,' she whispered, 'but I think Hamlet's forgotten to come on.'

The silence on stage was deafening as Gertrude, the queen, paced the creaking floor, obviously concerned as to the whereabouts of her proxy son. About twenty seconds after Polonius had hidden, Hamlet emerged looking flustered, but remembering his lines, the appropriate and, again, mirth inducing,

'Now mother, what's the matter?'

Even Harry, in his sanguine state, only just managed to contain his laughter. The queen continued,

'What wilt thou do? Thou wilt not murder me? - Help, help, ho!'

Again, there was silence.

Carol sat forward in her seat. 'What the hell. Don't say that Polonius has forgotten his lines too. He could have had a bloody script behind there. And there was me telling you how good I thought it was.'

The silence on stage was broken by Hamlet covering the lack of lines by drawing his rapier and making a pass through the arras with it.

Again, Polonius' line about 'being slain' was missing, so the other two stage-bound thespians carried on regardless.

'O, me, what hast thou done?'

'Nay, I know not. Is it the king?'

'Oh what a rash and bloody deed is this.'

'A bloody deed! - Almost as bad, good mother,
As kill a king and marry with his brother.'

'As kill a king.'

At this point, Hamlet carefully lifted the rather insecure bit of carpet and revealed Polonius lying, as if slain, at his feet. Before, however, the audience had time to really see the supposed 'corpse', Hamlet dropped the carpet again and, turning to the wings of the stage, his face drained of any

colour, he rushed off through the flats and, a few moments later, the curtains were drawn.
'Funny ending to the scene,' Harry murmured to Carol. 'Don't we get to see the body?'
'Something's wrong,' Carol replied ominously. 'This is nowhere near the end of the scene and the body's supposed to lie there for the audience to see for ages.'
'Are you sure?'
Harry didn't wait for the reply. Carol's face said it all. He leapt out of his seat and marched purposefully down the aisle towards the stage, oblivious to Carol's words of protestation. Flinging aside the velvet curtains, he jumped up onto the stage. The piece of carpet now lay crumpled up in a corner. Several actors were stood fixedly looking down at the still body of Derek King, still padded and looking huge in his Polonius costume. The body was lying on its front and a jewelled dagger stood erect in his back; he was obviously dead. Really dead!
Even with his duties in Manchester, Harry had only dealt with a few murders where stabbing had been involved and it still churned his stomach to see the loss of a human life in this way. Other members of the cast were slowly entering the stage area to see what the hold up in the show was. Some stood in stunned silence, as if unable to believe what they were seeing, whilst others looked as if they were going to be physically sick.
It was not usual for Harry to be first at a crime scene. Often, he would get a call at some unearthly hour and arrive once forensics and uniform had started their jobs. He realised, however, that this number of people in such a confined space would certainly contaminate the area and make it much more difficult for the specialist investigative teams to do their jobs effectively. It was, however, Lorraine from the lingerie shop that broke the silence first.

'Poor, poor Derek. Whatever could have happened?'
'I think,' said Harry, cautiously, so as not to give anything away, 'that someone should call the police straight away.'
'Who are you?' one of the other actors asked.
'Just a member of the public tonight, but I'm also a police officer and this doesn't look like it's part of the play. Please make sure that no one moves and, definitely, that no one goes anywhere near, that body.'
Harry turned back towards the curtains and pulled them aside so as to speak to the audience whilst keeping the body hidden.
'I'm afraid there's been an.... accident.' He spoke slowly and with as much gravity as he could muster. He felt the old lady, in row C, stare at him, as if to tell him to shut up and let the play carry on.
'I'm afraid the play will have to be called off for tonight, so, if you'd like to make your way out of the hall, we'd be most grateful.' He caught Carol's questioning gaze and gave just the slightest shake of the head to tell her there was more to it than a simple accident. He leapt down from the stage, pushed his way through the now standing, grumbling audience and made his way to the back of the hall where the front of house doorkeepers were looking as mystified as the exiting punters. Harry chose one that looked reasonably alert and gave her some instructions.
'Listen, it's a little more than an accident. Get these lot out and then seal the building. Is this the only exit?'
'There's an emergency exit behind stage.'
'Right, send one of the others to make sure no one goes out through it. Could someone have got out that way already?'
'I doubt it. An alarm would have gone off if it had been opened.'
'Good,' Harry thought. 'Did anyone go out this main door in the last half hour or so?'

'No way. I've been here the whole time.'
'Well done. Now, get these folk out as quickly as you can.'
Again, Harry pushed his way back through the audience and jumped back onto the stage.
'Has someone called the police?'
'I did.'
'And who might you be?' Harry questioned. The man looked to be in his fifties and, unlike nearly all the other people stood on the stage, or in the wings, he was not dressed in the obligatory Elizabethan attire, but, instead, a pair of dirty, paint splattered jeans and a dark polo shirt, again marked with splashes of emulsion.
'Stewart Manning, stage manager. Call me 'Stew', everybody does.'
'Right Stew. Did you give them any details?' Harry tried to place the name 'Manning', but his mind was racing and, for the present, the information eluded him.
'Just told them there'd been a problem and they should get here as soon as poss, which will probably mean about half an hour round here.'
One or two of the actors smiled faintly at this attempt to lighten the proceedings, but the moment was short lived as Angie King, dressed ready to play the mad Ophelia, burst out crying, for the first time, at her father's still form. The scene, Harry thought, was more tragic than anything Shakespeare could have conceived. Flower petals fell from her hair as she half ran, half fell across the stage to end next to Derek King's lifeless form. She had obviously been preparing for a forthcoming scene and had, just a moment or two before, heard about what had happened on stage. Harry's immediate instinct was one of pathos and empathy, but the policeman inside him almost instantaneously took over and he put his arms around the young girl and moved her back away from the body.

'I'm sorry, miss, but I can't let you touch him. Not yet.'
Through the tears welling up inside her, Angie managed to ask simply, 'Why?'
'That's what we've got to find out,' Harry stated.

ACT II

***There is no sure foundation set on blood,
No certain life achieved by others' death.***

CHAPTER 8

About three quarters of an hour had passed since the discovery of Derek King's body. The police had arrived somewhat faster than Stew Manning had anticipated; the first on the scene being Sergeant Pearson who remembered Harry immediately, as the person he had spoken to about litter earlier in the day. When he was reminded that Harry was, in fact, a superior officer in the force, Pearson's attitude did not change perceptibly and Harry was pretty sure that he was at the top of Pearson's list of possible suspects.

The Town Hall was now relatively quiet. A group of thirteen people, almost a last supper Harry thought, sat in the now, otherwise deserted, auditorium. The curtains had been left closed so as to keep the body hidden from view and a forensic team had just arrived from Shrewsbury to begin their meticulous and painstaking investigations.

Harry surveyed the group of thespians. He'd spent the last few minutes with Carol, trying to get to know who some of them were. Some, of course, were familiar to the two of them. Lorraine Davies sat on the front row of seats with her arm around King's daughter Angie, who, although obviously distraught, was not as visibly upset as Harry would have expected. To Angie's right on the front row, sat Roger Heart. He too was attempting to give physical support to the grieving Angie, but for some reason she seemed to be gathering more strength and comfort from Lorraine than from her boyfriend and her body language seemed defensive.

'Now, I wonder what that's all about,' Harry muttered and made a mental note to pursue that line of enquiry further. It took him several seconds to realise that this was not his case and that any line of enquiry would be followed by someone else. Even so, he continued to examine the gathering.

On the next row from the front, sat four actors that, until a few minutes before, had only been identifiable by their characters.

Mark Prince was nearest to Harry as he looked across the hall. He had been playing Hamlet's friend Horatio but seemed to be about fifteen years older than Roger Heart. The friendship, however, seemed only to be a performative one, as the two, as far as Harry could tell, had not spoken since the tragedy on stage. To Prince's left sat the pair of middle-aged twins that Carol had met in the local chemist shop, Arthur and George Mansfield, who were pretty much identical and Charles Blackwater's casting of the pair as the somewhat interchangeable - Carol's information, not his - Rosencrantz and Guildenstern, must have seemed inspired at the first casting meeting. Harry wondered how Blackwater must now be feeling. He knew from remarks that Carol had made about school productions, that a director always took responsibility for everything that happened in a production. He certainly looked as if the weight of the entire world lay upon his shoulders. He paced up and down the side aisle next to the outer wall of the hall, contemplating his footwear and the floor beneath.

Harry returned his attention to the seats and the rather rotund figure of a man called Mike Brown who had been playing the king, Claudius. Although his costume obviously helped with the overall effect, the man seemed huge. Both tall and broad he must, Harry thought, cut a striking pose in the pulpit on a Sunday morning, as Carol had whispered that he was the local vicar.

Near to the back of the hall, Stew Manning, the stage manager, stood in conversation with Steve Grey, the man who Harry had spoken to in the producer's office earlier. Sat near to them was Andrew Cross, the actor playing Laertes and, unlike the rest of the cast, a man for whom it seemed death was just another topic for humour. Almost everything that Stew, or Steve, mentioned became ammunition for yet another one-liner and, although they were obviously aware of the incongruity of the situation, some of the lines were funny enough for at least the occasional guffaw.

Harry, unlike some in the room, did not find the choice of laughing matter particularly strange. Everybody dealt with death differently and coffin humour was often a coping strategy as powerful as tears.

Carol was sat in the far back corner and, as Harry fixed his gaze upon her, she instinctively returned it with a weak smile. It seemed she, like Harry, had been taking the opportunity to examine the possible suspects. He walked over to her and sat down.

'So,' she said quietly, after a moment's pause, 'who did it then Sherlock?'

'Haven't a clue,' Harry conceded, 'but I know it's one of them sat in here. There is no way anyone else could have got in or out. I've checked.'

'Well, I reckon it's got to be one of those two at the front. King's daughter, or her boyfriend. Everything we've heard since we got to this town points to their relationship being the motive.'

Harry said nothing. He knew that what Carol was saying made a lot of sense, but he also knew that murder enquiries always uncovered a lot of dirty laundry.

'Who's top of your list then?' Carol persisted. However,

before Harry had time to reply, Sergeant Pearson entered through the back double doors and shouted Harry's name. He got up and went over to the uniformed policeman.

'Can I help you?' he said, in his friendliest manner.

Pearson's attitude remained business-like.

'I doubt that very much. In fact, I'm not entirely sure why yow're still here sir. I realise that yow are a police officer, but yow are also on holiday and out of your patch, so I think it would be best all-round if yow went back to your hotel and leave us to it.'

Harry only managed to get out a 'well' before Pearson continued.

'Just because we're a bit more rural round here doesn't mean we can't do our jobs, so if yow wouldn't mind.'

Part of Harry wanted to argue with the sergeant, but, as earlier that day, he recognised that it would be pointless and that, in fact, frustrating as it was, the man was right. He and Carol were on holiday and why on earth should Harry have any inclination whatsoever to get involved in work. He wandered back over to Carol and related the gist of Pearson's advice. Surprisingly, Carol was less than keen to leave.

'I've never been involved, close up, in a murder investigation,' she said, finally, 'let alone known the suspects. I want to try and do a bit of sleuthing.'

'Well, we can't, so let's just get back to the hotel and back to enjoying our relaxing break.'

'I know you, Harry Bailey. You're itching to get involved just as much as me.'

'I am not.'

'You so are.'

'Well, maybe just a little, but the issue is settled, so get your coat and let's go.'

Pearson stood waiting by the doors to escort them out, but,

as he went to push the door open, it was torn from his grasp by a tall man in his early forties who Carol had not seen before. Harry, however, knew him all too well.

'Harry Bailey, you old devil. What the hell are you doing mixed up in all this? Not gone over to the opposition and started your own assassination business, have you?' He shook Harry's hand vigorously before giving him a short hug.

'Not really Dan. I just happened to be in the wrong place on the wrong night.'

'Or the right one, eh?' The man's cool gaze turned to looking over Harry's shoulder and settled on Carol.

'Oh, sorry,' Harry said, 'Daniel Price, Carol Wainwright.' He turned to Carol. 'Dan and I worked on a couple of cases together up in Manchester before he got promotion and a nice easy placement in rural Wales.'

'Moved to Shropshire now. I'm heading up this enquiry, apparently. SIO,' Daniel continued. 'Don't get many murders round this neck of the woods. Thought they better put someone in charge who knew what they were doing.'

'So how come you're here then?' Harry quipped.

'Yea, yea, I remember your sense of humour. So, Harry, you going to give your old mate a bit of help on this one?'

Before Harry could reply, Sergeant Pearson, who had been hovering, ominously, nearby, interjected.

'Begging your pardon, sir, but I would strongly recommend that Mr. Bailey 'ere should not become involved. I believe him to be too closely connected with what 'appened here this evening. And, anyway, 'e's out of his patch so to speak.'

'Pearson isn't it?' Dan asked, winking at Harry and Carol without the sergeant seeing.

'That's right sir.'

'Well Pearson, I suggest you go and sort us all out a hot drink of tea, or coffee, and leave Mr. Bailey's involvement with me.'

'If yow say so sir,' Pearson said, defeated, and he made his way down the hall and into the kitchen.

'So, now the local constabulary are off your back, what do you say?'

'He says he'd be delighted,' Carol stated.

'Is she always this forthright?' Daniel asked.

'Oh no,' Harry mused, 'sometimes she can be really bossy.'

Carol nudged him in the ribs, but Daniel was already halfway down the hall.

'Come on then, let's have a look at this body.'

'Dan,' Harry called and Daniel stopped and came back down the hall. 'Careful what you're saying. The girl on the front row is the deceased's daughter. Go gently.'

'Bloody hell. No one tells me anything. I knew I needed your help. So, let's go see the crime scene.

CHAPTER 9

Daniel again marched purposefully up the hall, taking a second to glance over at Angie King before jumping up onto the stage and through the curtains. Harry and Carol followed and, judging that the forensic team were happy with their presence, joined Daniel over by Derek King's body.

Harry circled around the stage and tried to judge just exactly how the murder had taken place. It was clear that a real dagger had been used and its position in the small of the back meant that suicide was easily ruled out. Carol tentatively bent down and, without actually touching the murder weapon, examined the dagger. It could easily have been sat on the props table prior to its murderous use. It looked just like the various other weapons that had been used during the course of the performance, apart, of course, Carol thought, for the fact that this one could do real harm. Harry had begun to reconstruct the scene he had watched earlier. He picked up the piece of carpet and held it roughly where it had been hanging on stage, from what he could remember. Having got the position fixed in his mind, he dropped the carpet and made his way towards the wings. It became clear, immediately, that when the carpet had been hung, the area where King would have been hiding would have been accessible to anyone from off stage, but that, once on stage, no one could have seen what was happening there. It was, Harry thought, in some ways a perfect place to commit a crime, even though it would have taken nerves of steel. He returned to the stage and confirmed his findings with Daniel. Carol had already taken the opportunity of explaining the scene and it's staging to Daniel and had been impressed by his knowledge of 'Hamlet'. He'd referred to 'the closet scene' twice and had also questioned her as to the way in which the Hamlet-Gertrude relationship had been addressed during it. When Harry returned and began to discuss the placing of the 'carpet', Daniel was quick to correct him and call it an 'arras'. 'Are we here to solve a crime or study for a bloody English degree?' Harry asked, somewhat put out.

'Sorry, Harry, just fooling around,' Daniel countered. 'I think our next port of call should be the producer. What's he called?'

'Charles Blackwater,' Carol said before Harry had the chance.

'A bit full of himself,' Harry said quietly, aware that the producer was only a few feet away on the other side of the curtains.

'Any chance he could have done it?'

'As much as any of them,' Harry replied.
'Come on then, let's see what he's got to say.'
The three of them re-emerged through the curtains and Daniel, having ascertained that the still pacing figure was the producer, made his way over to him and asked if there was somewhere they could speak privately. Harry and Carol were way ahead of Daniel on this one and were already waiting by the doors to go into Blackwater's office. Harry was uncertain as to whether Daniel would actually want Carol present in a more formal interview situation, but, as it happened, Dan held the office door open for her and made it clear that her input would be appreciated. With four of them now squashed into the small room, the surroundings seemed even more cramped than they had been earlier that day. Blackwater sat at his cluttered desk and Carol sat across from him on the only other chair. The two policemen stood each side of the desk. It was Daniel who started.
'So, Mr Blackwater, can you tell us anything that might help us in finding Mr. King's killer?'
The final word hung in the now silent room before Blackwater began to reply.
'Do you know how much of my time and effort and money I have put into this production? This was going to bring culture to Pikesmere and North Shropshire. And now...'
He finished in mid-sentence and shook his head.
Harry tried a slightly different tack. 'Can you think of anyone who might want to kill King?'
'I'd find it more difficult to name someone who didn't. But wanting to kill someone and actually doing it are very different things. Derek King was almost universally disliked by the cast and, if I'm being totally honest, by most of this town, but I couldn't say that any of them, the cast that is, was capable of murder; and you've got to realise that I've been working with them all for months. I know them inside

out. His daughter, Angie, wanted to escape his control. Then Roger wanted to get her away from him; but they could've eloped couldn't they? Could she kill her own father? I doubt it.'

Harry caught Carol looking at him, reminding him of her thoughts earlier. He was, however, somewhat more convinced by Blackwater's take on the situation. Murder seemed a very extreme solution to the two young lovers' problems.

Daniel had now taken up the questioning again. He'd asked Blackwater whether any of the other cast members had a grudge against King.

'At one time or another, all of us have had a run in with him. He was, how shall I put it, a very forceful individual? Many would say bigoted! He would infuriate Mike, our local vicar, whenever they met on the church council. He'd tried to get Steve's garage closed down on health and safety grounds; he accused Stew of something or other, he'd reported Andy Cross to the council and so on and so on and so on. But it all seems so trivial in hindsight. None of its grounds for murder.'

'You'd be surprised what motivates murder,' Daniel sighed.

CHAPTER 10

There was, Carol thought, as the two of them left 'The Golden Pheasant' the following morning, more of a chill in the air than there had been the previous day. She was unsure as to whether this was a climatic feature, or more to do with the events of the previous evening.

After their interview with Blackwater had concluded, Daniel had felt that fresh minds and a new day would suit enquiries better, so all the suspects had been allowed to go home, on the strict understanding that none were to leave the town. No one seemed inclined to leave the hall, let alone the town, but, even so, squad cars seemed to be strategically placed on a couple of the main approaching roads and it was doubtful that anyone would wish to take the chance of admitting their guilt through attempted flight.

The one rather strange occurrence, it seemed to Carol, was that when they had finally managed to convince Angie to leave the site of her father's demise, she had asked to go home with Lorraine, rather than with Roger Heart. As Carol and Harry had walked back across The Green, towards their hotel, Carol had mentioned how weird this seemed.

'Perhaps she just wanted some female support and company,' Harry had ventured.

'Maybe.'

'But?'

'But, considering what Lorraine told us about how the group had had to cover for her and Heart and how much they wanted to be together, it does seem rather odd that, now they're free to be together, they're not.'

'A woman's prerogative, eh,' was Harry's only reply, but Carol had been too thoughtful and too tired to be goaded by him on this single occasion.

About two o'clock that night, however, during a rather broken sleep, partly due to events and partly due to being in a strange bed, Carol had again woken up with this separation of lovers uppermost in her mind and, although Harry's snores were a testament to the contrary, she had turned the light on and asked, 'Harry, are you awake?'

'I am now,' he'd murmured.

'What if Lorraine had been lying?'

'About what?'

'About those two being so close. It might have been part of

a very clever plan to make us think that Angie and Roger were lovers. We haven't spoken to anyone else to corroborate what she told us. She might be the murderer and be trying to pin the blame on Roger by making us think he would want King out of the way.'

Harry had, by now, been forced to wake himself up and he had proceeded to push his pillow further up the headboard and sit up.

'If we assume that Lorraine wanted to put us on some false trail,' Harry had replied, 'doesn't that also assume that she knew I was a police officer and that I would somehow be involved in the case?'

'Not necessarily. Maybe she drops it into conversation with anyone from outside the town in the hopes that some of them might be questioned after the murder she'd arranged.'

'But, the problem with that is that it's something that is easy to check. We can just ask someone else whether it's true or not.'

'Perhaps she expected us to leave and not have time to ask around.'

'But then we wouldn't be around to be questioned, or provide the motive you're suggesting.'

Carol had pondered this for a moment, had given Harry a look that had told him he had not been in the least bit helpful in her enquiries; had, without further ado, turned off the light and within a minute had fallen back to sleep. Harry, on the other hand, had restlessly laid awake for the best part of another half an hour before eventually returning to the blood splattered arms of Morpheus where his dream had revolved around daggers hidden in various items of lingerie and some extremely oddly shaped, Elizabethan codpieces. Freud, he felt, would definitely have been highly interested when he recalled these dreams the following morning!

Now, as he walked across The Green, he too felt the chill

that had disturbed Carol as they'd left the hotel and he, in turn, wondered whether it was truly a change in ambient temperature, or something rather more intangible.

'So, inspector, what...' Carol had begun to ask.

'Chief inspector to you, young lady,' Harry had grinned.

'So, chief, clever clogs who thinks he knows it all at two o'clock in the morning, inspector, what's likely to happen today?'

'I'd just like to remind you of who put on the light and who struck up a conversation at that unearthly hour.'

'Yea, yea, anyway.'

'Anyway, it'll be standard questioning of suspects and witnesses; setting up of an incident room at the hall, possibly more forensic work, and so on.'

'Do you think,' Carol asked uncertainly, 'that in the light of the new day, Daniel'll let me carry on sitting in on the interviews?'

'I've no idea, but you seemed to make a big impression on him last night. All that stuff about the 'arras' and 'the closet scene', It'll just be a bit irregular, that's all. Anyway, you can ask him yourself.'

As they had been approaching the Town Hall, a sleek, unmarked, black car had pulled up and Daniel Price had emerged.

'Morning Harry. Carol. Trust you're fully rested and ready for the day's exertions?'

'I would be if she hadn't had me awake in the early hours.'

'Lucky you,' Dan laughed.

Harry was happy to let the innuendo go, but Carol felt otherwise.

'Actually, we were discussing the murder. Did you notice that King's daughter went home with Lorraine Davies?'

'Yes! What of it?'

'She told us, yesterday...'

And with that, Carol outlined her theories to Daniel Price who listened intently, but then posed exactly the same problems that Harry had expressed earlier. Carol began to look a little dejected and Harry made it worse with another problem that he'd been mulling over through the night.

'Carol, you were watching the play more carefully than I was and you certainly know it better, so tell me something: during the performance, in the scene when King got killed, after he'd hidden behind the arras..'

'Yes.'

'Did Lorraine ever leave the stage, or go behind the arras? In fact, did she ever leave your eyesight?'

Carol thought back to the script and to the previous evening and, annoying as she found it, she had to now admit, with this new, crucial piece of evidence, that Lorraine was actually the only one of the whole cast who couldn't have been the murderer.

'Perhaps she was the mastermind behind it then,' she said after a long silence and in an attempt to save some face.

'Maybe,' Harry replied, but he didn't sound convinced.

It was Daniel, however, that made her feel a little better with his next statement.

'I like the way your mind's working, Carol, and you and Harry certainly seem to have a better slant on this town than I have. I'm pleased you're both on the team. Hopefully, you'll be able to act in a more informal way and, maybe, get more out of some of them.'

With that he turned and made his way through the glass doors into the Town Hall. Harry followed and, without looking, could tell that Carol was beaming from ear to ear.

CHAPTER 11

The murder scene had not changed significantly since the night before, although the hall seemed so much emptier without the rest of the cast sat in there. The curtains were still drawn across the front of the stage and a few muffled voices could be heard from behind the heavy velvet. Harry called Daniel over to the doorway.

'Listen, Dan, just before the murder took place, I was out here answering the call of nature. There were three or four actors sat out here playing cards. Any chance one of them could have got round the back to kill King?'

'Way ahead of you on that one. Someone else mentioned the possibility last night, so I got a couple of uniforms to time it. Couldn't be done because of having to go right round the building to get there without one of the other cast seeing and they didn't, according to the preliminary statements.'

'So, we're still looking at the principals,' Carol asked from inside the hall.

'Looks that way, yes.'

As if on cue, Sergeant Pearson entered the building, holding the front door open for Roger Heart who, Harry thought, looked as if he'd had a lot less sleep than even his own disturbed night. Carol was thinking the same and also whether this was because of a guilty conscience. His hair was dishevelled and, although no longer wearing his Hamlet costume, the jeans and sweatshirt he now wore looked as if they'd been slept in. He failed to make eye contact with any of the assembled gathering, preferring instead to gaze fixedly at the tiled flooring of the entrance hallway.

'Where do you want him? Blackwater's office?' Pearson asked.

'Let's keep it relatively informal and less squashed for the time being. We'll sit at the back of the hall. That alright with

you Harry?' Daniel asked.
'Yea, fine.'
Heart went first and sat nervously on one of the chairs in the next to back row of the auditorium, as Carol still thought of it. Daniel was first to speak, as Harry and Carol made themselves comfortable across the aisle, turning their chairs so as to be facing the interviewee.
'So, Roger. It is Roger, isn't it?'
Still no words were forthcoming from Heart, but a slight nod of his head indicated that this, at least, was a question he could answer in the affirmative.
'Well, Roger, I'd like to start by expressing my sorrow at your loss.'
Heart, for the first time that morning, lifted his head and looked at Daniel, an expression of disbelief crossing his features. Harry too looked across into those eyes and noticed the same vacancy that he had seen in Angie King's eyes the night before. His memory of her altercation with Steve Grey, in the producer's office was, however, cut short by the totally unexpected outburst that issued from Roger Heart.
'Sorrow? Sorrow?' He almost spat the repeated word at Daniel. 'I feel no sorrow for that bastard. I'm glad he's dead and I'm glad about the way he died. Do you think it was painful for him when the dagger was pushed in? I really hope so because he deserved to die in agony.'
The still glazed eyes continued to stare at Daniel for another few seconds before the head, as if his neck could no longer sustain the effort of holding it up, bent forward again and the young man returned to his vigil of the floor below. Daniel looked across at Harry and Carol, as if to ask for some divine guidance in questioning the obviously disturbed and, possibly, sick person in front of him.
It was Harry that broke the silence.

'Do you enjoy acting, Roger?'
Carol and Daniel both turned to look at Harry. Of all the questions he might have asked at that point in proceedings, this seemed the strangest.
'Yes, of course I do. I wouldn't have been doing all this if I didn't, would I?' He swept his arm towards the stage.
'No,' replied Harry, 'I don't suppose you would. You're pretty good at performing as well, aren't you?'
'If you say so.'
'Oh, I don't, but Carol here does and she knows what's good and what isn't, don't you?'
'I think so,' Carol said, wondering where all this was leading.
'Yes, a pretty good actor. You don't get to play Hamlet, even in an amateur production, without being pretty damned good.'
Heart had by now lifted his head again and was looking across at Harry with the same quizzical look as his colleague was giving.
'I don't see what this has got to do with…' Heart's voice trailed off as Harry stood up and walked across the aisle to sit next to him.
'What I'm saying, Roger, is that your little outburst just then was pretty well acted, wasn't it?'
'I don't know what you mean.'
'Oh, I think you do. You're a bright lad. What I'm saying is that, although you may be somewhat relieved at the death of your future father-in-law, the little performance you just gave was rather over the top. You're a pacifist. I can't imagine any pacifist revelling in the painful death of another human being, however disliked that person might have been.'
'How did you know I was...?' Heart began, but Harry was in no mood to explain his presence the previous day in the lingerie shop.

'What I want to know is why you felt you needed to put this act on for us? It's not as if we've paid to sit in these seats this morning.'

The weak attempt at humour seemed to make a difference to Roger Heart. His whole body seemed to change, almost imperceptibly at first and then, more noticeably, as he seemed to stop being the sullen, melancholic character that only a few hours earlier he had been portraying on stage and become a more confident and, Carol thought a little later, a wholly more likeable individual.

'Okay, you're right. I shouldn't have tried it on with you guys. I'm sorry. I just thought that if I sounded happier with the situation, it might take a bit of pressure off Angie.'

'Do you think there is some pressure on Angie? We haven't even spoken to her yet.'

'Yea, but you will and I reckon most of the time you lot suspect close family before anybody else; and seeing as how Angie's the only family he had, she must be pretty high up on your list of suspects.'

'Commendable as your feelings towards Angie are,' Daniel interposed, 'I really do prefer honesty to lying.'

'Technically, I didn't really lie. I just exaggerated emotionally.'

'Yea, well, technically, can you now answer my questions properly?'

'I'll try.'

'Good! Harry, do you want to carry on?'

'Okay. Roger, can you go over the few minutes leading up to the discovery of the body?'

This time Roger seemed almost happy to answer the question posed.

'Well, I was on stage with Lorraine doing the closet scene. We'd got to the bit when Derek was supposed to shout from behind the arras and, of course, nothing happened. We get used to that sort of thing, though, in our productions, so, after a few seconds, I just carried on and pretended I'd heard something. I got my sword out and pushed it through the arras.'

'What if King had been alive and was stood right behind it?'

'He knew not to and, anyway, he wouldn't have felt much. My sword had a button on the end and he was well padded, so there was no way he was going to get hurt.'

'What happened then?'

'I carried on with the way we'd rehearsed the scene. I lifted the arras and looked at his body. I'm supposed to drag it out a bit onto stage, but, as I bent down, I saw the dagger in his back. For a moment I thought someone had been having a laugh. We often try and make each other corpse, if you'll excuse the pun, on the last night, by playing tricks on stage, but I thought someone had started early in the run. Then I saw the blood and realised it wasn't a joke. I dropped the arras and ran into the wings to..'

'Now this is important,' Daniel interrupted. 'Who was stood at the back of stage?'

'That was the problem. There was no one there. The closet scene is quite a long one, so the rest of the cast have got a bit of time to check over their lines, have a drink and so on. Nobody was about to pull the curtains closed, so I ran right round the back to the other side of the stage and found Stew almost being knocked off his stepladder by Mike and Andy who were round there. He'd been trying to refix one of the lights that had blown, I think – they're always doing that!'

'Stew's the stage manager,' Harry informed Daniel.

'I know. I have been doing my homework.'

'Carol will be pleased.' And he smiled back across the aisle to where she was sitting. 'Sorry. Carry on Roger.'

'I got Stew to come round and told him to draw the curtains. He said it wasn't the end of the scene and I said something about murder, or a dagger. I can't remember. Stew might. He pulled the curtains and we went back on stage. By that time, most of the rest of the cast had appeared.'

Carol had listened intently to Roger Heart's words and had tried to check each memory with her own. Everything he had said seemed to fit, but she was concerned that the story had started at too late a point.

'What about your entrance?'

'My entrance?' Was it Harry's imagine, or had Heart suddenly begun to act again?

'Yes,' Carol said, 'If I recall, Gertrude had to wait a little while for you to come on.'

'I remember that as well,' Harry said, 'you whispered something to me about it.'

'I woke you up with the information.'

Roger Heart looked towards Harry.

'You fell asleep?'

'Busy day, no reflection on your performance, I promise,' Harry lied. He hoped his own acting skills were convincing enough.

Carol pressed her question. 'Gertrude had just sent Polonius to behind the arras. She was stood on stage waiting for your first line of that scene and you didn't come on. I'm not sure, but it seemed like at least ten seconds, maybe more.'

'Just about enough time,' Harry proposed, 'for you to be waiting behind the carpet, stab King, and then get to where you should have been for your entrance.'

'Now wait a minute,' Heart replied in a more nervous voice than had previously been evident, 'that's not what happened at all.'

'Then you tell us what kept you off stage.'

Harry kept his eyes trained on Roger Heart as the latter began.

'In rehearsal, Charles had decided that he didn't want Hamlet's speech at the end of the scene before the Closet, so I had a few minutes off stage before my entrance. I'd nipped round the back to use the loo, but someone was already in there. Just as I was about to go back to the wings, I heard the flush and the door opened. It was Angie. She looked as if she'd been crying, so I tried to find out what was wrong. She wasn't really in the mood to talk; certainly not to me anyway, but she obviously needed help. Let's just say that if she could have screamed, she would, but she was too professional to do that. She pushed past me and headed towards the kitchen. I ran round to the wings and made my late entrance.'

'You realise,' Daniel stated in a matter-of-fact tone, 'that we will check this out with Miss King?'

'Check all you want, that's what happened.'

Harry, by this time, had returned to Carol's side and she leant back and whispered, 'some corroboration, the word of his girlfriend. I think there was something else, but you can ask him about it another time when he's not so jumpy.'

Harry didn't reply, but instead mulled over in his mind what had just been said. It certainly seemed to fit with his memory of the evening: the fight he'd witnessed in Blackwater's office might well have been the cause of Angie King's upset backstage. Another thought was also forming. If Angie had left Roger in the way he was suggesting, then she could easily have been the one to have got onto the stage where King had been standing and killed him, whilst Heart was dashing in the other direction to make his entrance.

Daniel continued to ask Roger Heart another half a dozen questions, but none of them, Harry thought, added any more to their understanding of the previous evening's tragic events.

As Heart left the hall, Daniel told the two of them that he had

to return to Shrewsbury that afternoon to write his initial report, so they were free to enjoy themselves.
'Do you mind if we carry on with some discreet enquiries?' Carol asked.
'Carol!' Harry had interposed, 'This is Dan's case.'
'No, that's alright Harry. If you want to spend your holidays on a case, so be it. Just make sure it's all noted down and I get a full debrief.'
'It's a deal,' Harry said, as Carol, following him out of the hall, smiling behind his back for the second time that day.

CHAPTER 12

Carol, Harry and Daniel had just reached the outside doors when one of the forensic team, who had been continuing their work backstage, came running through.
'Chief inspector.'
Both Daniel and Harry turned, but it was Daniel to whom the call was addressed.
'Think you better see this sir,' the professional, young brunette said. 'Up on the stage.'
They all followed her back into the hall and onto the stage.
'I think we can have these curtains opened now,' Daniel shouted to a uniformed constable stood near to the wings.
A few moments later, the 'tabs' were drawn and Harry had a strange feeling of being caught in a play for which he knew no lines. He looked out into the empty auditorium and wondered, not for the first time, what possessed people to put on silly costumes and "tread the boards". If half the stories he'd heard from actors were true, then their lives were spent either 'resting' or throwing up from nerves. Then

again, he mused, maybe his life wasn't that different; hours of painstaking evidence gathering and form filling punctuated by moments of sheer horror.

'What do you reckon, Harry?'

Daniel's voice drew Harry back from his reverie. He looked down to see both Carol and Daniel peering at a crack between two sections of the makeshift stage.

'Is there anything in particular I should be looking at?'

Daniel simply nodded, pulled on some see-through gloves and proceeded to take a small pair of tweezers off one of the forensic team. Harry bent down further to watch, as a small, bloodied piece of screwed up paper was extracted from the crack. Daniel placed it on the stage and carefully used the tweezers to flatten it out.

What emerged was a yellowing page of typeface.

'That's a page of script,' Carol said and then, looking more carefully, exclaimed, 'a piece of the script of 'Hamlet''

'It says Act Three, Scene 4 at the bottom of the page,' Daniel said.

'That's the closet scene,' Carol informed Harry.

Daniel stood up and turned to the forensic officer that had brought them up onto the stage. 'Did you find King's script? Has it been bagged up yet?'

'There was a script near the body. It had slid under the curtains here.'

She pointed to the black drapes that hung between the wall flats as filler, so that the audience could not see into the wings.

'I'm not sure whether it's been shipped out to the lab or not.'

'Go and check, Jo, and if it's still here, let's have a look at it,' Daniel ordered and the woman made her way off the stage and into the kitchen area beyond.

'You reckon this has been ripped out of King's script?' Carol asked.

'The blood here might be his. We'll check it out. It seems odd that it's the scene he died in. Doubt if anyone else would have had this precise scene open and then tear a page out. Look at the frayed edge. Definitely a tear.' Daniel turned back to the fragile looking page of script and continued to examine it.

'But why would King rip this out as his dying act? If he had time to do this, why not cry out?' Carol mused.

'His cries might have simply been construed as part of the play at this part of the story, couldn't they?' Harry suggested.

'That's true. So, this might have been the only way for King to give us a clue to his murderer.'

'Hang on,' interposed Daniel, shaking his head, 'I fear you might have read too many crime novels. In my experience, clues do not tend to come from the victim.'

'In that case, how did this particular page come to have blood on it and be pushed down there, just where his hand was resting after he'd died?'

'I don't know, yet, but...'

Just at that moment, Jo returned from the kitchen clutching a plastic bag containing a script. Daniel carefully took it off her and, taking it out the bag, turned the pages of the script to the relevant page.

'Bingo,' he exclaimed. 'This page has been ripped from this script and...' He turned to the front cover. 'Guess whose name is written here?'

'Winnie the Pooh?' Harry facetiously suggested.

'Close, Harry, but not quite.'

'Derek King,' Carol stated, although knowing it was obvious from Daniel's face.

'Go to the top of the class.'

'So,' said Harry, 'we have a script and we have a ripped page and we have blood that will probably be shown to be

King's. How does it all help? Is there anything special about this last bit of scene?'
It was Carol that spoke before Dan had a chance.
'There's only one speech on this page and it belongs to Hamlet.'
'Was King telling us it was Roger Heart then?'
'Not necessarily,' Carol continued. 'Although the speech is by Hamlet, he refers in it to Rosencrantz and Guildenstern as his 'two schoolfellows' being 'hoist by their own petard'.'
'Petard? What the hell is that?'
'A small cannon for want of a better description. The saying has come into general usage to mean someone who gets their just desserts through their own evil actions.'
She looked at both of the policemen and smiled.
'I'm lecturing again, aren't I?'
The two men nodded, but it was Daniel that spoke first.
'Just a bit, but it might be incredibly important. Like I said, it's very unusual for dying people to have the presence of mind to leave a clue, but King might be the exception that proves the rule.'
'There is, of course, a further possibility,' Harry interjected. 'The killer might have ripped the page out, smeared some of King's blood on it and then pushed it down there to put us off the scent.'
'In other words,' said Carol, dejectedly, 'we're still at square one. This might be vital, or it might be worthless.'
'And that, my darling Carol, is the joy of police detection!'

CHAPTER 13

Rose Hubbard's garden was always immaculate. It wouldn't dare to be otherwise! The clematis that grew around the porch of her front door possessed deep purple flowers and the bulbs that grew on each side of the gravel path, leading from the small, front gate, had no fear of being overrun by weeds. Not in this garden. Small, rustic, stone tubs along the front of the thatched cottage, that Rose had called home the whole of her long life, were further testament to the time and effort she put into making this garden, one of the most beautiful in Shropshire. Indeed, it had been highly praised by the judges of the 'Britain in Bloom' competition that had twice chosen Pikesmere as a town of outstanding beauty; and Miss Hubbard's cottage as one of its best features.
As season followed season, a variety of colours and scents filled the garden and, on this, some might say, chilly afternoon, Rose was knelt with her trowel and small weed basket, near to the gate, attacking a particularly brave dandelion that had dared to appear between two small rocks that marked the border of the gravel path and the rose bed. After a remarkably lengthy fight to find the extent of its root system, the invader was dispatched to the basket and Rose, from her kneeling position, looked up to see the approach of two young people, one of whom she was not altogether surprised to again lay eyes upon. Using the gate as support, she cursed the arthritis that made her joints ache every time she tried to make any movement other than the gentlest of actions, she pulled herself upright and placed her left hand firmly on the wooden gatepost.
For Harry, making his way, after a particularly tasty lunch at the hotel, with Carol, across The Green towards the shops, the ascent of Miss Hubbard came just too late for any avoidance to be construed as anything other than obvious

and rude. Carol noticed her only a second or so later and the grip on Harry's hand indicated that she was there for him in what she was sure was going to be a most difficult meeting.

'Young man. I wants a word with you.'

Harry and Carol, ignoring the grammatically incorrect opening remark, put on their friendliest smiles and walked towards the old lady who Harry, less than twenty-four hours before, had offended so much by offering help up the steps of the Town Hall.

Carol's opening gambit, although wholly truthful, was intended also as an icebreaker. 'What a beautiful cottage and garden you have here. I noticed it when we first arrived. Have you lived here long?'

'Long enough to recognise when I'm bein' buttered up, young lady, so don't bother. Anyway, it's 'im I want to speak to, not you.'

Rudeness, Carol thought, and not for the first time, was not solely the province of the young. If any of her class spoke to her in this way, they would be seen as anti-social and disruptive. How incongruous it seemed here, in these surroundings, against the backdrop of thatched cottages, rose gardens and village greens. How incongruous to be coming from a wrinkled, old lady with a blue rinse hairdo and a pink striped apron.

'So, young man, what 'ave you found out about that bugger's death then?'

'It's Harry, and I presume you mean Mr. King's 'accident'?' Although the murder was not a secret, Harry still liked to keep people he felt had nothing to do with a case, as distant from it as possible. And his nemesis across the garden gate was definitely someone he wanted to keep as far away as he could.

'Don't give me any of that 'accident' rubbish, young man.'

Rose, obviously, had no intention of getting onto first name terms with the man. 'Pikesmere's a small town! Everybody knows everything what's going on. Just remember, I was there last night like you. I saw it all.'

Harry knew that, like Carol and himself, she had actually seen nothing, but he didn't pursue the point. Rose was now in full flow.

'I reckon you must be one of them plain clothed police fellows, but you're not from round here, which means you've got no, what's it called, *jurisdictication* or something like that. In other words, you can tell me all about it, can't you?'

'Much as I would love to discuss the case with you Mrs...'

'*Miss* Hubbard!'

'Miss Hubbard, I *am* involved, so it certainly wouldn't be right.'

'Oh, I see!' Miss Hubbard seemed genuinely disappointed. 'Well, what if I was to 'elp you with your enquiries then, as they say in all the best police dramas? I loves a bit of "Midsomer Murders", I does'

'What can you tell us?' Carol asked, intrigued and wishing to be seen, by Miss Hubbard, as equal partners with Harry in the investigation.

'Is she a policeman as well?'

Harry ignored the obvious gender problem with the question and informed Rose of Carol's invaluable help and support in his investigations. Carol beamed, but Rose still seemed rather dubious of her credentials. Even so, she leant a little further over the gateway, in true conspiratorial fashion, and said, 'I don't think we should talk, over the garden gate as it were. Why don't you both come in for a cup of tea?'

Before Harry or Carol could object, Rose Hubbard turned away from them, slowly bent and picked up her trowel and basket and made her way up the gravel path towards her front door.

'What if Old Mother Hubbard's cupboard is bare?' whispered Harry, mischievously.
Carol turned and winked at Harry who shrugged his shoulders in resignation, undid the latch on the gate and followed the old lady up the path and into the cottage.

CHAPTER 14

Ten minutes later, neither Carol nor Harry was regretting entering the abode of the 'she-devil'. Rose Hubbard had proved to be the perfect hostess. Not only had the tea been brewed to perfection, but the homemade scones and cakes that followed the liquid refreshment, were delicious in the extreme.
The room they were sat in was typical of a country cottage. Whitewashed walls and low, dark-stained beams gave the feel of being in Snow White's forest home and, in comparison to the modern, Manchester apartment that Carol and Harry lived in, there was almost an unreal quality to this woman's lifestyle. Sepia photographs stood along an old mantelpiece, brasses hung from the beams and crocheted squares lay on the backs of each of the two armchairs and the settee.
 As Carol gave Harry a look of disbelief at his acceptance of a third piece of chocolate cake, Miss Hubbard settled back in a well-worn chair and began to give them both the benefit of her local knowledge.
'I'm sure you're aware,' she began, 'that Derek King was not liked round 'ere. I reckon there'll be a few drinks knocked back in celebration, as news spreads of his death. He nearly ruined our town in bloom entry last year by complaining to the local plannin' department about where the flower tubs

and hangin' baskets had been placed around the streets.'
Harry and Carol smiled at the importance placed on this
particular action taken by King, but Rose seemed unaware
of their reaction to what seemed, to her, such an obviously
unsociable line of behaviour and continued.
'You must know about 'is daughter Angie and that lovely boy
Roger Heart. Everybody does.'
The two of them nodded, but what came next was far more
interesting.
'But did you know that she'd finished with 'im just before the
murder?'
Rose looked triumphant in her revelation and held the
silence like a true professional orator before continuing.
'I'm not one to gossip, as I'm sure you can tell, but yesterday
afternoon I was out in the garden there, workin' on that
border behind the front hedge. Stew had just delivered
some bags of John Innis for me and I wanted to get it down
before the rains came: which they didn't, even though that
nice chap on the tele said they would. Anyway, I'd just
started plantin' out some begonias for the summer when I
'eard footsteps out on the path and Angie King stopped right
there by the gate. Roger Heart was just the other side of the
hedge, but they didn't know I was there. I was going to stand
up and tell them of course, but I didn't want to disturb them.
Young love and all that.'
Again, Harry and Carol exchanged knowing smiles. It was
becoming clear that Miss Hubbard's denial of being a gossip
was not entirely true and that the chance of listening in on a
private conversation would have been unmissable for her.
'Anyway,' she continued conspiratorially, as if to draw her
younger listeners into the deceit that she herself had
perpetrated, 'Angie was obviously upset. She said, and
you'll 'ave to forgive me if I'm not word perfect, she said 'I
can't stand this anymore. All these lies are tearing me apart.

You've got to give me some space'. Then Roger started crying and he told her 'ow much he loved 'er and that he couldn't lose 'er. And then he said something really odd. He said, 'I know everything you know and I don't care'.'

Harry had taken more and more interest in Miss Hubbard's words and was now sitting on the front edge of the settee holding the small plate, with the chocolate cake crumbs, tightly on his lap.

It was Carol, however, that asked the question that was uppermost in his mind.

'Did Roger Heart say anything about what he 'knew'?'

'Not that I 'eard. They started to move away from the gate at that point, and Stew's bloomin' van drove off, so I couldn't rightly hear, but the last thing I 'eard was Angie telling Roger to keep away from 'er and that it was all over.'

'That's very interesting and very useful, Miss Hubbard and, if I may say so, made all the better by this delicious chocolate cake.'

'Would you like another slice? I've got plenty.'

'Well, if you're forcing me.'

Rose slowly pushed herself up from her chair and shuffled out into the kitchen.

'Another slice?' Carol looked amazed. 'You've never had that much cake at my mum's!'

Harry was not inclined to explain this anomaly, but instead whispered, 'If all that is true - and we've no reason at the moment to suspect otherwise, considering Miss Hubbard is not a suspect because she was sat directly in front of us when the murder occurred - then it explains quite a lot about Angie's behaviour, particularly why she went home with Lorraine and not Roger last night.'

'And also, why she didn't want to talk to him by the loo, just before the murder.'

'In the light of all this, I reckon it's about time we talked to the bereaved daughter.'

'And maybe another little chat with our favourite young 'Dane'.'

'There's someone else we also need to see.'

'Who's that?'

'Whatshisname from the garage. You know, the one I had to separate from Angie in Blackwater's office just before the killing. Grey, isn't it?'

'Steve Grey, I think.'

'That's him.'

'Yes, I'd have a word with Grey as well, if I were you.' Rose had returned with an enormous slice of cake for Harry and had obviously overheard the latter part of the conversation; impaired hearing was not one of Miss Hubbard's infirmities, Carol thought.

'Why would you say that, Miss Hubbard?' Harry's perception of Rose had changed considerably over the last half an hour, not least because of the seemingly endless supply of cake in this cottage.

'Because if you're lookin' for a killer, I wouldn't look much further than the garage. Steve Grey is a nasty piece of work. You ask Sergeant Pearson.'

Harry preferred not having to ask Pearson anything, so decided to try and elicit the information from Rose. 'He didn't seem too bad to me, when I met him last night,' he lied.

'Oh, he can be the charmer when he wants to be,' Rose took Harry's bait, 'but he's not a nice piece of work at all. I remember when he was in his mid-teens, he used to be a real thug. Spent some time in one of them borstals, or whatever they're called now.'

'Youth Custody Centres,' Carol corrected, thinking of a few of her pupils who had ended up in them. 'What was he sent there for?'

'Ah, well, that's where it gets a bit interesting. It was a few years ago now, but he was caught red-handed in Derek King's house.'

'What?' both Carol and Harry exclaimed.

'Oh, yes. King was supposed to be away for the day on business. Angie was about fourteen and was with a school friend of 'ers down the road. Anyhow, King came back early and found Grey in the house, presumably stealing the family jewels, or some such thing. Grey tried pushing past King to get away, but something happened and King banged his head. When Angie found him, he was unconscious and she called an ambulance and got him to hospital. He turned out to be okay, but they picked Grey up in Telford and although he always pleaded he hadn't done anything maliciously, he was sent off for eighteen months or so.'

'I can't believe he'd now be in a play with King?' Carol said.

'Whilst he was inside, they got him doing a bit of acting, so, when he got out, he carried on. He and King just kept to themselves and apart from each other, as far as I know.'

Carol thought about it. Grey played Fortinbras and King, Polonius. Neither was on stage at the same time as the other and if Blackwater had been warned aware of the history of the pair, it was possible that they might never have had to rehearse together the whole time. They'd have only been together on the nights of the performance. She made a mental note to mention this to Harry and Daniel later and to get them to question Blackwater on this.

'Miss Hubbard, you have been a fountain of information. Is there anything else you can think of that might help with these enquiries?' Harry looked at her hopefully.

'No, I don't think so. If anything comes to mind, though, I'll let you know.'

'We're staying at 'The Golden Pheasant',' Harry said, but, even as the words came out, he knew that they were totally unnecessary. Miss Hubbard's clear knowledge of town activities precluded the need for the information and she simply nodded to show that she was already aware of this. Even so, she thanked him for telling her and they all made their way to the front door.

'There is one last thing,' Rose said, as Harry and Carol crossed the threshold, 'You are aware that this isn't the first tragedy in the King family, aren't you?'

'What?' Harry realised that such information was probably being read by Daniel back at headquarters, at this very moment, but he cursed being somewhat on the side-lines of this case.

'King's wife was murdered.'

Carol gave a short gasp, as Harry looked at Rose Hubbard expectantly.

'It wasn't round here; it was somewhere away, before him and Angie moved here. Derek never really talked much about it, but it seems she was killed in their kitchen one evening when he was away on business. Angie was only little, but it was her what found her mum in the morning. Sorry, I don't know much else about it.'

Once outside the gate, Harry looked at Carol and let out a loud exhalation of air.

'Now that is one interview that I bet Dan will wish he'd been in on.'

'Does he like chocolate cake as well?' Carol asked, jokingly.

'You know exactly what I mean. We've certainly got plenty to follow up.'

'Where do we start? Angie? Heart again? Grey?'

'I think,' Harry mused, 'that we should start with Steve Grey. Some of the information he might give us may have a bearing on what we say to the other two.'

'Come on, then, let's get over to the garage.'

CHAPTER 15

As they walked back across The Green, Carol took Harry's hand in hers and looked across into his deep, blue eyes.
'Are you really alright about all this, Harry?' she asked.
'All this what?' he replied.
'This murder. Interviewing. This is supposed to be your holiday.'
'It's your holiday too. How do you feel about it all?'
'I'm loving it, but it's not a, how did you put it, busman's holiday for me. It's all new and quite exciting.' She thought for a second and felt something more was necessary.
'Not that the whole death of King isn't tragic. Of course it is. But...'
'I know. I felt the same the first couple of murders I investigated. Part of me felt like I'd lost a loved one as we interviewed relatives and friends. However, and I wouldn't tell anybody else except you, another part of me enjoyed the whole process of investigating a death; the searching for clues and the tracking down of a human being who was capable of taking someone else's life.'
'Exactly. I see the kids at school doing a lot of horrible things and I know they do even worse outside the school gates, but the actual act of killing somebody...'
'It's even worse than that, though, isn't it? With something like we're investigating here, we're talking about cold-blooded planning and execution of that plan, if you'll pardon the pun. Somebody, or somebodies...'
'I don't think that's a real plural!'
Harry ignored the grammatical complaint. 'Thought about where and when and how to kill King. This wasn't a spur of the moment, emotional outburst. This was cold, calculated and deliberate. That dagger was placed to cause a very speedy death and the way it pushed into the spinal column

was meant to make it very difficult for King to even move from where he was taken down.'
'Which makes it all the more interesting. Correct?'
'I suppose so. It also makes it dangerous. This isn't a game, Caz and if this whole thing starts to get any more sinister, we leave it to Daniel. Right?'
'Yes, sir.'
'I'm not kidding. This may seem like some rural beauty spot, with thatched cottages and village stocks, but there's a murderer out there and I'm not letting you get too close.'
'I can look after myself you know Harry. Don't start getting all male chauvinist on me. It's not in your character.'
'I stand reproached, but I mean what I say about the danger.'
'I know, but I've got my knight in shining armour to protect me, haven't I?'
And with that, Carol let go of Harry's hand and instead linked her arm with his, whilst making sure her head rested on his shoulder. She did feel secure in his vicinity and, perhaps oddly, so did he in hers.
Before they reached the far side of The Green, however, Carol stopped and turned to Harry with a look of revelation.
'Harry,' she almost shouted, 'I've just had another thought about that piece of script that we found stuffed into the stage. You know I told you that Hamlet mentions, on that page, being 'hoist by his own petard'?'
'Yes,' Harry said, tentatively. He had to admit that the whole Shakespearean angle of this case was causing him problems. 'Did you say it was some sort of cannon, or something?'
'Well remembered! But that's not important. It's what he says before that. He talks about 'the engineer' being 'hoist'.'
'Really?' Harry replied, not quite sure where this might be leading.

'But don't you see. Steve Grey is a car mechanic. That's a bit like an engineer. Maybe that's what King was trying to tell us. After all, he didn't have much time to make it a really good clue and I don't think Shakespeare mentions a car mechanic anywhere in 'Hamlet'.'

Harry ignored the obvious facetiousness of the remark, but responded by reminding Carol of Daniel's doubts about victims leaving clues. Carol was not impressed at Harry's rejoinder to what she thought was a really good clue and they continued their way, for a while, in silence.

They had reached the small chemists that Harry remembered primarily by the smell and they paused to let a rather elderly man pass by, somewhat precariously, on his bicycle, before crossing the narrow road to the garage that the detective had been perusing only the previous morning. How much water had passed under the bridge since then, he thought, as they entered the neon-lit interior. The floor was black from oil changes and spillages and towards the back was a pit and above it, on a hydraulic ramp, sat a rather tasty, red MG. Harry had been hoping to have a closer look at the Bentley that he'd spied the day before, but this had now disappeared. He had to admit, however, that the sports car in front of him, with its open top and veneered interior, was a worthy replacement. He'd always been interested in cars and yet, from the moment he had passed his test, he'd either been too skint or too utilitarian to buy one of his own. The public transport system was reasonable in Manchester and the pool of police cars was always available to an officer of his rank. Here, now, however, he could picture himself behind the wheel of this motor, racing round the country lanes of Pikesmere, the wind blowing Carol's hair as they sped towards an isolated beauty spot where they'd stop to eat strawberries and drink champagne.

'And what the hell do you want?'

The voice emerged from the pit below the car and belonged to an altogether oilier and less Shakespearean Steve Grey than the one Harry had met the previous evening.

'Detective Chief Inspector Bailey,' Harry said, extending his right hand in an act of reconciliation, 'I don't think we were properly introduced last night.'

Steve put out his hand, but to show the oil and grime rather than to take Harry's. 'Won't shake. Best we don't, for you I reckon. Who's the pretty bird then?'

Before Harry could rise to the bait, Carol stepped forward and introduced herself, making it clear that she did not appreciate being referred to as a 'bird', although the epithet regarding her beauty softened the political incorrectness somewhat.

'Sorry. Spent the first part of my life in East London and picked up some of the slang! Only moved up here when I was fourteen.' Unabashed by Caz' put down, Steve athletically jumped out of the pit and made his way across the garage to a sink at the back left corner, where he pulled the top of his overalls open and let it drop to his waist. He began to scrub his hands and that part of his now naked torso that had been splashed by oil; Carol was unsure as to whether this was his daily routine, or whether the partial nudity was part of his attempt to make the visitors, and particularly her, uncomfortable. He was only a little older than some of the students that she taught and this post-adolescent show of testosterone-induced peacock feather preening was more laughable than erotic. She had to admit, however, that he had a well-defined chest and a muscular frame and, were she a younger woman, say Angie King's age, he would definitely be considered 'fit'.

As if this thought had been transferred telepathically to Harry, the detective moved over to the mechanic and began his enquiries.

'So, Steve, do you want to tell me about that little scene with Angie King in the office last night?'
'None of your business. Made that clear last night, I reckon.'
'At that point you might have been right,' Harry conceded, 'but that was before Angie's father became a corpse and I was asked to help investigate. So, let's try this one last time, before we make this altogether more formal down at the station; what happened between you and Angie?'
Steve had finished washing and was now drying himself with a dirty towel that looked as if it was actually making his, now, clean arms, filthy again. He looked across at Carol, even though he was answering Harry's question.
'Angie just can't resist me, know what I mean? We've always been an item, off and on, ever since...' He faltered imperceptibly, but then continued.
 'Well, let's just say since we were at school.' He winked across at Carol. 'Can't help being irresistible, can I?'
In your dreams, Carol thought, but Harry was already pressing the young man.
'Angie seemed to be resisting quite a bit last night, from what I could see when I walked in on you,' said Harry.
'You know what girls are like, man. Sometimes they say 'no' when they really mean 'maybe'.'
'I locked a rapist up the other week who thought the same thing.'
'Hey, I'm no rapist.' He again turned towards Carol. 'Don't need to be, do I? Know what I mean?'
'Maybe not a rapist, but we do hear that you've done time.' Harry enjoyed seeing the inane, sexual grin drop slightly.
'I never went to prison. It was only one of them youth centres.'
'Holiday camp, was it?'
'Wouldn't say that. I didn't enjoy it if that's what you're getting at.'

'Still, you've got a record, haven't you? And it's all tied in with Derek King.'

'I never did it. I told that magistrate that I was innocent. She just wouldn't believe me. Preferred to listen to that fancy lawyer that King brought in.'

'Blamed him for it, did you? All those months spent inside. Did it make you angry? Angry enough to kill him?'

'Yea, of course I blamed him, 'cause I never did nothing, but I didn't kill him.'

Carol ignored the double negative and decided to get involved. 'From what we've gathered, King found you in his house. He caught you red-handed.'

'That doesn't mean I was stealing like what he said.'

'Then what were you doing in King's house, alone?' Carol continued.

Harry noticed that Steve's grin had now disappeared completely and a look of something approaching terror had replaced it. The man knew his past meant he was now a suspect for murder and this time it wouldn't be eighteen months in a Youth Centre. Harry mulled over what he was hearing. If Grey was telling the truth about his innocence, he'd certainly be aware of the shortcomings of the judicial system and, even if he hadn't murdered King, he was now contemplating the thought of being wrongly convicted of it, all the same.

Carol's question hung in the air and Steve Grey didn't seem to be inclined to answer it. Harry, however, suddenly had an idea of his own.

'The thing is, Steve, you weren't alone in the house that day were you?'

CHAPTER 16

'What? Of course I was alone,' Steve Grey replied.
'No, you weren't. There was somebody in the house with you,' Harry continued.
'Go on, then, clever clogs. Tell me who else was there.'
Carol had also turned to Harry, questioningly.
'I'd have thought,' Harry said, 'it should be obvious. You were there with Angie King!'
Carol looked at Grey and the narrowing of his eyes was enough to show that Harry had hit the nail squarely on its head.
'How did you know? Did she tell you?'
'No, we haven't spoken to her yet, but we will and I'm sure she'll confirm it now her father's not on the scene.'
'I never told anyone at the trial. I didn't want to get her into any trouble.'
Carol's disbelief was pronounced as she said, 'You were willing to be locked up for eighteen months for her?'
'Yes.'
'And she was willing to let you?'
'You didn't know King. She couldn't say anything. She didn't dare and I wouldn't have let her. I was seventeen and she was three years younger. All hell would have let loose.'
Carol and Harry's perception of the person they were talking to, not for the first time that afternoon, was changing considerably. Instead of an arrogant, self-centred narcissist, Grey had been willing to receive a criminal record and serve time, all in order to spare another human being's suffering. Harry was also thinking something else: Roger Heart had lied, or, as he had put it, 'emotionally exaggerated' for Angie King; Grey had lost eighteen months of his life. What was it about this girl that attracted such devotion?
'So,' Carol decided to pursue the questioning, 'you were in

the house with Angie. Was she your girlfriend?'

'I guess you could say that.'

'And she was fourteen then?' Carol's tone of questioning held no hint of moral indignation. As a teacher, she was well aware of what young adolescents got up to.

'Yes. But it wouldn't have mattered to her dad how old she was. She could have been thirty and he still wouldn't have approved.'

'Did he know you were seeing each other?' This time it was Harry who kept up the pressure.

'I don't think so. We kept it all pretty secret. We had to. He never said anything before or during the court case. He just thought I'd been in the house thieving and that suited me. We were both in Angie's bedroom when we heard the front door that day.'

Steve looked at both of them to see whether the revelation was met with any reaction. When it didn't, he continued.

'I told Angie to stay quietly in her bedroom while I went down to check it out. It seems a bit strange now, but because we thought old King was out for the day, we thought it might be an intruder. As I got halfway down the stairs, I was faced with King turning to come up. He was looking through some papers, so he didn't see me till he reached about the third step. I'll never forget the look of hate in his eyes as he recognised me. I panicked and tried to push past him to get out. He lost his step and the next thing I knew, he was lying at the foot of the stairs and he'd banged his head on a wooden chest as he fell.'

After the information they'd discovered about the death of King's wife in his own home, Harry could imagine how Derek King must have felt coming face to face with an intruder on his stairs.

'He was out for the count and I didn't know how bad he was. Just at that point, Angie came to the top of the stairs and, when she saw her dad, she started screaming. I think she had a flashback to her mum. I checked he was still breathing and then calmed Angie down. She phoned for an ambulance and I told her not to say anything about being there with me and that she'd just come home and found him like that. Then I made my escape.'

'To Telford?' Harry finished the story off for him.

'Yea. I was caught a day or so later. King only had a bump and had easily been able to identify me to the coppers. Angie pretended, as I told her, that she'd come back to the house early and found him there. I don't think he ever guessed the truth.'

'We've only got your word for that though, haven't we Mr. Grey?' Harry's use of his surname, and the formality of the use of the 'Mr', was purely intentional on his part. He wanted to see how much pressure the young man could take and whether there was any more to his story. His instinct was telling him that this was not their murderer, but he had learnt, to his cost in the past, not to trust solely his instinct. If King had, indeed, in some way, found out what had happened, Grey may well have decided to again protect Angie in the most final of ways.

'As far as I know,' Grey continued, 'King never knew anything about my 'relationship' with his daughter. I hadn't been seeing her for long and by the time I'd finished my sentence, she'd started seeing Heart.'

'Can't imagine that was very easy for you?' Carol said.

'What did you feel about Angie doing that?' asked Harry.

'I was cool with it.'

'Sure you were!' Carol said sarcastically. 'You'd just spent eighteen, rather unpleasant, I can imagine, months, locked away trying to protect this girl and, when you get out, you find she's deserted you for someone else. I can see how 'cool' that would make you feel.'

Harry was impressed with Carol's approach to questioning and the sarcasm was obviously having its desired effect on the mechanic. The anger he had seen the previous evening, at the production, was now there behind Grey's eyes and the clenching of his fists warned Harry that they must now tread a delicate path if the truth was to be elicited without the need for physical restraint, or someone getting hurt. He decided that if Carol was going to play 'bad cop', then he better be the 'good' one.

'Steve,' the previous formality was again dispensed with, 'we're not here to pry into your personal feelings or problems, but you must see that, from our point of view, it's important that we have a full picture of events leading up to King's death; anything in his, or Angie's past, could be relevant. So, tell us, how did you really feel when you found out about Roger Heart?'

Grey, although still tense, seemed to relax slightly at the gentler tone of questioning, but he turned to the workbench nearby and picked up a large wrench that was sat there. As he turned back, Harry too tensed and he went to step between Carol and Grey, beginning to take up a defensive posture.

Rather than brandishing the tool aggressively, however, Grey held it in front of him and said, 'You want to know how I felt. You see this. Well, I wanted to wrap something like this round Heart's neck and probably Angie's as well.'

He paused, put the wrench down and then continued, 'But I didn't! You see they do stuff to your head while you're inside. Even in them kiddie prisons, they mess with you and you're never quite the same when you come out as when you go in. I wanted to do something, but I couldn't... and I couldn't have done anything to King last night neither. Now you can either believe me, or not, but I've got an MG to finish, so if you'll just get out of here...'

Harry and Carol started to make their way to the garage entrance, but Harry suddenly realised that his initial line of questioning had still not been addressed fully. He turned, walked back over to the pit, and said, 'Just one last question before we go. What about the little scene I interrupted last night? If it was all over between you and Angie, what was going on there?'

'I wasn't completely joking when I said I was irresistible to the ladies.'

His cockiness had returned, Harry noted, and he again looked towards Carol as he said the words.

'When we started rehearsing the play, me and Angie never really spoke, but I watched her with Heart and I began to get the vibe that she wasn't too happy with him, so I thought I'd make another play for her. I took it slow and gentle like. No pressure, just the occasional comment now and again whilst Heart was on stage acting and so on. Anyway, let's just say that she couldn't resist and the other day she, uh...'

He stopped and tried to find the right words, but it was ultimately Carol that finished the sentence for him.

'She managed to show how much she 'appreciated' your previous sacrifices on her behalf.'

'I couldn't have put it better than the pretty lady herself.'

'Did Heart know?' Harry asked.

'Don't know. Don't care. Angie said she was going to tell him it was all over, but I think she wanted to wait till after the show had finished.'

Harry turned to Carol and said quietly, 'that all fits in with what Mrs Hubbard told us earlier.'

'Yes,' Carol continued, 'Roger must have been pushing Angie, so she decided to tell him earlier; on the afternoon before her father died, outside Mrs. Hubbard's garden.'

Harry turned back to Steve Grey and asked one last time, 'This all fits in with what we know, but what I saw, in

Blackwater's office, didn't look like the clinch of two lovers who were back together. It looked more like a fight to me.'
'Even when you're irresistible,' Grey grinned again, 'you can't always get what you want, when you want it. Ask Angie what it was all about, 'cause I've no idea what was happening and I haven't seen her since to ask. I met her in the foyer, dragged her into the office and went to have a quick snog. Like you do.'
Harry smiled, but Carol's face was fixed and hard as Grey continued.
'I knew King was waiting to go on, so I thought the coast was clear, but Angie wasn't up for it and she just started to push me away. I've no idea why. That's when you walked in and you know the rest.'
Yes, I know the rest, Harry thought, a dead father and another mystery to get to the bottom of. Why did Angie react to Grey in that way, that night, and did it have anything to do with the murder they were investigating? Like all crimes, the evidence you uncovered seemed, in the early stages anyway, to raise more questions than were answered. He took Carol's hand and they again made their way towards the doors of the garage.
'Thanks for your co-operation, Steve,' he called back to the mechanic, who was once again starting to climb down into the pit below the sports car. 'You won't go taking that MG for a spin to Telford, or anywhere else daft will you? I wouldn't want a prime suspect going missing.'
Harry didn't look back to see the worried face that watched their exit. He did, however, afford himself a wicked smile at Carol.
'Is he still a prime suspect?' she asked.
'We're no closer to the truth, really, than we were at lunch, even though we've got a lot more information about certain sections of Pikesmere society, so he's just as much a

suspect as he was before.'
'But not really a 'prime' suspect?' she pressed.
'Maybe not, but it won't do him any harm to have that grin wiped away for a while.'
'Just because he flashed his pecs at me.'
'Didn't notice you looking,' he lied.
'Don't worry, lover, your pecs are all I'm interested in.'
'Glad to hear it. Fancy investigating them back at the hotel, then?' Harry suggestively asked.
'Not until we've talked to Angie. Work before play, Harry Bailey.'
'But we're on holiday,' he whined.
'Just get up the street.'
'Why?'
'Lorraine's lingerie shop is up there on the left. Angie went home with Lorraine last night, so she's our best person to find out where Angie is. God, call yourself a detective.'

CHAPTER 17

The heavy scent of Lorraine's cheap, yet pungent, perfume assailed Harry's nostrils even before they had entered her shop. Carol had opened the door, just as Lorraine was about to see a customer out and her proximity to them made it impossible to avoid. As two days before, her attire would have suited a teenager far better and Carol, as well as Harry, noticed the beginnings of varicose veins on one of her, all too uncovered legs, as she turned to let them into the shop.
'I suppose you've come to ask me about the murder. I've been expecting you. I do think it was a bit naughty of you

not telling me you were a policeman when you bought your tickets.'

'Why on earth would I have done that?' Harry replied, annoyed that his profession should be of any concern to her when he was off duty.

Before Lorraine had a chance to reply and possibly upset Harry even more, Carol said, 'Actually, we were wondering where we might find Angie.'

'Oh, I see.'

The terse tone of Lorraine's reply was evidence that she was obviously put out by this piece of news. Unlike some of the Pikesmere inhabitants that they had already interviewed, it seemed that she was more than keen to share anything she could with them, particularly Harry, who had evidently become rather more attractive to Lorraine since his job and status had been made public. Ironically, as they had already discussed her possible guilt, or lack of it, at length, Carol had been convinced that there was no way that Lorraine could be the murderer and, therefore, her interview could wait until later.

A small pile of boxed tights suddenly became the focus of Lorraine's attention and, turning away from the pair, she continued tersely with, 'She's in the flat upstairs, but I'm not sure she's up to too many questions yet. She's still quite upset.'

Harry noted the use of the word 'quite'. Under normal circumstances, a daughter of a murder victim would be completely distraught and possibly under some form of sedation. Angie's relationship with her father, however, was, as they were continually learning, somewhat more strained and, thus, her reaction apparently rather more subdued.

'We'll take it easy with her,' Harry assured Lorraine. 'Where do we go to get up there?'

'The stairs are through that door over there.' She pointed to a light green door, almost totally hidden behind several rails of underwear.

'Do you live above the shop then?' Carol asked.

Lorraine seemed to take this as an act of criticism and, again, went onto the defensive. 'It's only in the short run. Just until the shop really gets going. It's so much more convenient to be on site. I've only been here a few years and it takes a while to get a good clientele.'

She seemed, Carol thought, to be convincing herself, as much as them, but they both nodded in agreement and made their way towards the door. Just before Harry could reach for the handle, they again heard Lorraine making a plea for leniency.

'She may give the impression that this isn't really affecting her, but I've spent half the night talking to her and there are feelings there. I could shut the shop and come up with you. After all, it's getting quite late, isn't it?'

'No,' said Harry, quickly, 'I prefer to talk to her in private.'

'Oh, well, in that case, you'll have to send Roger down.'

Carol now turned to look directly at Lorraine as well. 'Is Roger Heart up there?' She knew, as she said it, that the answer was self-evident and the question, therefore, superfluous, but, after what they had learnt that day, it also seemed an extremely odd turn of events.

'Oh, yes, he's been here since early afternoon. Angie was so pleased to see him. I stayed with them for a little while, but I thought they'd want some time together without me acting as a gooseberry.'

Harry looked at Carol and then back at Lorraine.

'Are you absolutely positive that Angie was happy to see Heart?'

'Of course! Why shouldn't she be?'

'It's just that we'd been hearing things weren't so good between them lately.'

'Oh, you know what these young folk are like. They can have broken things off one day and be in bed the next.'

Carol noticed that Lorraine's choice of phrase was accompanied by a rather charged smile and a twinkle of the eye which was directed solely at Harry. His composure, however, was unmoved and in a single movement, both of them turned back to the door, opened it, smiled at each other, unseen by Lorraine, and began to ascend the uncarpeted, wooden staircase, Harry making sure that the door at the bottom was securely closed behind them.

He was about to say something about their flirtatious shopkeeper, when voices above stopped him and, instead, he put his hand on Carol's arm above him and motioned to her that it would probably be prudent if they waited a few moments before making their presence known to the young couple whose conversation they were now eavesdropping upon.

It was Roger Heart's voice that first became audible.

'See,' he was saying, almost triumphantly, 'you're happy now aren't you. I told you I'd sort it and now I have.'

Almost dreamily, maybe euphorically Carol thought, Angie replied in the affirmative. Heart could then, again, be heard to boastfully assert his mastery in whatever activity he had been so obviously successful in.

'And if it wasn't for me, you'd still be feeling pretty awful, wouldn't you?'

Again, an affirmative response.

'So, let's not hear any more about Grey, shall we?'

'But, what about...?'

Heart interrupted, 'No buts. If I see you even talking to him again, you know exactly what'll happen, don't you?'

This time the 'yes' was almost inaudible, but it was followed only moments later by a maniacal laugh that had also, so far as Harry and Carol could tell, emanated from Angie. A few more seconds later and Heart, too, could be heard laughing and then, as quickly as it had started, the sounds stopped and so did everything else.

Harry waited a few moments more and then again touched Carol's arm to indicate that he thought they had gleaned enough from their eavesdropping and should now continue to ascend. Whether by chance, or by their own more careful footfalls, the rest of the steps were taken without creaking floorboards and they reached the top unheard by the occupants within the flat above.

The door into the first-floor room was slightly ajar and Carol, being in front of Harry, was the one to push it open and walk in on the young couple. By the time Harry entered the room, Roger Heart had managed to partially disengage his hand from the inside of Angie King's blouse and both, only slightly red-faced it had to be said, had turned to look towards the interloping adults that had, so thoughtlessly, interrupted their youthful engagement. Carol turned to look at Harry, suspecting that her face was somewhat redder than those they had surprised, but she turned back as the pair, seated, as they were, on a rather threadbare settee, now burst into similar laughter to that which they had heard only a few moments before.

Harry saw, in Angie's eyes, the same rather vacant, glazed expression that he had noted at the Town Hall on the night of the murder. Heart, although not showing such obvious signs of drug abuse, was, nonetheless, clearly under the influence of something. It only took Carol a moment or two longer than Harry to recognise the tell-tale signs and she turned to him with a concerned glance.

'Do you reckon we're going to get any sense out of these two this afternoon?'

'We'll give it a try, but I doubt it very much.' He lowered his voice to almost an imperceptible whisper. 'We don't want them together anyway. Take Heart back down to Lorraine and ask her to see he gets home safely. Try not to let him break his neck going down the stairs.'

'Roger,' Carol turned back to the two lovebirds, 'could I have a chat with you downstairs please?'

'You're not splitting us up. No one's going to do that ever again. Isn't that right Angie?' Heart, as if to accentuate his certainty, put his arm round her shoulders and drew her even closer to him.

Angie's reply was not what Harry, Carol, or especially Roger, were expecting.

'Get off me. I don't like being mauled and I don't like being taken for granted.'

She pulled away from his grasp and went, somewhat unsteadily, to stand by a small bookcase that evidently held Lorraine's small library of books, a few old videos from the 1980s and DVDs from the late '90s. For a brief moment, Roger Heart looked as if he might pounce upon her once again, like some wild animal that needed to prove himself the pack leader, but, without warning, the fire that burnt in his eyes was extinguished and he slumped back into the folds of the settee cushions. The change was incredible to watch and to Harry and Carol it seemed that he had been shrunk by some supernatural tumble dryer. Carol walked over to him, helped him to his feet and led him over to the stairs.

'Won't be a minute,' she said, hopefully, and they disappeared into the gloom of the passageway below.

CHAPTER 18

'Want to come and sit back down now?' Harry ventured, after the other two had departed.
'Not really,' Angie replied tersely. 'Happy here thanks.'
The final word was spat out rather than it being a civil reply, so Harry wandered around the room, allowing the silence to perhaps, he thought, unnerve the seventeen-year-old. After a few steps, he felt in his pocket and found his packet of mints. He got them out and unwrapped one. The action had its desired effect.
'Give us one,' Angie asked, petulantly, and then, almost as an afterthought, 'Please.'
'Here you go.'
He stepped towards her and she moved to meet his outstretched offering. He stood back and then let her choose her territory. She moved around to the back of the sofa and stood looking out of the small window. Harry took a moment to squat down and peruse Lorraine's bookshelves that Angie had, a moment or two before, been stood by. An eclectic mixture of books met his gaze: trashy, modern pulp alongside copies of 'Moll Flanders', 'Mill on the Floss' and 'Women in Love'. The almost ancient videos were no less consistent in style, ranging between several Quentin Tarantino blood-fests to a copy of 'The Sound of Music'. He was about to stand and begin his questioning, when a thin DVD case title caught his eye. He pulled it out and looked at the back sleeve, then he carefully reinserted it back on the shelf, in exactly the same position as he had found it. With a slight grin, he stood back, just as Carol returned from the shop below.
'So,' Harry broke the silence, 'you get your gear off Heart, do you?'
'Don't know what you're talking about!' Angie's attitude was

hard and aggressive and Carol wondered how much of this character was her and how much was some drug-induced persona. 'I'm just upset, that's all. Don't I have a right to be emotional? My father's dead, in case you've forgotten.'
'No, we haven't forgotten, although we were concerned that maybe you had.'
'No!' Tears began to well up in Angie's eyes and she at last turned from the window and, unsteadily, made her way to the settee and sat down.
'Angie,' Harry said softly, 'we need to know some more about last night.'
'I didn't do it, if that's what you think.'
'At the moment, we're looking at a lot of possibilities,' Harry replied.
'What do you want to know from me? Coz I want to help, really. I want to know who killed, dad!'
'Even if it's Roger?'
Angie's eyes seemed, for the first time that afternoon, to clear. 'It wasn't him; I promise you of that.'
'Well, a few minutes ago, as we were coming up the stairs, we happened to overhear him saying to you that he'd sorted everything out. Sounds like a possible confession to..'
'Christ, bloody coppers. How long were you out there perving and listening before you came in here? Christ!'
Angie's outburst was understandable, Carol thought. She had, herself, felt uncomfortable on the staircase.
'Sometimes,' Harry began, 'to get to the truth, we do some pretty horrible things. But you did say you wanted to know the truth as well.'
'Yea, I do,' Angie muttered, 'They never found out who murdered my mum and now dad's gone as well. I hope you lot can do a bit better this time! But you won't find the murderer here.'
'Then what was Heart talking about?'

'Nothing to do with you.'
'You're not being very co-operative, Miss King.'
Angie's eyes were glazing over again and she sat back into the cushions of the sofa.
'Sorry,' she murmured, 'I would give you some violets, but they withered all when my father died.'
Harry looked over at Carol for explanation.
'A line from 'Hamlet'. After Polonius' murder, Ophelia goes mad and comes on stage strewn with flowers which she hands out to her brother and the king and queen.'
'They say he made a good end.'
With this, Angie sat upright and burst into a fit of laughter. Carol sat next to her and, as she did so, Angie turned and the laughter became tears as her head fell onto Carol's shoulders.
Five minutes later, Angie seemed more able to continue with Harry's questioning, although Carol had suggested that they should leave things and get Lorraine to come and sit with her.
'I won't push her, but we need to try and find out a bit more about last night,' Harry whispered. They were both over by the bookshelves and wary of how much Angie was able to understand.
'Go gentle on her, then. You can see what a state she's in. She might not even be seeing things straight anyway!'
'Then again, we might get more truth this way.'
He walked back over to the sofa and sat next to Angie. 'How much can you tell us about last night, Angie?'
'My father began the evening alive and ended it dead. What else do you want me to tell you?'
'What about your meeting with Steve Grey, in Blackwater's office? The one I walked in on.'
'Oh, that was nothing. Nothing to do with you, anyway.'
'You keep saying this, Angie, but unless you can be a bit

more forthcoming with your answers, how can I judge whether you're telling me the truth or not?'

'Careful,' Carol interrupted quietly, 'don't push it too much.'

'Sorry!' Harry retorted, but continued, 'Angie, have you been seeing Steve Grey?'

"Seeing Steve Grey'. Yes, you could put it that way. I have been 'seeing Steve Grey'. I have been going out with Steve Grey. I have been involved with Steve Grey. But...'

Her voice trailed off and she turned away from Harry and stared at a point on the far wall where the wallpaper was starting to peel due to damp.

'But?' Harry pressed.

She turned back with cat-like speed and almost spat, 'but, not anymore!'

'I sort of got that impression in the office. Why?'

'None of your business.'

'Will you stop saying that? This is a murder enquiry. Your father's murder. Everything is my business, particularly yours and Grey's and Heart's.'

Angie held his stare for several seconds before returning to gaze at the wallpaper. Harry looked at Carol, but she shook her head as if to indicate that he had said enough and should just wait.

After what seemed an interminable amount of time, Angie turned and asked, 'Any chance of another mint? It helps me concentrate!'

Harry found his packet and gave her one.

'Steve and I used to be really close. A couple of years ago, though, he got put in prison.'

'We know!'

'You do? Oh, well it was all a misunderstanding and I could have got into big trouble, but Steve was cool and helped me out.'

'By going to prison!'

'Yes! I know I should have said something, but I was really young then.'
Carol was always amazed at how young people, of whatever age, could feel so grown up at the age they were, but then refer to a relatively short time before as being 'very young'. The irony, however, was not evident in Angie's tone of voice as she continued, 'By the time Steve had come out, I'd sort of hooked up with Roger. I know it was bad of me, but, well, there were reasons.'
'Which were?'
'Steve's good-looking and everything, but Roger's more...' Angie seemed to be having trouble finding the right words and Harry couldn't tell whether this was because she was trying to hide something, or just because she was still reticent to discuss her private life with the police.
'He's more interesting, I suppose. And he's a really good actor, you know!'
'Yes, I'd noticed.' Carol replied, truthfully.
'This still doesn't explain what was going on in the office.' Harry was starting to tire of the conversation, or was it an interview? He really wanted to return to the hotel, have a long, relaxing bath and then a pleasant evening's dinner in the restaurant. In short, he was on holiday and wanted to get back to enjoying it.
'During rehearsals, Steve kept flirting with me. He's pretty confident in himself and can be very, uh, persuasive.'
'I've noticed that as well,' Carol said.
'You've spoken to Steve already? Then why are you asking me all this? Didn't he tell you what happened?'
Harry threw Carol a glance and she knew immediately that she had given too much away. Her amateur approach to police interrogation procedure had become evident and she just hoped it wouldn't spoil what Harry was trying to accomplish.

'We'd like to hear your side of the story,' Harry replied. 'It's always best to get each person's point of view.'
'Well, Steve can be very persistent and with Roger on stage so much, he had a lot of time to try it on with me. To cut a long story short, he pestered and cajoled and even did a bit of moral blackmail until he broke down my resistance and I, uh, started 'seeing' him again.'
'When?'
'A bit ago.'
'Did your father know?'
'Christ no. He thought I was still going out with Roger and that was bad enough. If he thought I was seeing both of them and that one of them was the person he had put in prison, or whatever you call it, I hate to think what he'd have done.'
Harry thought for a moment before asking, 'I'm sorry to have to ask this, but we keep hearing about your father as if he was some kind of monster. Was he?'
'I..I..I really don't want to say anything bad about him now he's gone. Whatever you've heard is probably only the half of it, though.'
Carol could see the tears beginning to again form in Angie's eyes, so she returned her attention to the love triangle that she had been discussing before. She knew what the answer would be, but she still asked,
'Does Heart, uh, Roger, know about you and Steve?'
'I told him, the day before yesterday.'
'How did he take it?'
'How do you think? He was angry. He was upset. He told me how much he loved me and that he didn't want to lose me.'
Harry thought back to their conversation at Miss. Hubbard's. 'Did he threaten you in any way?'
Angie's reply was sharp and not, altogether, unexpected.

'No, of course not. Listen, I'm feeling really tired, can we leave all this for now?'

'Just one last question and I'm sorry to keep coming back to it.' Harry pressed, 'If you'd got back with Grey and finished with Heart, why the fight in the office last night?'

Angie's eyes were becoming more and more glazed, as she replied, 'Let's just say that Steve doesn't have as much love of County Lines as I do!' And with that, she slumped further back into the cushions and started to quietly laugh again. Carol and Harry both knew what she meant. The threat of drugs to rural communities was becoming a bigger and bigger issue and something that was taking up a considerable amount of police and school time. What perhaps did surprise them was the fact that the 'ex-con' Grey was the one that found Angie's habit uncomfortable; enough presumably to cause the ugly fight that Harry had witnessed the previous night.

'A reasonable explanation, I guess,' murmured Harry.

'Come on then,' said Carol. Let's head back to the hotel and try to relax. This sleuthing takes it out of you, doesn't it?'

'Before we do,' replied Harry, 'take a look at this DVD I found on Lorraine's shelf whilst you were downstairs.' He took it out again and passed it to her. She looked at the cover and grimaced slightly.

"Lingerie Ladies'? Really? Lorraine using it to decide on new stock?'

'A little more than that. Have a look on the back. The pictures are a bit grainy, but the name of one of the 'actresses' gives you a clue.'

'Lorraine *Lovebomb*. No, it can't be. You don't think..?'

'The date would be about right. I reckon that picture, to the bottom left, is a somewhat younger Lorraine Davies, who is still into her lingerie to this day! Made in Soho by the looks of it!'

'Put it back. Quickly. This really is none of our business!'
Harry did so, ensuring it was returned to exactly the same spot on the shelves, but did wonder to himself whether Caz' last statement was absolutely true. He didn't voice these doubts, but instead murmured, 'Almost as if she wanted people to see it, don't you think? Leaving it out on display like this.'
'Perhaps she's proud of it. Maybe that's what got her into acting!'
Angie's continued laughter from the sofa was now joined by Harry's, as he and Carol descended the rickety staircase once more. Nothing was mentioned to Lorraine as she took her coat off from escorting Roger Heart back home and they left the shop in order to return, once more, to their lodgings.

INTERLUDE

CHAPTER 19

'When sorrows come, they come not single spies, But in battalions.' Now why should that line suddenly come to mind? Two deaths now! No sign of the police having a clue about either of them – or, indeed, that the first was in any way linked. No 'sorrows' then! Rather, it feels good that they are now both dead! Justice seems to have been done. Does murder become easier the more one does it? Not sure… yet! There may have to be more… from what has just been said on the phone. Perhaps the police are 'all at sea', but it seems that there is at least one person that might have some suspicions – and that would not be good. Not good at all! Far too astute that one! Definitely not as stupid as they might seem. What had they said again? 'I've worked it out and I think it might be you. What have you got to say for yourself?' Not a lot to say is there? Especially when you know their suspicions are correct.
Dangerous!
For them!
Yes, it's going to be interesting to see how easy - and perhaps habitual - murder can become!

ACT III

*As in a theatre, the eyes of men,
After a well-grac'd actor leaves the stage,
Are idly bent on him that enters next,
Thinking his prattle to be tedious.*

CHAPTER 20

The early morning sunlight began to make the ripples on the water glimmer and sparkle, where the great-crested grebe had just re-emerged from catching her breakfast below the surface. The dawn chorus was almost at an end and shadows were beginning to form, created by the trees at the water's edge and the rising sun. In the distance, a heron glided lazily back to its nest on an island, while a lone fisherman sat in a rowing boat waiting for his first catch of the day.
Harry had not been able to sleep very well – not this time due to Carol waking him in the early hours - so had left her slumbering while he quietly threw on the clothes from the night before and ventured out into the new day. He had hoped that a brisk walk around the town might clear his head somewhat, but, turning the corner of the street near to the old Norman church, he had come across the mere, as it was known locally, which constituted one of the main tourist attractions of Pikesmere. A tourist sign, near to where Harry now sat taking in the beauty of his surroundings, had informed him that there had been a settlement on this site since Saxon times and that legend had it that, during a battle, one of the soldiers defending, what was then a village, from attack had, with his dying breath, thrust his pike into the ground, whereupon water began to gush forth,

drowning the enemy and forming the mere by which the town now stood. A rather less prosaic paragraph informed passing tourists that it had actually been created by glaciers receding at the end of the last Ice Age, well before anyone owned a pike!

However it had been formed, Harry sat and pondered how much more beautiful the scene in front of him seemed to contrast his usual morning journey to work, but how, behind the serene façade of rural England, evil still lurked, needing to be unmasked; and with a somewhat uncharacteristic, egotistical moment, he knew that he was the person to do just that.

He considered what the previous day had brought to light: lovers' arguments, drug abuse, past murders and soft-porn DVDs. What an eclectic mix of oddities and not at all unexpected in a murder enquiry, although strangely, here, in this rural idyll, it all was. What on earth was the motivation behind the gruesome murder that he and Carol had been a party to? He really would have been so much more comfortable back in the city where he thought he knew what was going on and where to start an investigation. Here, he was out of his depth: amateur dramatics, Shakespearean plays, thatched cottages and tree-lined meres. What would another day bring, he wondered?

He began to wend his way back along the somewhat muddy track that circumnavigated the water's edge, continuing to watch the coots and mallards play and the swans gracefully gliding along, when he saw, in the distance, Sergeant Pearson's lumbering form approaching. 'Just what I need before breakfast,' he thought.

Rather out of breath, Pearson began to call to Harry whilst there was still a little distance between the two men. 'Glad I managed to catch up with yow, sir.' The use of the final 'sir' still seemed to grate a little in the sergeant's voice, Harry thought, but he ignored it. 'The receptionist at your 'otel told me that she'd seen yow walking off in the direction of the mere. Chief Inspector Price has been trying to get 'old of yow for a while, but you weren't answering your phone.'

Harry checked his pockets. 'Must have left the damned thing in the hotel room. What's the problem?'

'Best you come and see for yourself, sir. Seems there's been another murder.'

'You're joking.'

'Yow may joke about such things in the big city, sir, but we don't round here.

'Who is it?'

'Mr. Blackwater, that there play's producer.'

'Christ almighty!'

'No need to blaspheme, is there, sir, but it is a bit of a shocker, isn't it?'

Harry ignored the rebuke and his mind started to race ahead of itself. Two murders were never wished for, but it often meant two sets of clues, two lines of enquiry, linking of evidence and suspects. He began to follow Pearson back towards the town, finding the sergeant's pace somewhat lacking in immediacy. 'Where did he die? At home?'

'Yes sir. His cleaner pops in twice a week and she decided to start early today. Found 'im in 'is study and it isn't a pretty sight, I can tell yow. Brenda's in quite a state!'

'Brenda. Is that his wife?'

'The cleaner. Try and keep up, sir.'

Harry ignored the further jibe. 'How long's he been dead?'

Doctor was with him when I came looking for you, sir, but he was still dressed. Not in 'is pyjamas or anything!'

'I see. So might have been there all night.'

'Wouldn't like to hazard a guess, sir. Beyond my pay grade is guessing!'

They had been walking up from the mere, towards the

church, and as they turned a corner, Harry saw a large, imposing Georgian House with several police cars and a forensic van parked outside. Daniel's car was also there and, as they approached, his colleague emerged, talking animatedly to a grey haired, bespectacled man in a tweed jacket which sported leather arm patches. The detective in Harry deduced this to be the aforementioned doctor. Daniel said his goodbyes and hurried over to Harry. 'Where the devil have you been? Never mind! At least my search party was able to find you. Aren't you told about always keeping your phone on you?' He laughed.

'Funny thing is, I had this odd idea that I might be on holiday and not need to be contacted!'

'Yea, yea. Okay! I hope I didn't worry Carol too much when she answered though. She didn't seem to know where you were!'

'Left before she woke up. Thought I might just take a stroll round the local beauty spots before breakfast.'

'Right! Well, I apologise for Blackwater upsetting your early morning ramble. Most inconsiderate of him dying like this! The residents of Pikesmere certainly have a way of spoiling your fun: first the play and now a sightseeing walk! Come on in and take a peek at the corpse before they take him away.'

The two entered the large house, elegantly decorated in a style that matched its eighteenth-century grandeur. In a spacious drawing room off to the left, lit through a large bow window by the rays of the rising sun, an elderly lady sat sobbing, a young police officer trying to tempt her to drink a cup of, no doubt, highly sweetened, tea.

'Brenda, I presume?' asked Harry.

'Yes, poor dear. Not what you want to find as you go about your chores!'

They entered Charles Blackwater's study and Harry could immediately see why Brenda was in such a state of shock.

Not only was her employer dead, but the body, and the desk behind which he sat, immobile and staring, was covered in copious amounts of blood. The amateur producer's neck had been cut, or more accurately slashed, and a large kitchen knife, presumably the culprit, lay, almost innocently, next to the man's hand.

'Whoever did this couldn't have been trying to pretend that he committed suicide, surely?'

Dan shook his head. 'I don't think so. I reckon he, or she, is so callous and sure of themselves that they just killed him in cold blood and then left the knife because it had fulfilled its purpose. No more, no less!'

'Killed last night?'

'That's what the doc reckons. Body's cold and so on. That's who I was talking to when you arrived.'

'I sort of guessed.'

'Tweed jacket a giveaway?'

'That's the one!'

'Anyway,' Daniel continued, 'he obviously couldn't be precise – they never want to commit themselves, of course – but he thought late yesterday evening was about right, maybe after about 9 or 10.'

'And the knife'

'Forensics will make sure, but there's a rack of exact same handled ones in the kitchen, one of which is absent. They're those sort that are magnetic and you can just grab the one you want off the strip attached to the wall.'

'No sign of a break in?'

'None whatsoever. Again, everything's being checked, but I'd bet on whoever did it being invited in. The front door's a Yale lock, so they'd just have been able to leave afterwards and pull the door closed behind them.'

Harry thought for a moment. 'Bit dangerous. They'd be able to be caught on CCTV leaving the premises!'

Dan let out a short guffaw. 'Harry, mate, this is Pikesmere, not Moss Side! There might be one or two shops with cameras and a couple near the main square, but nothing round here. No, whoever did this knew what they could and couldn't do. And the fact that they must have been invited in..'

'Implies pretty strongly that they were known to Blackwater.'

'That and the fact that he was the play's producer strongly suggests a link to the previous murder.'

'Indeed!'

'What did Blackwater do? Before he retired, I mean. This is a big house to be living in all by himself and it's been kept very well.'

'He used to be a doctor. GP I think, but not local. I'll find out more and let you know anything that might be pertinent to the case.'

'Where's the kitchen?'

'Through here.' Daniel took Harry out of the blood splattered study, down a small step and into a large, modern kitchen with an island set in the middle of the room where two half empty wine glasses sat, one white and the other red.

Harry glanced at the glasses and then over to the kitchen knives where a glaring space made it fairly obvious where the instrument of death had come from.

'So,' said Harry, 'not just known to Blackwater, but friendly enough to have been offered a drink and to have sat chatting while partaking. They talk, drink and then Blackwater suggests they go through to his study. He leads the way and, while his back is turned to exit, the murderer quietly takes the knife off the wall and follows.'

'That's what all the clues seem to indicate.'

'The use of his own kitchen knife might suggest that it wasn't premeditated though?'

Daniel nodded. 'That thought had crossed my mind, but the

links to the previous crime would tend to preclude that. I had an idea about that, however.'
'I thought you might.'
'If they did know each other – and, seemingly, quite well - the killer would possibly be well aware that there were knives readily available in the house and have planned from the outset on using one of them, making it impossible to trace the murder weapon back to them.
'Very clever!'
'Oh yes! We're dealing with a vicious, almost sadistic, murderer, who know exactly what they are doing and how to cover their tracks. Think about the death at the play: no one around and yet everyone is nearby and anyone could have done it. As you say, two very clever murders!'
'What do you reckon? Man, or a woman? What's your gut telling you?'
'Nothing at this time. Could easily be either. Both killings were done with a very sharp blade which can do the deed without vast amounts of force.'
'Thought you might say that! I was thinking pretty much the same thing. Anything else I need to see. I'm starving and they stop serving breakfast at ten.'
'Really? After seeing that body?'
'First rule of detective work, Dan, mate: never work on an empty stomach. Stops the 'little grey cells' from working, as Hercule might say.'
'The Greek bloke?'
'No, the Belgian! Caz got me reading a couple of his novels.'
'Oh, he's a writer, is he?'
'Philistine! I'll see you later. I better go and bring Caz up to speed.' Harry started to head for the door.
'Plans for today? Another walk round the mere?'
'Thought I might salve my immortal soul and see the vicar.'
'Good call. I'll keep you up to date with anything I turn up.'

'Likewise! See you later.' He left the charnel house that had once been Charles Blackwater's beautiful home and headed back for what he felt would be a well-earned full English and further revelations to tell Caz.

CHAPTER 21

Carol had already eaten breakfast when Harry returned to the hotel, but she offered to join him and watch him tuck into a hearty meal of bacon, sausage, fried eggs, mushrooms and toast, whilst he explained everything that had happened that morning. At the end of his lengthy narrative, Carol sat back in her chair, exhaled audibly and watched Harry devour the last triangle of toast. She mused on what she had heard and then asked the question that neither policeman had considered.
'Why did they stop drinking their wine, leave half in their glasses, and move to the study?'
Harry pondered this for a moment. 'Who can tell?' he finally replied, having been unable to come up with any answer that would be useful. 'Do you think it might be relevant?'
'Don't you? What do you normally do when you're having a chat with a mate over a pint? Stop halfway through and then just leave it, or finish it off before you move on?'
'Finish it off; and several more, probably, before even considering moving.'
'Exactly. So, what was so important that they left to go into the study? Why didn't they take their glasses with them?'
'Because they thought they were only going to be a short time?'
'Possibly, but then Blackwater would probably have just told

them to stay put while he fetched whatever it was in the study that was important.'

'So, what else might it be? You've obviously got something in mind.'

'I reckon they were having an argument. Obviously not at the start – you don't open two bottles of wine, white and red, if you've already started rowing – but during the conversation in the kitchen. The killer argues about something and Blackwater says that he can prove his point with evidence in the study. The wine is forgotten and they make their way to look at whatever it is Blackwater has.'

Harry again mused over what Carol was suggesting. Eventually, as he wiped the last crumbs of toast from his lips, he said, 'I think you're probably right, but I'm not sure that it gets us very far. The killer, whoever he, or she, might be, presumably would have taken whatever incriminating evidence they were being shown and disposed of it. We're no closer to knowing anything new.'

'But you said Blackwater was a doctor: an intelligent chap who liked to ensure his home was clean and tidy. Someone used to keeping records and with an orderly mind. Surely, he wouldn't just have one copy of whatever it was he was arguing over? Not if it was something he thought might be important. Surely, he would have another hidden away somewhere?'

'I reckon you're right again.'

'I usually am!'

'We'll nip back up to the room. I'll message Dan to get on to trying to chase up any hidden files that Blackwater may have had and then take a quick shower before we head off to the vicarage.'

'Vicarage? Are we planning on getting hitched?'

'You wish!'

'I don't, actually. Not until you've had a shower, anyway.'

'No, we're going to have a chat with the Reverend Brown. He played the king in the play, didn't he?'
'Oh yes. Claudius! "The play's the thing, wherein I'll catch the conscience of the king".'
Harry looked confused. 'What play?'
'Were you taking any notice of 'Hamlet' the other night?'
'Some.'
'You sound like one of my GCSE students that has been caught gazing out the window instead of listening in class!'
'As if I'd ever dare to do that in your lessons!'
'In the play of "Hamlet", young Hamlet finds out from his father, old Hamlet, that..'
'That's a heck of a lot of Hamlets in one sentence.'
'Just pay attention! His father is called Old Hamlet and..'
'That was the ghost. I remember that bit.'
'Good boy! You were paying some attention then. And what did the ghost tell his son?'
Harry groped for an answer. 'He had to leave because it was getting light?'
'Before that! He tells Hamlet that he had been murdered in a garden!'
'Yes?'
'By his brother!'
'Yes?'
Carol's look was one of exasperation. 'His brother, Claudius! In the play, Claudius is a murderer. The first murderer: the crime committed even before the play has begun. He's so power hungry that he's been willing to kill his own brother, steal the crown and marry his sister-in-law!'
'So, Charles Blackwater decided that the local vicar would play this blood-thirsty character really well? Interesting! You are definitely firing on all cylinders this morning.'
'Thanks, I think! Claudius even goes off to pray at one point because he says the killing of his brother is 'the primal

eldest curse'.'
'You going to enlighten me as to what that means?'
'It goes back to Cain murdering Abel.'
'Right!' Harry looked at Carol as if to plead for just a little more.
'In the bible! It's supposedly the first recorded murder: Cain kills his brother Abel.'
Realisation spread across Harry's face at last, as a moment of epiphany dawned. 'So, Blackwater, as producer, gave the part of this brother killer to the local vicar knowing the character used biblical references, but maybe, also, because he knew something about him that may have been the basis of the argument last night?'
'It's a big jump, I know.'
'Sometimes those jumps are the things that solve a crime.'
'Doesn't really help with King's death, though, does it?'
'No! But that may emerge when we get to the vicarage. Let's head up to the room. I definitely need that shower!'
It was only a short walk to the vicarage, but the final part of the journey was up a steep, high-walled street which ran alongside the ancient graveyard that surrounded the church. It was a beautiful, warm, sun-drenched day that showed off the town in all its Spring glory: a far cry from the rain and showers of previous days. Carol, ever the English teacher, had remarked, as they strolled along, that had this been in a novel, the weather would have been cold and dreary, in sympathy with the deaths that had occurred. Pathetic fallacy she'd have taught her students! A background that sympathises with the developing tragedy. Harry listened, relatively attentively, but his mind was on the next round of interviews and the need to solve these murders before there were any more. As they reached the top of the road, two large stone pillars and open, iron gates marked the entrance to the vicarage.

'Wow,' was all that Carol could muster as they stared up the short drive to the house. Actually, 'mansion' might have been a better word for it: three-stories high and built in red brick, with numerous windows that indicated the large number of rooms that were contained within.

'Ever fancied becoming a vicar, Harry?' Carol asked, as they crunched their way up the long, winding, gravel drive. 'I could get used to living in a place like this, if these were the perks of the job!'

'Somehow, I don't think I would be the sort of person they'd want to ordain, let alone get given a parish like this!'

As they continued to muse over alternate career paths, they heard whistling coming from their left and saw ladders leaning against the side of the house and the local window cleaner attempting to reach up to some of the higher ledges.

'Mr. Cross, isn't it?' Harry called up.

'Yeah! That's right! Who wants to know? Oh, wait a minute! You were at the play the other night when old King snuffed it, weren't you?'

'Murdered, Mr. Cross,' Harry retorted, 'and I'm helping to look into that crime, along with certain other events.'

'Blackwater's murder, eh?'

'And how might you come to know about that?'

'News travels fast in a small town. Can't hide nothing round here.'

'They certainly liked their double negatives as well,' Carol thought.

'I'd prefer not to have to keep up this conversation with a crick in my neck,' Harry shouted. 'Any chance you might come down the ladder and continue this on the ground?'

'Can't see why not. Time for a cuppa, anyway. Mike said he'd put the kettle on a while ago!' Andrew Cross began to descend his ladder, making sure that his bucket and sponges did not tip as he did so. He was obviously adept at

his job and was soon down and facing Carol and Harry.
'Always bring your missus on interviews, do you guv? Not that I mind, of course!'
'I am not his 'missus' if *you* don't mind,' Carol interjected before Harry could reply, 'and we're only here for a pleasant little chat, isn't that right, *dear*?' She looked over to Harry and he recognised that she had very quickly ascertained that Cross was the sort of character that would respond to more gentle questioning than full on interviewing. He looked to be in his late twenties or early thirties and held a lazy stance in front of them that seemed to confirm that he would not be intimidated into revealing anything he didn't want to disclose if put under pressure. However, if a nice chat over a cup of tea was on offer, then possibly plenty of juicy gossip might be forthcoming. Window cleaners hear and see a lot as they move from house to house and Carol was sure that, with the right sort of persuasion, some useful morsels of information may well come their way.
'Now then,' said Harry, trying to sound at his friendliest, 'just remind me of what you were doing in the play and where you were at the time Mr King was stabbed.'
'Laertes, Ophelia's brother, and I was in France when the 'wicked deed' occurred.' He gave a wry smile, as Harry turned to Carol for some clarity.
'Early on in the play, Laertes "begs leave" to go back to France and doesn't return until after his father is dead and his sister has gone mad.'
Cross looked impressed. 'Now I see why she's with you for these 'chats'. A very good summary of what I do. A bit at the start and a bit at the end, that's my character in a nutshell.'
'So,' Harry continued, 'you had a lot of spare time to get around behind the carpet..'
'Arras,' Carol reminded him.
'Arras.. and murder Derek King!'

'Yes I did, but no I didn't.'
'Sorry,' both Harry and Carol said in unison.
'Yes, I did have the time to do it, but no, that's not what I did. I was in the lady's dressing room at the time, if you must know, behind the stage.
'What on earth were you doing in there?' Carol asked.
'Wouldn't you like to know?'
'Yes, we would,' Harry pressed.
'Well, perhaps Mike here will enlighten you. They turned to see Reverend Brown coming round the corner of the vicarage with two mugs of tea in his hands.
'Oh, I'd have brewed extra if I'd known we had visitors. Mr. Bailey, isn't it? And you must be his charming…?
'Carol. You can call me Carol, reverend.'
'Of course. I didn't mean to make you feel uncomfortable. Many of my parishioners would still be shocked, even in this day and age, to learn that you were sharing a hotel room 'out of wedlock', but I'd like to think that I do not harbour any such antiquated thoughts, other than to consider what a lovely couple you seem to be.'
'Thank you, I think,' murmured Carol.
Harry attempted to pick up the threads of the previous conversation. 'Mr. Cross here seems to think that you might be able to explain why he was in the lady's dressing room at the time of Mr. King's murder. Is that right?'
'Oh yes. Most certainly. He and I were having a little drop of the hard stuff together. We both realised that there was a brief period of the play when neither of us was on for a while and that a little Dutch courage would help us to get through to the end of the production.'
'So, each of you can vouch for the other when the crime took place?'
Reverend Brown looked over to Cross, smiled and replied, 'it would seem so.'

'Can anyone else corroborate what you are saying? Any of the ladies that might have more plausibly been in their own dressing room?'
'Come, come now detective. Don't say it like that. 'Hamlet' is a play with a lot of male characters and very few females. We didn't want to be seen drinking backstage, so went into the empty dressing room: Lorraine was on stage as Gertrude and poor Miss King was elsewhere, getting her make-up redone ready for Ophelia's mad scene probably. So no, we were alone in our secret, alcoholic assignation. Now, before you ask any more questions, why don't I invite you into the vicarage and we can take the weight off our feet? I'll brew some more tea, or maybe I could even entice you to partake of the demon drink. A small sherry before midday, perhaps?'

CHAPTER 22

'Cream sherry alright? Or I think I may have an Amontillado hidden away somewhere?'
'Tea will be fine, thank you reverend. But, before you do that, can we go back to the night of the murder?'
The three of them had been shown into the sunlit drawing room that overlooked the magnificent old church and, slightly further into the distance, the mere, where Harry's day had started somewhat more peacefully. Much of the furniture in the room seemed to be almost as old as the vicarage itself and both Carol and Harry had the same feeling that they were in one of those National Trust properties where there should be roped off sections everywhere and signs saying not to sit on the chairs or

chaise-longue, of which there happened to be one. Instead, the vicar had offered them a plush, well-cushioned sofa, whilst he ensconced himself in a nearby armchair. Just behind him, a bookcase indicated an eclectic mix of reading material, ranging from classics to what looked like a set of early publication Ian Fleming novels and a few science fictions. Not a bible or ecclesiastical text in sight, Harry mused, as he scanned the room for any signs of religious iconography. It seemed totally bereft of anything that might suggest the house was a vicarage at all!

'But which night and which murder, Harry? Do you mind if I call you Harry? When talking with anyone, I do so like to be on first name terms. It does, I think, make any conversation more relaxed, don't you think?'

Harry was not so sure of that, but let it pass for the time being. 'Harry's fine. Let's stick with the night of the play and King's death for the time being, shall we?'

'As you wish. But I'm not sure I can tell you much more than we discussed outside. Andrew, uh, Mr Cross, and I were in the dressing room. He'd got a hip flask and we were having a little chat whilst imbibing, when we heard the commotion and thought we better see what had happened. We came out of the dressing room, along the corridor that runs around the back of the stage and nearly knocked Stew Manning off his stepladders. Most of the rest of the cast were milling around by then and, at that moment, you burst through the curtains!'

'Was Angie one of those 'milling' around?' Carol asked.

'No, I don't think she was. I seem to recall her entering a little later.'

'Yes. That tallies with what I seem to remember happening,' Harry said, but he knew that it would have still been easy enough for her to have murdered her own father and then feigned a late entrance. None of it helped! He decided to press a little more. 'And you're positive that neither you, nor Mr. Cross left the dressing room in the minutes leading up to the body being discovered?'

'Not that I can.. Oh, wait a moment. Andrew did pop to get his script from the men's changing room at one point. He wanted to check a couple of the lines in the later scenes. But he was only gone for a moment or two.'

'Long enough to slide a dagger into someone and then get back?'

'Harry, please! I've known Andy for a few years now. He had moved here a year or so before I was sent to this parish. He wouldn't..'

'I didn't necessarily mean Mr. Cross,' harry interrupted. The same applies to you, reverend. You could have slipped back onto the stage whilst he was out 'looking for his script' and got back before he returned.'

'Yes, I suppose I could. However, as a man of the cloth, I prefer to nourish the soul in life rather than condemn it to the flames.'

'You think Mr. King will be in Hell?' Carol asked, a little shocked. 'I wasn't sure the Church of England still believed in such things!'

'Oh, I fear Derek King's soul will be in torment even as we speak. He was one of foulest human beings I have ever had the misfortune to call a parishioner and there are many who will be glad to see him out of their lives. As to the teachings of my church, let's just say that Hell can take many forms and it is only to be hoped that it still exists for some!'

'You've shocked me, reverend, I must say,' Harry said, expressing what Carol was sensing, 'and the strength of your feelings may make me wonder at how far you might, yourself, go to ridding the world of such a person.'

' "Thou shalt not kill", Harry, but also, "Thou shalt not bear false witness". My faith precludes me from murder just as much as it stops me from lying about the depths of my distaste. I hate myself for feeling that way towards another human being, but I do feel that way, nonetheless!'

'Thanks for the cuppa, Mike. I've left the mug on the side.'

'Mr. Cross. Another quick word if we may?' Harry asked, as the window cleaner entered the room.

'Of course, guv. Just remember, though, this house has got one hell of a lot of windows.'

'There's a lot of Satanic imagery around this morning!' Carol murmured. 'Some stronger than others.'

'We won't keep you too long.' Harry stated. 'We just wanted to clear up a little detail that the reverend here has just mentioned.'

'Oh yes. And what might that be?'

Did Andrew Cross show an ever so slight moment of doubt as he looked over at Brown? Carol seemed to think so and she reckoned that Harry would definitely have noticed it if she had!

'Apparently, at some point before Mr. King's death, you left Reverend Brown alone whilst you went to get your script?'

'Did I? I can't remember. Oh, yes, you're right, I did. I've got a longish speech in Act Five and I wanted to check whether I said "Whose reason is the case" or "Whose motive" when I talk to Hamlet. It's 'motive' by the way.'

He had recovered his poise almost immediately, but that moment was enough to make both Harry and Carol cautious as to how much of what the young man was saying was actually the truth.

'How long would you say you were out of the dressing room?' Harry asked.

'Not sure really. When I got to the men's changing room, it was an absolute tip – as usual! Clothes piled up everywhere and my script had been moved from where I left it. Probably took me about a minute to find it. Maybe a bit longer.'

Or, thought Carol, it was where you left it and that gave you enough time to get to the arras and back. This detective work was a lot harder than it looked and her respect for Harry went up just a little, even though she would never admit it!

'When you got back, was Reverend Brown here still in the ladies' changing room?'

'Yes, just where I left him.'

Which proved nothing, Harry thought, other than the fact that, as he had thought, either of them could have done it; or even have both been involved and were covering for each other's involvement. He decided to move on.

'Let's talk about last night. About 'Ninish' onwards. Where were you both? Mr. Cross, you first; then I can let you get back to your windows.'

'I was in the pub - as usual.'

'Which one? I've seen a couple around the town.'

'The Lion. It's the one down by The Green. Near to the stocks. Ask anyone in there. They'll all vouch that I was there.'

'Do you think you need vouching for?' Harry asked.

'Do you? I'm not used to being accused of murder, you know Guv!'

'No one's accusing you of anything, at the moment. We're just trying to sort out who was where. Now, were you there all evening, until closing?'

'Left about 10, I reckon. Maybe a bit after.'

'Did you leave with anyone?' Carol asked.

'No, just me. So, no alibi after that. Went straight home. I try to get up about 7 and start my round early on you see.'

'Thank you,' Harry said. 'That'll be all for the time being. We'll let you get back up your ladder!'

Andrew Cross gave another look across to the vicar who had remained still and silent throughout the exchange; he

then left. Harry turned back to Brown.
'Can we turn again to what you were saying about Mr. King? What exactly had he done to infuriate you so much? It must have been pretty awful to make the local vicar feel so angry?'
'I'm not sure how detailed I can be, Harry. Quite a lot of the things I have been told are covered by my beliefs in confidentiality between parishioner and minister.'
'Yes, but Mr. King is dead, as I'm sure I do not need to remind you.'
'Indeed he is. But it is some that are still alive to whom I refer.'
'His daughter by any chance?' Carol asked.
'You are very astute, Carol, but I couldn't possibly comment.'
'Look,' Harry interjected, 'you're not a Roman Catholic priest. I presume there are no confessional boxes in that church over there.'
'Harry!' Carol could see that Reverend Brown had given him a withering stare.
'It's alright Carol,' Brown continued, his composure reinstalled, 'often it is difficult to appreciate the nuances of faith if you are a layperson.'
'Or a heathen!' suggested Carol.
'Surely not!' replied the vicar. 'It is true, Harry, that you will not find any confessional boxes in my church, but Anglicans can still make their 'confessions' whilst kneeling at the altar rail. In essence, they are confessing to God, not to me. They can discuss their worries, doubts, anxieties and, yes, their sins, but forgiveness comes from the divine, not from me. Even so, what has been said in my hearing, over there at the altar, is still not open for me to discuss with you.'
'Very well, vicar, let's try a more circuitous route.'
'If you wish, but you won't change my mind over my

responsibilities.'

'You've made that crystal clear, but let's just suppose that the daughter of Mr. X had spoken to you about her father, what might Miss Y have been worried about?'

'Suffice it to say that Miss Y might often have spoken to me about her father, but not solely her father. Other men might well have been the cause of her anxieties and more! Now, that is all I shall say on the matter, except..'

There was a slight gleam in the reverend's eye thought Carol.

'Except?' asked Harry, leaning forward for what he hoped might be a nugget of information.

'To change the subject entirely: Hamlet is a very complex character, wouldn't you agree Carol? Multi-faceted? Prone to long periods of melancholy and introspection.'

'Most certainly,' agreed Carol. 'But also, great violence and passion when aroused.'

'Indeed he is. An incredible character!'

'And a character played very effectively by Roger Heart!' stated Carol, slowly.

'Oh, I'm not a theatre critic. I couldn't possibly say.'

Harry had to admit to himself that the man of God sat in front of him was a very confusing character. On the one hand, he seemed the epitome of a modern vicar, forward-thinking and a reader of Isaac Asimov rather than the Good Book. On the other, he had been talking about the fire and brimstone of eternal damnation and making confessions to the Almighty. He decided to move on.

'Thank you, Reverend Brown. That has been most enlightening.' Harry said. 'Now, same question to you as I asked Mr. Cross earlier. Last night, about nine: What were you doing?'

'I was working on my sermon until about quarter to and then Mrs. Wilson, one of the old dears that helps with the flowers for the church, phoned and, once she starts on about her delphiniums, she never stops. I probably finished talking to her about half an hour later and..'

'That's a long time to discuss delphiniums!' Carol suggested.

'As I say, she does like to go through the minutiae of floral arrangements. After that, I watched a bit of television and then went to bed to read a chapter or two.'

'Old or New Testament?' Harry enquired.

'Harry Potter, actually. Still trying to plough through the last couple of books!'

'So, no alibi either, after about nine-fifteen?'

'I'm afraid not. The problem is that one never knows when someone might need one, does one?'

'How very true, reverend; how very true! Anyway, we'll leave you in peace.'

'But you never got to have your tea!'

'Another time, perhaps.'

Harry went to stand, but Carol remained seated.

'May I ask you something? Completely different line of thought,' she said.

'Of course, Carol. Anything at all.'

'How did you come to play Claudius in the production? I was telling Harry about the character earlier and just wondered about what made Blackwater think you were right for the part.'

'Funny you should say. He didn't at first! I was pencilled in, at the first read through, to play Derek King's eventual role, Polonius; he was going to do Claudius.'

Carol was intrigued. 'So, what happened?'

'Well, I shouldn't like to blow my own trumpet, but King wasn't the best at the first read through. He was alright when we did pantomimes and so on, but getting to grips with Shakespeare's blank verse caused him a few problems.'

'Blank verse?' Harry asked.

'I'll explain later,' said Carol, knowing that could be a very long conversation.

'That was one issue. There was something else though!'

'Yes?'

'Charles had a quiet word with me a day or two later. Said that he'd been chatting with a couple of the society's members and they were unanimous in thinking that I should play Claudius because of the number of scenes the character had to do with Hamlet. Do you begin to get my drift?'

'I think I do,' said Carol. 'King and Roger Heart were not seeing eye to eye over Angie and putting them together for rehearsals could be rather difficult.'

'Exactly! That isn't to say that my acting ability didn't have a large part in the decision-making process, but other factors did have to be considered.'

'Not to blow your own trumpet, of course,' murmured Harry.

'Indeed,' retorted the vicar, somewhat testily.

Carol began to explain the number of scenes that Claudius had to do with Hamlet and Harry saw just what the problems might have been. 'Polonius,' Carol concluded, 'really only has one main scene with Hamlet and their dislike for one another off-stage would have only helped with the portrayal. I'm beginning to think that Blackwater might have actually known what he was doing.'

Before Harry could speak, Reverend Brown interjected. 'Oh, he did. He really did! He was a wonderful addition to our society. He'll be a great loss to the Arts in the area.'

This time, Carol rose, along with Harry, and, thanking the vicar for his hospitality and time, they made their way back down the hill towards the centre of the town, unsure as to whether the morning's questions had thrown up anything of value, or had, otherwise, been a complete waste of their time.

CHAPTER 23

'So, our reverend suspects Roger Heart of being prone to violence and possibly murderous intent,' Carol said, as they got far enough away from the vicarage not to be overheard by the window cleaning Cross, or anyone else.
'That was the implication,' replied Harry, 'but a word of warning. Suspects can often throw shade onto somebody else in the hopes of taking the spotlight off them. Angie may well have said something to him about Heart, but she might equally have not; and because it was done in the way it was, there's no way of verifying any of it.'
'We could ask Angie.'
'Yes, but she might have other motives as well and therefore be an unreliable witness. This is the big problem with what I do: you lose trust in everything that anybody tells you.'
'I hope you trust me.'
'Of course. You were sat with me. You can't be a suspect!'
'Thanks a bunch,' said Carol and she punched Harry on the shoulder.
'However, I did go out shortly before the murder, so you could have crept round the back and done it!' He laughed and received a somewhat harder punch to the shoulder.
'Come on. Let's go and browse some lingerie.'
'It's no good feeling frisky when you've offended me,' Carol joked.
'Shame! But I would like another little chat with Lorraine.'
'But, like me, she couldn't have done the murder. She had

been speaking to King earlier in the scene, before he hid behind the arras, and she stayed on stage with Hamlet until the body was discovered. She's one of the very few people who absolutely couldn't have done it.'

'That's very true, but it doesn't mean that she hasn't got some vital information to impart. The innocent can be just as useful as the guilty!'

They retraced their steps from a day earlier, passing the stocks on The Green and the family run chemists. Steve Grey was still working on the MG as they passed the garage and headed towards 'Lorraine's Lingerie and Linen.' The small, hand drawn poster, for the production of 'Hamlet', still sat in the window of the door, but a strip of fluorescent paper was now emblazoned across it stating: 'Postponed until further notice.'

'Only postponed,' queried Harry. 'Surely cancelled?'

They entered and, as the little bell above the door finished marking their arrival, Lorraine Davies again emerged from her office up the steps and beyond the iron railings. Immediately, Harry noticed that the acrid aroma of Lorraine's perfume was not as pungent as on the two, previous occasions that they had visited the shop and, as the owner descended the short flight of steps to the ground level, her dress was slightly more conservative and altogether less obscene; almost sober.

'If you've come to speak with Angie, she's gone home. There's nobody here except me.'

'That's great,' said Harry, 'because that's just who we've come here to see.'

'Oh, right,' replied Lorraine, a little taken aback, Carol considered. 'I thought you'd made it clear on your last visit that you didn't want to talk to me. I was on stage at the time it all happened. You were there. You were watching me. I couldn't have done it.'

'It's alright. Don't get so worried,' Carol said. 'We're just here to get a bit more background on what might have been going on before the death.'

Lorraine looked relieved and leant against the counter, attempting to strike a relaxed, but slightly provocative pose. 'How can I help you then?' Her eyes stayed fixed on Harry, even though it had been Carol speaking, and the old, in both senses of the word, flirtatious Lorraine returned. Now why, Harry thought, had she so wanted to be interviewed before, but not so much now. Something must have happened to change her mind. Something to do with King's death on stage, or Charles Blackwater's the previous evening? Whatever it was, it had shaken her.

'Harry!' Carol whispered, 'Are you going to ask Ms. Davies some questions?'

Harry realised that he must have been staring at Lorraine whilst he mused about her change in personality and this had only encouraged her to change her position further and allow the conservative skirt to ride up a little more. Definitely on purpose, he realised!

'Sorry,' Harry said eventually, 'We were just wondering whether you could enlighten us a little more on the relationship between Derek King and his daughter. You're obviously close, to Angie, that is, and we witnessed the way in which you dealt with her father's rather public altercation with Roger Heart in the shop when we visited for the tickets.'

'As I told you before, I think all of us were rooting for Angie and Roger. Derek could be, how shall I put this, rather forceful in his paternal duties. I don't know whether you remember Scene 3 of the first Act of 'Hamlet', but Polonius is rather heartless when telling Ophelia not to continue her relationship with the prince. Several of us remarked that Charlie had an easy time rehearsing that scene because Polonius' speeches mirrored King's own feelings towards

Angie and Roger. And he could be physically rough as well!'
'In what way? Surely not with his own daughter?' Carol asked.
'I really shouldn't be speaking ill of the dead, but she's been in here once or twice to buy tops and I've seen some nasty bruises on her arm which looked very much like finger marks. One rehearsal, Charlie even had to step in to make the scene I've just been talking about a little less physical. He didn't think Polonius would grab Ophelia quite as harshly as King was portraying him!'
'That's horrible,' said Carol, forgetting that they were supposed to stay dispassionate during interviews.
Harry continued. 'Were you sure that it was King that had caused the bruising?'
'That's certainly what Angie suggested, although she would never come out and directly say it. To be fair, I guess it must be hard being a father and bringing up a daughter without her mother.'
'What happened to Angie's mother?'
'Not entirely sure. They didn't live round here, but I know that she's dead. Angie and Derek both told me that on different occasions. Neither elaborated! The mother's never turned up and something in the way King spoke of her certainly seemed to imply that she wouldn't be any time soon.' It was clear that Lorraine was unaware of the mother's murder and it was not their place to reveal that fact.
'So, what will happen to Angie now? I presume she'll inherit the house where they've been living?'
'Oh yes! And the rest! Has nobody told you yet?' Lorraine's eyes sparkled as she held Harry's attention with something juicy that she could disclose to him. 'Angie King will be a very wealthy woman. When King left the armed services, he invested heavily in land somewhere down south, relatively

close to London. It became very sought after once the M25 had been built, as commuter belt. He made a small fortune and continued to reinvest a lot of it. I'm not sure how much she'll get, but Angie once said it would be like a big win on the lottery, so I assume it will be in the millions!'

Harry gave out a long whistle and thought about what sort of motive that might give to either Angie King, Roger Heart, or both. 'That has been incredibly useful, Ms Davies. Thank you for being so candid in your responses. Just one more thing; I noticed your poster for the play says it has been postponed. Surely you mean cancelled in light of both King and Blackwater's deaths? You had heard about what happened to Charles Blackwater, I presume?'

'Yes, poor Charlie. That's a much bigger shock than the loss of Derek King. Charles Blackwater has turned our little band of thespians from a disorganised group of pantomime players into a society that was having a go at 'Hamlet'. We couldn't have done any of it without his drive or passion. Okay, he could be a bit full of himself at times and storm out of rehearsals if it wasn't going as well as he wished, but he was really making a difference!'

'Unlike Derek King?' Carol suggested.

'Oh, he had his moments too, but, yes, I suppose you're right; we can continue without him rather more easily than without Charlie.'

'And the term, postponement?' Harry asked again.

'That was Charlie's idea. He'd had a word with Stew Manning, our stage manager, to see if he'd be willing to go on as Polonius, in a sort of tribute performance. He just didn't want to see all our hard work go down the drain over Derek's death. I'm guessing it will now and I'll soon be changing the sign to 'cancelled'!'

'Interesting!' Harry said. 'Well, thank you again for your help.'

Lorraine's eye lashes fluttered. 'Anytime I can be of help, just pop in. Anytime at all'

INTERLUDE

CHAPTER 24

Well, there was certainly a lot more blood this time around. Good choice of knife though: cut across the throat very nicely. The wine was nice as well, good quality, not cheap plonk! It was pleasant to have a bit of a chat before the deed. He seemed a bit surprised that his call had led to such a quick meeting. Looked really shocked when he opened the door. Should have kept it locked and just gone to bed! Bet he was even more surprised that the problem was resolved so quickly, though! The look on his face! But what did he think was going to happen? Threatening me: most unedifying and the egotistical way in which he started to congratulate himself for working it out didn't go down too well at all.

'Foul deeds will rise,

Though all the earth o'erwhelm them to men's eyes.'

Let's hope not. There's probably going to be more 'foul deeds' before this is over and it would be such a shame to be found out too early. Funny how these quotes from 'Hamlet' keep coming to mind. Clever chap that Shakespeare: words for any occasion, especially murder!

CHAPTER 25

As Carol and Harry emerged from Lorraine's shop, Carol turned to walk back towards The Green, but Harry stopped her.
'Fancy a look around the garden centre?'
'Last time I was at home, our flat hadn't got a garden!' she joked.
'True! But I presume that the brightly coloured sign up the road suggests that it belongs to Stew Manning, the stage manager, and he's someone we haven't had much chance to chat with yet.'
'Lead on Macduff,' Carol replied.
'Another line from "Hamlet"?'
' "Macbeth" actually, but we'll make a Shakespeare scholar of you yet!'
They began to walk up the street towards the large building that the sign declared was 'Manning's Horticultural and Agricultural Supplies'. It consisted of what, for Pikesmere at least, looked a pretty modern, central brick building with, to either side, large glass conservatories which seemed to house a variety of plants and small trees. The automatic doors swished open as Harry and Carol approached, and they entered a world of compost bags, pet food, kitchenware, bathroom fittings and, oddly, a few racks of books, which Harry wondered at, until he realised that they were entirely devoted to making your garden more beautiful.
'What an eclectic mix of items,' mused Carol. 'I guess he tries to cater to all the needs that are not provided for by the other, smaller shops in the town.'
'Yes! Quite the entrepreneur I would say. Now let's see if we can find the man in question.'
They started to make their way along an aisle lined with toys for cats and dogs, items to put in your aquarium and

hamster wheels. A young girl, with a nametag indicating that her name was Mandy, was restacking a section of the shelves and Harry asked if the manager was available to chat to.

'If you've still got the receipt, you can exchange the item, or get your money back, at one of the checkouts.'

'No, you misunderstand,' countered Carol, 'we haven't brought anything back to exchange. We just want to have a chat with Mr. Manning.'

'I think he's free at the moment.' Mandy replied, 'I haven't seen him take anyone through to his private office yet today, so I guess he must be. Makes a change!'

Before the girl could continue, a loud booming voice from the end of the aisle made the assistant jump and Carol and Harry to turn quickly around. Filling most of the end of the row of squeaky toys, was the almost comically tall, yet slightly rotund, figure of Stewart, 'Stew', Manning, dressed in a three-piece suit that was finding itself difficult to stay buttoned up, his tie also seemed to be struggling to hold his neck inside his shirt.

'Call me Stew! Everybody does!' he continued to boom. 'Let's go to my office if you fancy a chat.'

He led them through several more aisles of taps and pipe fittings, cutlery and cleaning products and eventually emerged by a door marked 'Private'. He ushered them through it, closing the door firmly behind them, down a corridor and through into another room which was remarkably plush: the carpet was a relatively thick pile, the walls were wood panelled halfway up and various paintings hung above this with scenes of the countryside, a herd of cows grazing, and a fly fisherman stood in the middle of a river. Manning manoeuvred himself to behind his desk, rather like a tanker attempting to make port and indicated that they should sit on the other side.

'So, what can I do for you? Is it about the murder at the play, or Charlie Blackwater last night? Not sure I can be much help with the latter, but fire away.'
'Thank you,' said Harry, 'I'm..'
'You're the chap who got things moving at the show, the night of King's demise. I know. I remember you coming up onto the stage. Very professional if I may say so.'
'Thanks, again. We're helping the lead detective with some questioning if you've got a few minutes to spare. I realise you must be a busy man with all this to keep going.'
'Runs itself! Almost!' he replied, self-deprecatingly. 'Been here about four years now. Started as a small pet shop and grown to what you see now. Quite a journey.'
'Impressive,' stated Carol. 'Have you always been in retail?'
'Pretty much.'
'Round here?'
'No! Travelled wherever the opportunities arose. Never had the urge to settle down you see. No ties. No wifey to make a home with. Like I say, though, this has been a dream project of mine and I think I'll probably stay around here now. Getting on a bit, so it's nice to grow some roots as you get older.'
'Very true,' agreed Carol. 'You've certainly found a lovely spot to do so.'
'Nicest town I've ever lived in.'
'Yes!' said Harry, wishing to move the interview along a little. 'So, could you take us through what happened on the night of the play, before the death was discovered?'
'Certainly. How far back would you like me to go?'
'Whatever suits you, Mr. Manning.'
' 'Stew' please. Well, as you know, I was stage manager. Did last year's pantomime and one of the previous plays. When Bill left the society – he'd been manager for years - Charlie thought it might be useful to get someone involved

who could lay their hands on various bits and pieces and ease the costs of production; so, he asked me.'

'Weren't you a bit put out that you were asked for that reason?' Carol asked.

'Not at all. Not at all. I'd been helping backstage for a while anyway, so I thought I could make a good go of it. Never been lacking in confidence, me!'

'I can tell,' said Harry, without realising how rude that might sound.

Manning laughed. 'Obvious, is it? Don't you worry! Takes a lot more than that to offend old Stew! Anyway, when Blackwater said he was going to tackle 'Hamlet', I relished the opportunity of getting to grips with some of the staging. We met quite a few times and he explained the sorts of sets he wanted and, hopefully, that I'd be able to oblige. Clever chap was Charlie; had a vision and knew what he wanted. He'll be sorely missed by the society. Any clue yet as to what happened to him?'

'Shall we get back to King's murder first?' Harry said, not wishing to lose track of the main reason they were there.

'Oh yes. Well, once rehearsals got going, I didn't have much to do with the cast, including King.'

Carol thought back to their earlier conversation with Reverend Brown. 'But you did discuss his casting with Mr. Blackwater, didn't you?'

'Did I? Can't remember that.'

'Reverend Brown said he was originally cast as Polonius, but after a discussion between you, Blackwater and others, he got swapped into playing Claudius;

King was somewhat relegated to playing Ophelia's father. Is that correct?'

'As I said, it's possible I was at the meeting, but probably to discuss any implications of cast changes for the overall production.'

'So, you didn't have any grudge, say, against King, to want to see him lose a major part?' asked Harry, seeing where Carol's question was leading and again impressed at how easily she was falling into the detective role.

'Nothing more than anyone else had against King. I'm sure people have told you the horror stories about his behaviour. I'll add to the list if you like.'

'Please do,' said Harry.

'Second dress rehearsal night I think it was. I was up my ladders as usual, trying to secure a cross beam that we use to hang backdrops from. I don't think King knew I was up there, but he was behind one of the flats with Roger Heart. I'm not sure how it started, but after some swearing, he grabbed him by the arm.'

'Who grabbed who?' interrupted Harry.

'King grabbed Roger. Heart pulled back, went to go, and then turned and said, 'I'll see you dead before I let that happen to Angie!''

'You realise that you are suggesting Roger Heart had a motive to kill his prospective father-in-law?'

'I would have thought, by now, that it is fairly evident that few people liked King and I'm pretty certain that you must also be aware that he and Roger did not, shall we say, see eye to eye over his daughter. Surely none of this is new to you?'

'Not entirely! But you're telling us about something that happened reasonably soon before the death, so we will most certainly be following it up with Mr. Heart. Now, is there anything else you can tell us? Let's move forward to the opening night.'

'Bloody shambles!'

'Really? We were in the audience and I was really impressed how good the production seemed to be; for an amateur group that is.' Carol wasn't sure whether that had come out as praise or not, but she needn't have worried. Stewart Manning took it in his stride.

'Thank you. So long as it seemed so from the audience's viewpoint.'

' "Seems, nay it is, I know not seems", or something like that,' Carol blurted out, as Harry gave her an askance look which showed total obliviousness to what she had just said. Stew noticed though and seemed to be impressed with Carol's knowledge.

'If we could return to the night in question? Why did you think it was a "bloody shambles"?' asked Harry.

'People not where they should be, drinking of alcohol backstage – a definite no, no in my book – backcloth sticking, halfway down, for the ghost scene; Andrew Cross moving props about that aren't even his to need to be moved.'

'Props?' questioned Harry.

'Properties,' replied Carol before Stew could continue his tirade. 'Items that actors carry on with them, or use whilst on stage. Like books or swords.'

'Or daggers?' asked Harry.

'I guess so.' Carol could see where he was heading.

'Did Andrew Cross move any daggers as far as you know?' Manning thought for a moment and then replied slowly, 'I can see where you're going with this. I wouldn't like to swear either way and certainly couldn't testify to it in court. Have you met Andrew?'

The other two both nodded.

'He's a bit of a joker is our Andy Cross. The sort of chap who will swap cold tea for real whisky in an onstage decanter on the last night of a play. Likes to get a reaction from other cast members. He was definitely messing about round the props table, but, as to the daggers, I really couldn't say.'

'Very well,' said Harry. 'What about the moments just before King's body was discovered? Did you see anything that might be useful?'

'I've gone over this a hundred times in my head and have been kicking myself ever since it happened, but it just so happened that at that moment, I wasn't at the side of the stage by the curtain ropes, where I might have been able to throw some light on what happened. In the previous scene to Polonius' murder, the reverend, as Claudius, has to kneel and pray.' Manning laughed for a second or two.

'Yes, Carol and I have remarked earlier over the suitability of his playing this scene out,' said Harry.

'Nice casting by Charlie. Perhaps that's why he swapped characters around, coming back to what you asked earlier. I do seem to remember something being said about that, now I come to think of it.'

'So, you were explaining why you weren't where you were meant to be?'

'Well, where I might have seen something. As SM, that's stage manager, I'm meant to be everywhere at any time! Anyway, I noticed that when Mike went down onto his knees, he was in shadow and I knew damn well that I'd positioned a spotlight to catch his expressions as he raised his head at the end of his soliloquy.'

'And?' Harry prompted.

'I made my way round to the other side of the stage and saw that the bulb in the spot that I'd positioned must have blown. It was too late for that night, but I didn't want to forget about it, so I went to get a bulb and got my ladders out. I'd just changed it when all the shouting started. I came down my ladders and immediately got told to close the curtains; and then you appeared; I phoned for the police as you requested.'

'Did you see anyone at all, near the area where King was,

whilst you were up your ladders?'
'There're quite a few spots up there and, although the one bulb was out, the others were still very bright and right in my face. I couldn't see a thing while I was up there. The first time I really knew something was wrong was when Reverend Brown nearly knocked me off my ladder. It was a good job I was nearly down at the bottom by that point!'
'Yes, he did say that he'd done that!' Harry confirmed. 'Can I ask you about last night? Where were you when Charles Blackwater was killed?'
'What time did it happen?'
Carol was unsure whether this was a trick that Harry often used to get people to incriminate themselves, but, despite its cleverness, Stewart Manning hadn't fallen into any trap that might have been laid for him.
'Sometime after nine,' Harry stated, as if any nefarious trickery was the furthest thing from his mind.
'Oh right,' said Manning, 'I reckon I'd have just about been finishing up some paperwork here and then heading home. I only live just down the road, so it doesn't take long.'
'Did you meet anyone as you walked back?'
'No, sorry.'
'Does your walk take you anywhere near Charles Blackwater's house?'
'It's in that direction, but before you get to it; and, before you ask, I didn't see anyone else walking that way.'
Harry started to rise and Carol joined him. 'Well, Mr. Manning, uh 'Stew', if there's nothing more you wish to add, thank you for all the time you've managed to give us. I'm sure you've got plenty of other things you should be getting on with?'
'Always pleased to be of help, if any help I have been.'
He showed them back through the shop floor and just before they left, Harry turned and asked, 'Just one more

thing. We've recently come from Lorraine Davies' shop and her poster for the play suggested that it was merely postponed rather than cancelled. In the light of Charles Blackwater's demise, can we assume that the latter is now the case?'

Manning looked a little taken aback. 'I should hope not! This play was Charlie's pride and joy. He put so much effort into it and now it's up to the rest of us to do him proud and finish the run.'

'But you have no Polonius,' interjected Carol.

'I shall be proud to stand in for Derek King; probably play it a damn sight better than him even when I have to read from a script, actually.'

Nothing more seemed to be needed to be said and Stewart Manning ushered them out of the automatic doors and stood for a while watching them as they walked back towards the town.

CHAPTER 26

'What do you think? Truth? Lies? What's your gut telling you?' asked Carol, once they were out of earshot.

'What my gut is telling me is… It's definitely time for lunch! Come on! I know just where we should eat while the sun's shining.'

'What did you make of our stage manager? He seemed very open to me.'

'Yes, very much so. However, he also threw a lot of shade on others which can sometimes mean deflection from guilt.'

'So, we're still miles away from solving these crimes?' Carol asked, looking somewhat despondently.

'We've only been looking into it for a day or two. You know

as well as I do that these cases can often take months to resolve.'

'But we're only here for a week!'

'Crime doesn't work to the school holiday timetable.'

They both laughed and made their way towards a café that Harry had seen close to the water's edge of the mere. It was called 'The Heron's Nest' and as well as tables inside, it had several picnic benches laid out between the main building and the sandy slope that led down into the murky blue depths. Quite a few ducks, Canada geese and a pair of swans waddled about, hoping to feed on some bread or other goodies, despite a number of signs that warned guests that feeding the waterfowl was detrimental to their health. A couple of small children, who seemed to have been brought out for the day by their grandparents, were obviously oblivious to these warnings and were merrily throwing large chunks of bread towards the birds, who were gobbling them up, unaware of any harm they might be doing to themselves!

Carol and Harry sat at a bench a little way from the feeding frenzy and a young waitress quickly came to take their order.

Whilst they waited for the food and drinks to arrive, Carol returned to her favourite topic of the moment.

'Do you have any suspicions yet then, Harry?'

'Oh, plenty of suspicions. Almost every single one of them is suspicious in one way or another and, for a close-knit community and drama society, they certainly like casting aspersions at one another. I'm used to gang culture, where people are, misguidedly I fear, driven by loyalty and fear to snitch on each other. I reckon this lot would shop their own granny if it got them off the hook. Not sure which type I dislike the most.'

'Really?'

'I'll tell you something else: we've got one death where almost every person on that stage could have done King's murder and another where that same group of people could all have been legitimately at Charlie Blackwater's house the night he died and not one has an alibi between them. It's really frustrating.'

The drinks arrived and they stopped talking 'shop' while the girl put them down and said that the food would be with them soon. Once she left, Carol continued. 'Where do we go from here then? There must be strategies that you employ in these circumstances.'

'You just keep questioning and digging and correlating the answers until something clicks. That's usually the way these things get sorted.'

'Let's do that then. While we're sat here, in this idyllic spot, watching the ducks and the ripples on the water, why don't we see whether anything we've learnt so far helps at all?'

'Can't I just enjoy my ploughman's lunch in peace?'

'No!'

'I knew that'd be your answer. You're tenacious once you've got the bit between your teeth.'

'You know it!'

'Okay, let's start with King's murder,' suggested Harry.

'Everybody hated him. Suspected of at least physical, if not emotional, abuse of his daughter Angie. Nasty piece of work!'

'Which gives her a motive and, like all the others, she had the opportunity.'

'She's also going to inherit what sounds like a large sum of money now.'

'Do you think she's capable of murder, especially of her own father?'

'From what I see at school, I think it is very dangerous to think that teenagers aren't capable of many things. We also

know she isn't the strongest person mentally speaking and that can make a big difference. She also lost her mother at a really early age and had the shock of discovering her body. That must have had a terrible, psychological effect on her.'
'You're definitely right on that score. What do we make of her off and on boyfriend then? Is he just as capable of murder for pretty much the same reasons?'
'I'd say so. Constant arguments with King over the safety of the love of his life. Actual overheard threat to kill him.'
'Unsubstantiated, as yet. We've still got to question him about that.'
'We'll park that to one side until we've seen him again, then. However, we, ourselves, were witness to the way King spoke to him whilst we were at Lorraine's shop the first morning we got here; so some of that we can be sure of.'
'True! And Lorraine is always looking out for Romeo and his Juliet.'
'Oo,' said Carol, 'look at you starting to come out with the literary allusions!'
'Just trying to impress! We are pretty certain, however, that Lorraine is the one person who can't have actually plunged the dagger into King.'
'Absolutely! He was alive on stage with her at the start of the fatal scene. He went to hide behind the arras and was then found dead and she never left the stage the whole of that time.'
'But you thought Hamlet's entrance had been delayed, didn't you? I remember you saying that Roger Heart should have entered earlier than he did.'
'That's right,' agreed Carol, 'he didn't make his entrance on time and Lorraine looked a bit flustered waiting for him, so it definitely wasn't a dramatic pause, which is what he sort of suggested as well as using the excuse that he was consoling Angie.'

'So that gave him the opportunity to kill King and then enter.'
'I guess so.'
It was at this point that their lunches arrived and very tasty they both agreed that the plates looked. They again paused until the waitress was gone before continuing.
'Right then,' began Carol, 'let's carry on with our friend at the garage.'
'Loverboy Steve Grey. Yes, I'd definitely like him to be the culprit in all this. I'd take great pleasure in banging him up!'
'There speaks the voice of blind, yet balanced, Justice. Just because he showed me his pecs.'
'The thought never entered my head!'
'Not much! Now, you had to break up his altercation with Angie before the murder, didn't you?'
'Yes, but like all the others, he'd have still had the time to get backstage before the murder took place. I was back with you before the previous scene finished, so, like Angie, he could have got round the back if he wanted to. Also, we know he liked to mess with the, what did you call them, props? Nobody would have noticed if he'd got a real dagger in his hand!'
'And he certainly didn't like King after being locked up before because of him.'
'Like Heart,' continued Harry, 'he also has a thing for Angie and wouldn't have wanted to see her hurt by her father.'
'I see what you mean about motive and opportunity,' said Carol, as she mused over all these factors.
'Moving on,' said Harry, as he bit into a piece of rather tasty crusty bread on which he had spread, what looked to Carol to be, half a pack of butter. 'The vicar and the window cleaner!'
'Sounds like a new West End farce!' joked Carol.
'They were both backstage, close to the murder scene and both were alone for enough time for either to have done it.'

'Opportunity, but what about motive?'

'Same with our larger-than-life stage manager, "call me Stew", Manning. Up a ladder, but near the scene of the crime. Seemingly, no motive though, other than a dislike for King which only narrows the suspects down to the whole town! He gave us another line of questioning in terms of Roger Heart, so, like we already said, we need to talk to him again.'

'The reverend's dislike was bordering on paranoia didn't you think? All that talk of Hell and damnation.'

'Of the three of them, his altar-based talks with Angie and, as you say, his outburst with us, might indicate the most motive, but it's all very circumstantial.'

'Who else do you think we need to talk to?'

'You tell me. You're the one with the knowledge on 'Hamlet'. Which of the other main characters haven't we caught up with yet?

'Well, there's Horatio, Hamlet's friend from university.'

'He was played by Mark Prince if my memory serves me correctly. He's definitely kept a very low profile since it all went down. Anyone else off the top of your head?'

'Just Rosencrantz and Guildenstern.'

'That's a mouthful. Who are they?' asked Harry.

'Another two of Hamlet's friends. They betray him in the end, but he turns the tables on them and they get killed by pirates.'

'Pirates? You must be kidding me.'

'Not in the least. It's a shame we didn't get through to the last scenes. I know you liked 'Pirates of the Caribbean'!'

'Only the scenes with Keira Knightley in.'

'Be that as it may - and I'll pick that up with you later – I think they work in the chemists on the high street. I remember seeing them in there when I popped in on the first morning here. The identical twins that I mentioned to you.

Didn't realise at the time that they'd be in the production, but it was more clever casting by Charlie Blackwater.'
'Why might that be?' Harry asked with a quizzical look.
'In the play, the two are interchangeable. Claudius gets their names wrong and Gertrude has to correct him. Tom Stoppard wrote a really clever play about them a few decades ago. In it he..'
'Let's just stick with one play for the time being. I'm just an old-fashioned, simple copper remember.'
'Simple, definitely,' Carol retorted, amused by her own wit. 'Have you finished polishing off that plate then? Any room for dessert?'
'Not a chance. You?'
'No. I'm full. There's one other clue that we haven't gone back over yet.'
'The scrap of script that was found by King's body? Yes, I was thinking about that as well. I'm still not sure that we should pay too much attention to it. Might be a red herring! We'll keep it in mind though. "Hoist by" - what was it?'
' "tis the sport to have the engineer, Hoist by his own petard."'
'And a petard was a bomb?'
'That's right. The idea is that of poetic justice. The bomber is blown up by his own device.'
'So, if King did rip it out on purpose, as a final revelatory act, what might he have been trying to tell us?'
'I've no idea. You're the 'simple, old copper'. You tell me.'
'Leave that one with me.'
'Wait a minute. You know I mentioned pirates? Rosencrantz and Guildenstern are sent, by Claudius, to have Hamlet killed when he gets to England. The prince turns the tables on them and they get killed instead.'
'And?'
'Don't you see? It's an example of poetic justice: they're

'hoist by their own petard', sort of!'
'I guess so.'
'And if the two of them were working together, they could have more easily overpowered King, who was not a weak looking bloke. One could have held him while the other plunged the dagger into him. Case solved!' Carol again laughed, but she was keen to hear what Harry thought of her deductions.

He thought for a moment, not wishing to dampen her enthusiasm too much. He called the waitress over and asked for the bill before continuing. 'Certainly sounds plausible, but that's just another couple of suspects that could have done it. Let's not get too carried away, especially since we haven't even spoken to them yet!'

'Spoilsport! Thought I'd got it all wrapped up! Are we going to go through Blackwater's death in the same way?'

'Don't think we can say much there yet. It must be related to the first murder, but, unlike King, no one seems to have much of a bad word to say about him.'

'Apart from Lorraine who thought he was a bit pompous.'

'If you killed producers for being pompous, they'd be an endangered species, don't you think?'

'I hope you're not referring to when I put on the school productions!'

'Oh, Heaven forbid!' Harry smiled.

'Anyway, that aside, everybody else seems to think his casting was very clever, that he'd improved the standing of the society no end and provided much-needed Arts in the town.'

'He must have known or seen something that he shouldn't have and the killer found out. That's the usual reason in cases like this.'

'That makes sense. I wonder if Daniel has found any of those files that you asked him to look for?'

'Don't worry. I'm sure he'll let us know if anything turns up.'
The waitress arrived with the bill and once it was paid, they left their picnic bench and started to walk back around the mere's edge towards the town.

CHAPTER 27

As the couple made their way towards the point where the Mereside ended and the town proper began, Carol noticed, in the near distance, a lone figure sat on one of the swings in the children's playground that sat in the park, near to the water.
'That isn't Roger Heart sat over there on the swing, is it?' she asked Harry.
'Certainly looks like it. Fortuitous, I'd say,' he replied. 'One of the suspects that we needed to catch up with after our little chat with Mr. Manning. Come on, let's go and see if he's in a chatty mood.'
Strolling through the open five bar gate that marked the entrance to the park area that formed part of the mere locale, the two headed along the gravel path that led towards the playground. As they approached, Heart's head was down and he seemed lost in thought. He didn't really notice their presence until they were almost on top of him and, even then, as he looked up, there was no greeting or any real sign of recognition at their being there. His eyes were somewhat bloodshot, but not, Harry thought, from anything he might have taken; more from tears this time.
'Are you alright?' Harry asked, as they stopped close beside him.
'Yeah,' Roger Heart replied and then added a belated, 'Thanks!'

Carol sat on the adjacent swing and said, 'This takes me back. I don't think I've been on a swing since I was a teen. Holiday in Torquay, I think it was.'

'Knew how to live it up, didn't you?' Harry joked, picking up on Carol's astute assessment that the young man needed coaxing into any discourse this afternoon, rather than Harry's usual brusque approach to questioning.

'Do you often come down here?' Carol asked Heart and, before he could answer, added, 'It's a beautiful spot to sit and think, isn't it? You're so lucky to have all this right on your doorstep.'

'That's right. I'm such a lucky person me!' and tears again began to form in his eyes.

'Want to chat?' Carol continued. 'Sometimes it's easier to talk to a stranger than to a friend.'

'Better be. Haven't got many friends if I did want to!'

'What's happened?'

Carol guessed the answer before he started.

'Angie says she doesn't want to see me again. She blames me for her dad being...' he tailed off.

'Murdered?' Harry said, rather too bluntly for Carol's liking and she gave him a look that said, 'Please let me do this one.'

'Of course, murdered. What else might I be talking about?' He looked down at the floor again and started to go back into the shell that he obviously built around himself when depression got the better of him.

'She'll come round,' Carol said, unsure as to whether that might be true or not, but knowing that it was what Heart wanted to hear. 'Did she say why she blamed you?'

Roger Heart looked up and stared at her. 'Because I did it. Don't you see, I murdered him.'

Carol quickly glanced over at Harry before returning eye contact with Heart, not sure now how to deal with such a

forthright confession. 'Do you mean..?'
'I killed him as surely as if I had plunged the dagger in myself.'
'So, you didn't actually murder him? Physically?' Carol's cognitive faculties were whirring. 'What do you mean then?'
'I'm guessing that by now you know what Angie's father was like. I reckon he must have been one of the most hated men in the town, if not the county. Ever since Angie and I started going out together, he's been trying to split us up and lots of people have been trying to help us stay together.'
'Like Lorraine?' Harry couldn't keep silent.
'Yeah! She's one of the good ones! She always had our backs. Even let us use her rooms at the shop if we wanted to, you know..' He blushed slightly.
'Go on,' Carol said, not wanting to put a stop to what was starting to sound more like a stream of consciousness outpouring than the earlier confessional.
'Well, anyway, Angie reckons that it's someone that's been trying to help us stay together that bumped the old man off and now she hates me for being the cause of it all.'
'I think she's probably just grieving for her father and taking the pent-up anger that she feels out on you.'
'But she hated him.' The tears began to well up in his eyes again. 'She hated him. She should be glad he's dead. He did and said the most horrible things to her. Even Reverend Brown called him a wicked man. She told me that, one evening after she'd been up to the church to talk to him.'
'He was still her father, Roger. You've just got to give her time to come to terms with what has happened. He hasn't just died. He hasn't been ill, or had an accident; he's been killed and in a pretty gruesome way. Any daughter's going to feel something for her father in that situation.'
'I guess so!' Heart did not look convinced, but at least, Carol thought, the tears seemed to be receding a little. She

nodded to Harry that, if he was careful, he might be able to take up the reins of the questioning.

'Roger,' Harry said, squatting down in front of Heart's swing, so as to be at eye level with him, 'do you mind if we go over the night that it all happened? We're just trying to piece together whether anyone saw something that might help us to identify who really did murder Derek King.'

'I'll be as much help as I can, but I didn't see much. I was on stage when it happened.'

Was he trying to quickly give himself an alibi, Harry wondered. The statement had been just that bit too quick to come out of Roger Heart's mouth only seconds after his tears and teenage angst.

'We'll get to that in a moment, but can I ask you about something that we've been told happened earlier?'

'Oh? What's that?' He began to sound a little less self-assured.

'Did you have an altercation with Derek King that very night?'

'Probably. We did almost every time we were in the same space and, as you can probably remember from when you joined us on stage, that space is pretty small behind the scenes. Luckily, we didn't have to rehearse much together, so it was only when the show was coming together that things started to get nasty.'

As he said it, the look on his face showed that he knew he shouldn't have said it. Roger Heart, thought Carol, had an extremely expressive face both on and off stage! 'Nasty?' she repeated.

'Well, fraught I suppose would be a better word,' Heart answered, attempting to backpeddle a little.

'Fraught then,' continued Harry. 'What might that mean?'

'Rows, threats; all the usual stuff that I got used to hearing from him.'

'I bet you could give as good as you got, though,' said Carol.
'I tried not to rise to the bait. I knew it didn't do any good with him.'
'So, what about the evening of the production? We have heard that you might have "risen to the bait" on that occasion?' Harry suggested.
'Really? I honestly don't remember. I must admit that evening is a bit of a blur now.'
'You were overheard saying to Mr. King, 'I'll see you dead before I let you do that to Angie."
Carol was impressed at Harry's recall of the words Stewart Manning had used, but tried not to show it and awaited Roger Heart's reply.
He took a few seconds to consider his response. 'I don't recall saying that exactly, but, now you mention it, I think I might have said something like that.'
'And can you remember what it was in response to?'
'Yes! King said he was going to take Angie away from Pikesmere. Take her somewhere that I would never find them!'
'That sounds like a pretty good motive to stop him in whatever way you could.' Harry continued the pressure.
Heart began to look flustered and his head started to fall to the ground again. 'But it wasn't me, I promise. I could never have done that to someone. Even him!'
Carol thought that he was beginning to sound like a young boy, rather than the adult he was growing into. She thought she would go gentle again. 'It's alright, Roger. We're just trying to get to the bottom of what happened. Okay?'
'I guess so. I was onstage when it happened, anyway. Like I said before.'
'About that,' Carol continued, trying not to sound accusatory, 'can you tell us again why you were late coming onto the stage in the Closet scene? I know you told us about finding

Angie in the loo, but I think there was more to it than that. You hadn't forgotten your entrance, had you?' She laughed, trying to make it sound light-hearted. 'Although you said you were consoling Angie, that would have been a little bit before your entrance and I reckon you're professional enough not to be late.'

'No, you're right, I was back in the wings and all ready to enter when I realised I hadn't got my rapier. I ran round to the props table, grabbed it and then made my entrance. That's all.'

'I see.' said Carol, 'Well at least that's got that sorted.' She looked over to Harry and tried to suggest that it was probably best to leave things at that for the time being. He understood the look all too well, having been in several arguments with her when the same look had told him it would be to his advantage to shut up and stop talking.

'Well,' he said, turning to Heart, 'that'll be all for the time being, I think. Glad we've had that little chat and got things sorted. Hope things turn out alright with Angie. I'm sure they will.'

Roger immediately seemed to brighten up again. 'I'll give her a bit of time, like you suggested.' He jumped off the swing and without another word, or backward glance, walked quickly away towards the town.

Harry sat down on the newly vacated swing and looked at Carol with a raised eyebrow. 'So, what did you make of all that?' he asked.

'That is one troubled young man, but I wouldn't say he was the homicidal type.'

'Met many have you?'

'Not as many as you, no doubt of that. He obviously hated King; and him taking Angie away certainly gives him a strong motive, but doesn't the death of King seem a bit too calculated? Not a spur of the moment act?'

'Not sure,' replied Harry, 'the jury's still out on that one. But I agree that Roger Heart does seem almost too scared to kill anyone. He seemed physically traumatised by the very thought of doing anything like that.'

'We keep coming back to Charlie Blackwater's clever casting, don't we?'

Harry gave her his quizzical look.

'In the play, Hamlet is exactly the same. He is a thinker, not a doer. He finds the act of killing repugnant, even though he's promised his father's ghost that he will take revenge. He just can't bring himself to do it until the very end when he is forced into a corner and has no choice.'

'I see.'

'While we were chatting to Heart, I did think of something that might be important, though.'

'Go on. Your hunches in this case have seemed to be pretty good so far.'

'And what we were just saying about the play seems to confirm it. In the scene before Derek King got killed, Claudius is praying.'

'That's the bit that Stewart Manning said the spotlight wasn't working for.'

'That's it. Anyway, whilst he's praying, Hamlet enters and has the chance to kill him, but can't because he thinks about it too much and doesn't want to send Claudius' soul to heaven instead of hell. Well, don't you see?'

Harry didn't. He shook his head and look plaintively at her for the answer.

'Hamlet draws his sword to kill Claudius and then can't.'

Harry was still rather in the dark. 'And?'

'His sword. His 'rapier'! Hamlet already has his rapier in the previous scene. Heart wouldn't have needed to get it from the props table.' She looked triumphantly at Harry.

'He lied to us. He lied about his delayed entrance. Well,

well!'

'And if he's that good at lying. Who knows what else he might be trying to conceal or obfuscate?'

Carol's question hung in the air as they got up from the swings and followed the same route that Heart had taken a few minutes earlier, back towards the town. Harry didn't like to ask what 'obfuscate' meant, but he was pretty sure it didn't bode well for Roger Heart.

CHAPTER 28

What was left of the afternoon passed relatively uneventfully. Carol and Harry returned to their hotel where Carol spent an extremely pleasant hour lying in the bath reading a novel that she had been saving for this holiday, but which, so far, she had only managed to get through one chapter of. In the meantime, Harry spent some time messaging Daniel and then, eventually, phoning him because his fingers had got tired texting. He brought his friend up to speed with everything that happened so far that day and Dan agreed that it didn't really open any new lines of enquiry. Indeed, it seemed to close several and they both came to the same conclusion that the usual mantra of 'means, motive and opportunity' was not being particularly helpful on this occasion.

Carol called from the bathroom to ask Dan about Charles Blackwater's files, which Harry subsequently did, but again they seemed to be heading down a dead end on that murder as well. No papers, pictures or other incriminating items had been found in his study, or anywhere else around the house, including the loft space and, although the tech crew were still working on his computer, they had managed to find his password protection – unsurprisingly, Dan laughed whilst telling Harry, it was 'Blackwater58', name and year of birth – so far, there didn't seem to be any hidden files, or anything that might give a clue as to who might have wanted him dead. When Carol was relayed this unhelpful news, she asked what files were on there. Harry went into the bathroom and put his phone on speaker so that Carol could join in the conversation.

'Mainly stuff to do with his play producing,' said Daniel, 'as well as downloaded, critical pieces on 'Hamlet' and an annotated copy of the script. There were files going back over several of his previous shows, pantomime posters, photos and so on, as well as copies of reviews from the local rags and elsewhere round the country.'

'Can we have a look at any of the reviews?' asked Carol.

'Can't see why not, if you've got the time and the inclination. I'll send some over to you.'

'Do we really want to spend our time reading those?' asked Harry.

'Might be something in them,' replied Carol. 'Some of these local critics can be pretty vicious. Might give us another angle on his death.'

'Nice thinking,' said Dan and Harry could almost see him smiling on the other end of the phone call.

'That it then?' he asked.

Daniel paused before answering as he thought over what he'd been sent. 'Pretty much, unfortunately. We found a few historic files on an old memory stick which was in his lap-top bag, but again it was all pretty innocuous. Pictures of him getting awards at a medical seminar, some of his wife and presumably friends; he didn't have any children.'

'Can we look at some of those as well?' Harry asked, pre-empting the same question from Carol.

'Of course. I'll get a copy of them made and send them round to the hotel.'

'We haven't got a lap-top here,' said Harry. 'We're on holiday, remember?'

'Nothing but trouble, you two! Okay, it's getting late: why don't you pop into the situation room we've set up at the Town Hall, tomorrow, and I'll show them to you then?'

'Sounds like a plan,' Harry replied and after a few final pleasantries, he rang off, noticing he had been on for so long that his battery life was almost exhausted. He plugged in his charger and decided that there might just be time for a shared bath with Carol before they headed down for dinner. He began to remove his clothes.

****

After another delicious meal, courtesy of The Golden Pheasant's restaurant, Harry suggested that now might be a good time to take a stroll to the Lion public house and see if Andrew Cross' alibi for the previous night stood up. They grabbed their coats from their room and headed across The Green, past the medieval stocks and towards the welcoming arms of the local hostelry. The building looked to be quite old from the exterior, like much of Pikesmere, and, as they entered, it was nice to see, Harry thought, that the interior had attempted to maintain an 'olde worlde' feel about it. Exposed timbers, painted black, were everywhere, with horse brasses hanging from them. Pictures of Eighteenth-Century rural life were dotted about on the whitewashed walls and the furniture was dark and wooden. It being midweek, the lounge area was reasonably quiet and, after ordering their drinks, Carol and Harry quickly found a free table in the corner near the window that overlooked the path they had just taken to get there. Harry had decided not to go in all guns blazing in his search for confirmation of alibis, but, instead, to bide his time and see who turned up that evening. He didn't have long to wait!

As Harry was raising his pint to his lips, the door opened and Steve Grey entered. He was no longer dressed in his oil and grease covered garage overalls, but instead had opted for a tight white T-shirt and even tighter jeans.

'Enter Fortinbras, stage right,' whispered Carol and, just to make Harry a little bit jealous added, 'and looking every bit the prince!'

Unwilling to rise to the bait, Harry asked, 'Prince? I thought Hamlet was the prince?'

'He's the prince of Denmark. Mr. Grey over there is prince of Norway. His character is used to contrast Hamlet: similar princes, but Fortinbras is a man of action.'

As if to underscore what Carol was relating to Harry, Steve Grey went across to the bar, grabbed another young man by the arm, twisted him round to face him and said, in a voice loud enough for the whole room to hear, 'So, Timothy, are you going to pay up for that job I did on your Corsa, or am I going to have to get angry? Like the Hulk used to say, "you wouldn't like me when I'm angry" I reckon.'

Grey was nearly a head taller than the man he had referred to as Timothy and could, fairly obviously, have carried out whatever threat he was making.

'I told you, Steve,' said Timothy, altogether more meekly than his opponent, 'I'll get it to you by the end of the week. Promise! I'm just waiting to get paid, myself.'

'Make sure you do then. I don't like to be made to look a fool. I've got a reputation to maintain.' He turned back to the young barmaid that had served Carol and Harry just a few minutes before. 'Pint of Shropshire Brew, Holly luv, and a smile if you've got one for me?'

Holly declined to give him his smile, preferring instead to

turn her back to get a glass, before pulling his drink of choice.

'Charming!' said Carol.

'Aggressive!' replied Harry. 'Just the sort of person who could easily plunge a knife, or a dagger, into someone, just for crossing him.

'Prejudiced again?'

'Not at all. Merely putting together all the evidence and forming a conclusion.'

'Of course,' said Carol and she took another sip of her drink. A few minutes later, as the room had returned to its conversations and Steve Grey had made several more attempts to chat up the underworked Holly, who seemed desperate to find any job that might take her away from the mechanic sat on his bar stool, the door again opened and Angie King walked in. It was quite an entrance: she was heavily made up and wore a short summer dress that certainly did very little to hide any modesty she might have wished to keep hidden. She held an empty bottle of Prosecco in her left hand, but Harry, as he looked across, thought it was likely that she had been on something rather stronger than the alcohol that was in evidence. She half walked, half staggered over to the bar, placed the empty bottle next to one of the pumps and ordered a drink from Holly. Carol, nor Harry, could hear what she had asked for, as her back was turned to them, but they overheard the barmaid's relatively terse reply.

'Sorry, Angie, you know I can't do that. You're underage.'

'Oh, come on, Holly. We went to school together. You're only a bit older than me, so don't be like that. Just one.' She slightly slurred the word school.

'No can do. It's because we went to school together that I know you're seventeen. I'd lose my job.'

Angie turned to Steve who was still sitting on the barstool a few feet away. Although she must have seen him the moment she walked in, she reacted as if he was being observed for the first time. 'Steve,' she slurred the 's' again, 'my favourite mechanic. Fancy buying me a drink?' To emphasise her request, she let her finger casually stroke his white T-shirt.

Before Steve Grey could reply, Holly again spoke up. 'That isn't going to help either, Ange. I can't sell to him if I know it's for you.'

'Perhaps it might be best if I get you home,' Steve said to Angie, stepping down from his perch and making a step towards her. Before he could take her arm, however, her whole persona seemed to metamorphosise before everybody's eyes. She glared at Grey and then at Holly, took a step or two back and her fingers tightened into claw-like shapes that accentuated her long, sharp fingernails. It was as if she had become a dangerous tiger or, perhaps, given her petite stature, a leopard or cheetah. She leapt at Steve Grey with a ferocity that could have taken an eye out, had he not been more spatially aware, at that moment, than her and swerved to avoid the onslaught. Angie fell towards the barstool that he had recently vacated and went down, almost in slow motion, to the barroom floor, slightly winded, but still very much in attack mode. She twisted her body to look up at Steve Grey and almost spat out the words, 'You'd like that wouldn't you? Take me home and get me into bed again. Well, it's not going to happen. I hate you.' She began to stand and slowly turned to face the rest of the lounge bar. 'I hate all of you. I wish you were all dead, like my father.' As suddenly as she had turned savage, she changed again; her body slumped and she began to make languorous, almost sensual movements around the room.

'He is dead and gone, lady, he is dead and gone; At his head a grass-green turf, at his heels a stone.' The voice was sweet and melodic, tinged with so much suffering and despair. Harry turned to Carol for an explanation.

'You're witnessing one of the scenes that we didn't get to watch in the play,' she whispered, 'Ophelia's famous madness, brought on by her father's murder.'

'Do you think Angie's gone mad?' he asked.

'More the booze and drugs, I'd say, but who knows what effect all this has had on her?' Carol stopped as Angie King approached their table. The actress dropped to her knees in front of Harry and said, rather than sang, 'I cannot choose but weep to think they should lay him i' the cold ground.' Tears seemed to well up in her eyes, but her transmuting was not complete. The next sound she made was a maniacal laugh, as she looked up at Harry and said, 'that's a fair thought to lie between a policeman's legs.'

'That's sort of another quote from the play, if you were having any doubts as to her intentions,' Carol interjected. 'One of Hamlet's lines, actually.'

Harry stood and drew Angie up to a standing position. He had to hold her so that she didn't drop to the ground again. 'I think, young lady, that despite Mr. Grey's possible intentions..'

'What's that meant to mean?' shouted Grey, already tense from Angie's failed attack.

Harry ignored him but softened his tone. 'Despite what you may have thought Mr. Grey's intentions were, I do think he was right in saying you should be at home right now. Would you like me to accompany you back?' If he had had eyes in the back of his head, he would have seen a slightly raised and arched eyebrow from Carol.

Angie King pushed herself away from Harry, stood up as tall and straight as her present state allowed and started to move back towards Steve Grey. Halfway across the room, she paused and turned. It was as if all the sadness, all the

pain, all the anger and performed insanity had instantly left her. She said, 'No thank you, Mr. Policeman, sir, I think I will take Mr. Grey up on his kind offer to escort me back.'
As she approached the mechanic, he visibly tensed in preparation for another attack, but it didn't come; instead, she linked her arm with his and, with almost a flourish, walked him out of the main door.
Harry sat down and exhaled audibly. 'Never a dull moment in Pikesmere! Fancy another round?'
'I thought you'd never ask. I wonder what's next on the cabaret programme?'
'Do you think all that was an act?'
'Not all of it, no. She's certainly a very vulnerable and highly strung teenager, but, yes, I do think there might have been a performative element to what we just witnessed.'
'Interesting!' said Harry and he rose to buy some more drinks.
It wasn't long after he had sat back down and they had started to run over what they had just witnessed, that the door swung open again and Andrew Cross came in. Like Steve Grey, he was no longer wearing his occupational garments, but, instead, was in a tank top and chinos.
'Scrubs up well,' said Carol.
'Could you stop eyeing up all our suspects?' Harry pleaded.
'Sorry. Just saying.'
Harry walked back over to the bar just as Cross was ordering his drink. 'Drop of the usual, please Holly.'
'Mr. Cross.'
The window cleaner turned to see who was addressing him. 'That's my name. Don't wear it out. Come for a pleasant drink, or to check out my alibi for yesterday?'
'Both,' Harry admitted. 'Perhaps the barmaid here can sort out the latter. Holly, were you behind the bar last night?'
She nodded, not really wanting to become involved and not

having a clue as to who the man asking the questions was.
'Did you see Mr. Cross in here last night?'
She looked for a moment at Andrew Cross and then gave the same non-committal nod.
"She's not usually this quiet, guv. Must be your effect on the ladies.' He laughed and turned to the barmaid. 'It's alright, luv, he's helping to investigate them murders in the town. Don't worry about me. I know I'm innocent; I just need to convince him.'
'When was Mr. Cross in here, last night?' Harry asked.
Holly seemed somewhat happier to speak now she knew who she was dealing with. 'Always comes in about this time, does Andy. Just before nine usually.'
'And what time did he leave?'
'That's a bit trickier as we get busier towards closing time, so I can't say for certain, but probably some time after ten; maybe quarter past.'
'There we go. Just as I told you this morning. Can I have my drink in peace now?'
'There is one more thing I'd like to discuss with you. Why don't you join Carol and me over at the table there?'
He looked somewhat reluctant to do so, but still made his way slowly across and sat down on the spare stool opposite Carol.
'Hello again,' said Carol. 'Pleased you could make time for a chat.'
'Exactly what I came out for this evening,' Cross answered sarcastically. 'Now what can I add that I didn't tell you this morning?'
'Since we met up with you at the vicarage,' began Harry, 'we have been told that you are a bit of a joker when you're backstage at the shows.'
'Stew been complaining about his precious props table, has he? It's only a bit of fun. Never does any harm. The cast

love it! It's only him as stage manager that gets his hair off when I do it.'

'Be that as it may,' continued Harry, 'on the night of Mr. King's murder, did you tamper with any of the daggers or rapiers?'

'No chance. I know what's a joke and what isn't. Mess around with something like a dagger and someone could get hurt.'

'They did Andrew!' said Carol. 'Someone ended up dead.'

Cross stared at her for a moment and then took a gulp of his drink. 'Yeah! Well, I never touched any of them.'

'But you did something to the props?'

'Okay, listen. If you must know, I put a note in the book that Roger reads when he goes on stage. It was only a joke.'

'What did the note say?' asked Harry.

'Nothing important,' Cross replied.

'Look, this conversation will end a lot quicker if you answer my questions properly.'

Carol put a hand on his arm to remind him he was not in an interview room and heads around the lounge bar were turning in their direction.

'Sorry, Mr. Cross. Could you please be kind enough to tell us what was on the note you placed for Roger Heart to read as he went on stage?'

'Alright. I put something about his girlfriend.'

'Like what?' Carol questioned.

'Like that I'd, you know.. with her. I hadn't mind. I just wanted to put him off his lines, nothing else. He knows I fancy her and he always has that smug look on his face when they're together and they see me.'

'Bit young for you, isn't she?' remarked Carol.

'I'm only twenty-five, you know. I'm not ancient.'

'Still, eight years between you is still quite a lot.'

'I guess, but I can still fancy her, can't I? No actual law

against it, is there?'

'No, so long as it doesn't lead to trying to help her by getting rid of an allegedly abusive father.'

Andrew Cross started to turn pale as he began to see where the conversation might be headed.

'That'll be all for now,' said Harry, 'we'll let you get back to the bar.'

Cross began to stand up and then said, 'I didn't murder King and I didn't murder Blackwater, so you'd be best to look elsewhere.'

He turned and made his way back to the bar to drop back into conversation with Holly who was right about the pub starting to fill up as late evening arrived.

Carol and Harry finished their drinks and headed back to the hotel for a well-earned night's sleep.

ACT IV

My words fly up, my thoughts remain below,
Words without thoughts never to heaven go.

CHAPTER 29

Carol and Harry were sat in the same seats as they had been on the night of Derek King's murder. The set, the costumes, even the audience looked exactly as they had done that fatal evening. Carol couldn't help but wonder at how similar and familiar it all seemed. Even the elderly Miss Hubbard, that was so annoyed with Harry before, was sat in front of them again, this time munching on a piece of chocolate cake. The strains of the National Anthem faded away; the curtains opened. The actors creaked their way around the stage once more, the 'wall' did its customary wobble. However, incongruously, this time the audience did not suppress their laughter and the actors had to pause while hoots of derision filled the hall. Carol couldn't begin to comprehend how people could be so tactless at a homage to those who had died so recently.
'Who's there?'
'Nay, answer me. Stand, and unfold yourself.'
'Long live the king!'
The famous opening lines filled the stage once more, but almost immediately the soldiers seemed to morph into Roger Heart, standing alone, in a grave, holding a skull. Somehow, the grave had been made to look realistic and the set was suddenly incredible, with what looked like a real moon shining down on a foreboding, misty churchyard.
'They've made it look like the one at Pikesmere church,' Carol said, as she turned to where Harry had been sat. He

had, however, again left her alone to watch the play unfold. 'Alas, poor Yorick! – I knew him, Horatio,' intoned Heart, as he held the infamous gleaming, white skull in his hand. There was no Horatio though to hear, as Hamlet stood alone in the moonlight. Strange, thought Carol. Why have they done that? Hamlet dipped down into the grave and as he rose again, Heart's face now resembled the very skull that he held in front of him. That's clever, she thought. Suddenly, though, he was surrounded by almost the whole cast. Mike Brown and Lorraine Davies stood to one side, looking regal and aloof as Steve Grey and Andrew Cross, dressed as Fortinbras and Laertes, dragged Roger Heart from the grave and drew their rapiers. Carol began to doubt the validity of this new interpretation, but her thoughts were interrupted as Angie King entered, dripping wet. It was not, though, her appearance that shocked Carol – after all, Ophelia was supposed to have just drowned – it was the fact that, standing next to her, gripping her arm more tightly than was necessary, stood her father, Derek King, glaring at the amassed ensemble.

'What on earth?' she tried to shout, but the words seemed to stay in her throat and no sound escaped. She tried to rise, in order to fetch Harry, to tell him that King was still alive, but her legs were like jelly and unable to support her.

On stage, the cast had forced Polonius to the centre of their throng and, slowly and deliberately, each was thrusting a knife, a rapier, or a dagger into his portly frame. And then, just as she thought that it couldn't get any stranger, the entire audience stood and applauded, whistling and cheering the brazen murder taking place there in front of them.

Carol awoke with a jolt and sat upright in the hotel bed. There was indeed moonlight, but it filtered in through a crack in the curtains that Harry hadn't quite closed properly when they'd rolled in from the pub. He, however, was not disturbed by nightmares, or by moonbeams. He lay snoring next to Carol, blissfully unaware of the horrific scene that Carol had just witnessed in her dream. For a brief moment she contemplated waking him, to narrate all that she thought had been happening, but that seemed just a little too sadistic, so she rolled over onto her side and spent a fitful hour attempting to return to her slumbers.

CHAPTER 30

'I think I might like to visit the library this morning,' announced Harry as they concluded their breakfast.
'Now there's a sentence I never expected to hear coming from your lips,' replied Carol.
The memory of the night's dream was still nagging in the back of her mind and she had related it to Harry over the meal. He hadn't laughed, or made a joke of it, as she'd half expected him to, but, instead, had listened intently, before explaining that, quite often, in murder cases particularly, but not exclusively, the intensity of emotions was difficult to exclude from one's nightmares. She was glad it was not just her who had to deal with what she considered to be a particularly unpleasant set of images.
'I think it's time we had a little chat with Mark Prince. Prince! There're definitely too many princes in this case!' said Harry, as he swallowed the last morsel of his croissant and jam.
'There are more things in Heaven and Earth, Horatio.'
'Come again.'
'Nothing! It's just something Hamlet says to Horatio which is the character that Mark Prince was playing.'

'Hamlet's friend from university?'
'Well done. We'll make a student of you yet.'
'We'll see. Me going to the library is a bit like a vampire entering a church. I might turn into a pile of dust, or burst into flames.'
'Don't worry, Nosferatu. I'll protect you from all those evil books!'
Half an hour later, they were again wandering along the high street, heading towards where the hotel receptionist had told them that they would find the library. She did warn them, however, that it didn't open every day, so they might have to take their chances. As they walked along, they passed, on the other side of the road, Steve Grey's garage and Harry stopped and motioned to Carol to wait a moment. She glanced across to see what had brought them to a standstill; inside, Grey, back in his overalls, was obviously having another heated conversation, this time on his phone. His anger was intense enough for his voice to have been raised so that they could overhear pretty much everything that was being said whilst they were out on the pavement on the other side of the street.
'Yeah, I took her home last night. Yeah, wouldn't you like to know. Perhaps you should have been there to take care of her then. Huh, that'll be the day.'
Harry had walked across the road and was standing at the entrance to the garage, silhouetted against the light from the street outside.
'Yeah! Who's that?' asked Grey, as he glanced across, his phone conversation obviously aborted by the person on the other end. 'Oh, it's P.C. Plod. Checking up on me again, are you?'
'Just passing,' replied Harry. 'Did you manage to get Miss King home safe last night? Was she alright? Seemed a little distraught, I thought.'

'She was fine. As far as I know, anyway. Saw her to the door and then went home.'
'Very chivalrous of you, Steve,' said Carol, coming up behind Harry.
'That's me down to a tee. Chivalrous Steve they call me!'
'I'm sure they do,' she retorted, unconvinced.
'Funnily enough, I was just telling Roger Heart that very same thing. It was him you presumably heard me chatting to.'
'I wouldn't have used the word 'chatting', would you Carol?' replied Harry.
'Sounded a bit like goading, to me,' she said.
'As if I would do that to sweet, little Roger.'
'I get the feeling you and he aren't on the best of terms,' said Harry.
'Now whatever gave you that idea?' Grey wiped his grease covered hands down his overalls. 'I just think Angie deserves better, that's all.'
'Someone like you perhaps?' asked Carol.
'Well, now you mention it, I reckon I'd be a better choice. I'm sure you'd agree.'
Grey was going back into provocation mode, but Harry was having none of it. 'Any reason that you don't get on with Mr. Heart, other than rivalry over Miss King?'
Grey turned his eyes reluctantly away from Carol and back to Harry. He seemed to be considering what he should, or should not, say to him. Eventually, he made his mind up.
'It's not just that. I don't think he loves her at all. I reckon he's just after her money.'
'And what makes you think that?'
'Just little comments he's made about what they'd be able to do together, once old King was out of the way. I reckon he thinks she'll fund his acting career and a whole lot more.'
'But, of course, you're not interested in any money that

might be coming her way,' stated Harry, innocently.
'I'm doing alright for myself, here. At least I've got a business and some money in the bank. Doubt Heart has!'
'Thank you,' said Harry, as he started to turn away and leave the garage.
'Don't mention it,' returned Grey, 'always glad to see a pretty face round here.'
Before Carol could say anything, Harry replied. 'Why thank you, again. I didn't think you cared!' Even Steve Grey had to grin as the couple left.
'Library, then?' asked Carol, as they continued up the street.
'If it's open,' said Harry.
Luck, however, was with them and, as they reached the entrance to the library, the opening hours displayed informed them that today was, indeed, one of the three days in the week when the facilities were available to the good folk of Pikesmere. The civic building was not of a similar design to the monstrosity that was the Town Hall that they had visited a few days before. Instead, the library took up the ground floor of what looked, from the outside, to be an old Victorian structure that had been refurbished to accommodate several activities. Signs in the foyer suggested that rooms upstairs were used for community interests such as senior citizen yoga and Pilates, Masonic meetings and adult learning, the last of which made a lot of sense if the library was situated below. Carol and Harry pushed through the glass, double swing doors and made their way into the library.
As Harry had intimated earlier, a library was not his natural habitat and he had many unpleasant memories of trying to study for exams in them: the very particular odour of old, musty books with their Dewey Decimal numbering sellotaped to the spines filled him with something akin to loathing. However, despite them entering what might have

been considered a rural backwater of academia, Pikesmere library held none of the horrors that Harry was anticipating. The air smelt fresh and what books he could see were relatively new, with colourful, modern sleeves and displayed to attract, rather than discourage, the act of reading. Soft, colourful easy chairs were dotted about, alongside a suite of quite modern looking laptops which seemed to be the focus of most of the clientele that morning.

As Harry began to feel more at home, Carol nudged him gently and pointed in the direction of a light, pine counter, behind which stood the diminutive figure of Mark Prince. He was staring at a computer screen whilst scanning several children's books for a lady who was attempting to keep her two, very young offspring quiet and follow the signs on the counter that requested the library be kept reasonably silent for those wishing to read in peace. She was not succeeding that well!

'That'd be me at their age,' whispered Harry.

'That's you now, given half a chance,' retorted Carol with a grin. 'Come on, it looks as if our young Horatio is free.'

As the mother and children made a hurried retreat from the room, Harry and Carol walked over to the desk and greeted Mark Prince. At first, he didn't seem to recognise them, but then, he swapped his glasses, and identification dawned.

'Sorry,' he said quietly, 'blind as a bat if I'm not wearing the right ones!'

'Is there somewhere we can talk without being shushed too often, Mr. Prince?' Harry asked.

'Oh, yes, of course. You're here in an official capacity, are you?'

He didn't seem flustered by this realisation, but, instead, stepped out from behind the desk, walked quickly over to a greying, elderly woman who seemed to be helping an equally aged man with the laptop he was on and pointed over to the desk, to which she nodded. Prince came back over and led them through a door marked "Librarians Only", explaining that they weren't allowed to leave the desk unattended due to data protection laws governing the information on the computer.

'Who know what could happen if someone got hold of all the addresses and so on that we have for the residents of the town? Happened once when I was working as an apprentice librarian in Hemel Hempstead. Terrible uproar.'

He seemed genuinely worried, despite everyone probably knowing where everybody else lived anyway.

The three of them entered a small staffroom which had a couple of similar easy chairs to the library, a microwave and a kettle, and a trolley with, what Carol assumed, were books that had not yet been scanned, to be put on the lending shelves.

'Please sit down,' Mark Prince said. 'Can I offer you a cup of something?'

'No, thank you,' replied Harry, 'we've just finished our breakfasts.'

Carol looked across at the chipped and caffeine-stained mugs that sat on the side by the kettle and decided to decline the offer as well, despite, being a teacher who was almost always willing to grab a hot drink whenever and wherever time and place allowed.

'So, how can I help you? I presume it's to do with the murders and not to loan a book.'

He almost laughed at his own little joke, but managed to suppress it.

Harry smiled. 'Yes, we'd like to take you through the events leading up to Mr. King's death, if that's alright.'

'Of course,' replied Prince, 'Fire away.'

'Could you tell us where, exactly, you were, at the time the murder took place?'

'Well, it's a little bit embarrassing.'
'In what way?'
'I think that during most of Act 3 – that is when it happened, isn't it?'
Harry nodded.
'Well, through most of the latter part of that Act, I was in the loo throwing up.'
'Something you ate?' asked Harry.
'Or stage nerves?' countered Carol.
'Yes, the latter, very astute of you. That's why it's so embarrassing. Don't get me wrong, I love being on stage, but I suffer awfully with my nerves. I've tried taking pills and done yoga and so on, but nothing seems to help. I was fine at the start. Got through all the ghost stuff in the first act and thought I was going to be fine. Watched the Players and then it hit me. I didn't want people to hear what was happening, so I went round to the toilets in the foyer and kept my fingers crossed that none of the audience would come in.'
'Someone did though, didn't they?' said Harry, stifling a grin.
'I think so. I heard the door go. How did you know?'
'It was me.'
'Really. So, you're sort of my alibi, then?' This time it was Mark Prince's turn to hide a smug grin.
Harry was not going to provide an alibi that easily, though.
'Not really. You see, I was back in my seat and watching the play when the murder took place. That means you also had the time to get back round to backstage to commit the crime.'
'Oh.' Prince's smile faded for a moment, but then it returned. 'Wait a minute, though. You weren't the only one who heard me in the cubicle. I heard the door open again and this time I knew who it was because he called out to me.'
'Really? Who was it?'

'Bloody Steve Grey. It would be him, wouldn't it? "Is that you, Princey boy" he says, right cocky as usual and calling me "boy" even though I'm about ten years older than him! "Throwing up again, are you?" and he laughed. I tell him to leave me alone – or words to that effect – and a second or two later he goes out again.'

'Strange! He hasn't mentioned this encounter when we've been questioning him,' Harry says.

'Probably doesn't even remember it. Would mean nothing to him, but it's etched on my memory as yet another embarrassing moment that I'll have to live down for years to come.'

Carol was again moved to think about the similarities between actor and character. Here was Mark Prince, acting in a very similar way to Horatio; the introspective, intellectual university friend of Hamlet who, so movingly, is willing to act "the antique Roman" and commit suicide in order to support his dying friend. Only once Hamlet stops him, does Horatio regain his composure enough to talk of "flights of angels" taking his companion away from him to Heaven. Yes, if the play had been allowed to reach its conclusion, Carol was pretty sure that this young actor would have delivered his final lines both eloquently and with real emotion. His was definitely another tormented soul, but did that mean he should not be a suspect? Like the other young actor at the centre of this tragedy, Roger Heart, did the raw emotion actually screen murderous intent?

As she returned to the conversation taking place in front of her, Harry was continuing to ask Mark Prince about the night of the stage murder.

'Let's assume, for a moment, that your alibi sticks and you were, how shall we say, indisposed, at the time of Mr. King's death, could Mr. Grey have still got back in time to do it?'

Prince's eyes almost twinkled at the suggestion, but kept his

answer low key. 'Possibly. He wasn't in the toilets for much more than a few seconds and it doesn't take long to get round the back. I was still in there for a while and when I came out and got back round, everything had happened.'
'Okay! Assuming that is true, who do you think might have done it?'
'Oh, I've no idea. I mean, no one liked Derek, uh Mr. King, so the list is quite long.'
'So we keep finding,' said Harry.
Carol decided to follow a little hunch. 'What about Mr. Heart? Do you reckon he could have done it?'
Prince's face changed a little and seemed to glow slightly redder. He considered the question for a moment, seemingly weighing up the best response, before committing to it.
'No, I wouldn't say Roge, I mean Mr Heart, could be a murderer.'
'Really?' continued Carol, 'He seems to have a lot to gain from Mr. King's demise, not least of which is having more freedom to pursue his daughter.'
'Nothing will come of that,' replied Prince quickly. 'He and Angie aren't suited. He'll realise that, now the thrill of meeting up with her behind her father's back wanes. He's a marvellous actor you know. He'll go to London and take the West End by storm and forget all about little Angie.'
'I see,' said Carol and she thought that she did. Was it just hero worship in Mark Prince's voice, or was there real angst and perhaps love? What lengths might a young man go to in order to help the target of his 'affections'? She could see that Harry had recognised this as well.
'What about Miss King, then,' ventured Harry. 'Might she be capable, in your opinion, of killing her own father?'
Prince was definitely not so reticent to release his venom about her. 'She's an out and out bitch. I wouldn't be

surprised by anything that Angela King does and certainly don't doubt that she could kill her own father if she was in one of her moods. The number of times I have tried to talk to Roge about how he is far too good for her and that it was time to call it a day on their relationship. She is definitely bad for him. And the way she flirts with other men. That Steve Grey for one. It's obscene!'

'Does she flirt with you, Mark?' Carol asked.

'She used to. Tried it on once or twice after rehearsals. She soon got the hint that I wasn't interested. Far too old for her. I made sure I told Roger, though. Didn't want him to find out and think it was anything to do with me.'

Carol nodded, making so many connections in her thought processes.

Harry decided to move things along from Angie King.

'Obviously, there is little love lost between the two of you, Mr. Prince. What about others in the cast? Anyone else you have reason to suspect?'

'Well, it's hard to think of anyone who wouldn't have wanted to have got rid of King.'

'Except you, seemingly?' Harry smiled. Mark Prince chose to ignore the implication of this remark and spent the next twenty minutes throwing shade on almost every member of the cast and crew, including the town hall caretaker, who, Harry knew, was at home during the performance, watching a boxset on Netflix. Just as he was beginning to lose his patience, the conversation turned to Charles Blackwater.

'Charlie shouldn't have died, though,' mused Prince for a moment. 'Everyone liked Charlie in the society. Not like old King!'

'Everyone?' asked Harry. 'No backstage gossip that might be enlightening?'

'Not really,' replied Prince. 'There'd be the odd argument over who he'd cast as who, or a bit of a row over how he wanted something staged, but only the usual stuff you might get in any drama society. We were lucky he moved here and that we got the benefit of his enthusiasm and creativity. Mind you, I don't think the twins got on very well with him.'

'The twins?' interjected Harry.

'Arthur and George,' responded Prince, as if this was all that was needed to be said.

'Rosencrantz and Guildenstern,' helped Carol.

'Ah, right,' said Harry. 'And why do you say that, Mr. Prince?'

'I overheard an almighty row going on between the three of them, in Charlie's office the other week. They were really going for it. I've never heard Blackwater swear so much!'

'And what did it seem to be about?'

'I couldn't really tell. The door was closed, so I only got the occasional word or two. You'll have to ask them.'

'We will,' replied Harry. 'We most definitely will.'

CHAPTER 31

As Carol and Harry left the library building, Carol looked at him expectantly.

'What?' Harry asked.

'You know what!' she replied. 'Is he another suspect, or can we cross him off our list?'

'We don't cross anyone off the list unless we have a cast-iron alibi for that person and, unfortunately for Mark Prince, me hearing someone vomiting a few minutes before a murder does not constitute anything of the sort.'

'Thought so,' murmured Carol. 'Chemists next then? Talk to the twins?'

'In a few minutes,' agreed Harry, 'but first we'll pop to the

garage again.'
'Really? Steve Grey will be starting to get a persecution complex.'
'Good!' was all Harry deigned to reply.
'Mr Grey', called Harry as they re-entered the garage for the second time that morning.
'I am blessed,' said Grey. He turned and fixed Carol with a stare. 'Can't keep away, eh?'
Harry ignored him, but Carol gave one of her best teacher looks that could wither anyone at twenty paces. 'After our little altercation during the production, where did you go when you left the office?'
'I went for a quick p.. to urinate. Why? Is there a law against that now?'
'No,' replied Harry, 'but you haven't mentioned it at any of our previous encounters.'
'Pardon me for breathing! I didn't realise I had to account for all my bodily functions. Do you want me to make you a list?'
'That won't be necessary, I'm only interested in this one toilet visit. While you were in there, did anything happen that you might want to get off your chest?'
'You've been chatting with Marky boy, have you? Saw you heading in the direction of the library when you left here. Yeah, he was in there, throwing up as usual. Don't understand these people who put themselves through all that just to get on stage.'
'Might have been useful if you'd told us this before,' pushed Harry.
'What, and spoil your fun at him having to tell you it all himself? No way.'
'You are a rather nasty piece of work, aren't you?' Carol couldn't stop herself from addressing him. She'd dealt with too many playground bullies to just let it go, but Grey wasn't fazed at all.

'Just the way I am, luv. Just the way I am!'
'Nasty enough to commit two murders?' countered Harry.
'Probably,' came Grey's reply, 'but I didn't, so I suggest you keep up your enquiries. Now, if there's nothing else, I've got a couple of filters that need changing.'
Before Harry could reply, he turned his back on the two of them and returned to the car he had been working on. Carol took Harry's arm and they walked out without looking back.
As they returned to the street, Carol guided him across the road and pointed to the poster in Lorraine's shop window. The previous banner had been removed and, in its place, was a new, fluorescent one announcing that the following evening would see a further performance of "Hamlet" in commemoration of its producer, Charles Blackwater. In smaller print, underneath there was also mention of Derek King's demise and that the role of Polonius would now be filled by Stewart Manning.
'I guess Daniel must have given the go ahead for this?' suggested Carol.
'He must have opened the stage up from being a crime scene.'
Just at that moment, Harry's phone buzzed to announce a WhatsApp message had arrived. He opened it and smiled. He turned to Carol. 'You know when strange coincidences occur in real life?'
'Yeah, I guess. What is it?'
'This is from Daniel saying that they've opened up the Town Hall and he's allowing the actors to go ahead with their tribute performance.'
'Anything else?'
'Yeah. He wants us to attend and see if there's anything we spot that might help with the investigation, seeing as we were there on the night of the murder.'
'Can't wait!' said Carol excitedly.

'Me neither,' replied Harry, with rather less enthusiasm. Their last night of the holiday in Pikesmere was going to be so much fun!

CHAPTER 32

The family run chemist was only a couple of shops down from "Lorraine's Lingerie and Linen". Carol remembered visiting on their first day in the town and also recalled how slow service had been then. She also retained a pretty good image of the identical twins that had been serving in there. George and Arthur Mansfield seemed indistinguishable from each other and, as she had thought so many times these last few days, such a great casting for the roles of Rosencrantz and Guildenstern who were, themselves, difficult to separate in Shakespeare's play.

Over breakfast, assuming they would be making a visit to see these two thespians, Carol had again explained to Harry how they were minor characters that pretended to be friends of Hamlet's, but were actually spies. He'd assured her that he could remember their previous discussions and that they fitted the idea of being caught out by their own plotting, or, as the ripped-out quote had said, "hoist by their own petard", which made them definite suspects. Carol had been impressed, but obviously hadn't shown it. She hated Harry when he was able to be smug! Which wasn't very often! All the same, she was pleased that her literary knowledge was being listened to, absorbed and possibly being found useful in helping to solve this case.

The doorbell tinkled as they went inside. Luckily, no one was being served, but only one of the twins was behind the counter.

'George or Arthur? Any idea?' Carol whispered.
'Your guess is as good as mine,' returned Harry.
They approached the twin, behind whom, and on a slightly raised level, seemed to be a pharmaceutical area, no doubt used for preparing prescriptions. For the present, it looked to be empty.
'Mr. Mansfield?' Harry asked and the chemist looked up for the first time, in order to greet them.
'Yes, what can I do for you?'
'I'm Harry Bailey. I'm with the police and…'
Before he could conclude his introductions, he was somewhat rudely interrupted.
'I recognise you from the night of poor Derek King's murder. How can I help? I've already given my statement on the night.'
'That's fine. We're just following up on a few points of interest.'
'Very well. Fire away. As you can see, it's not our busiest time for customers. That's about 10 o'clock on a Monday morning, if you're interested. Once they've all been to the surgery after getting ill over the weekend.'
'Fascinating!' murmured Harry, under his breath and then continuing. 'We'd like to discuss the night of "poor Derek's" death in a bit more detail, but first, there's an incident that occurred a few weeks ago that might have some bearing on the case. Is your brother about? It might be useful if we talk to you together.'
'Of course.' He opened a door to the side of the counter and shouted up a narrow flight of stairs, 'George, have you nearly finished? We've got visitors.'
'This is Arthur, then,' Carol again whispered, whilst pretending to look at some toothpaste on a nearby shelf.
'Amazing powers of deduction!' Harry stated with his best dead-pan face.

'He's on his way,' Arthur stated, but with no necessity, as his brother's heavy footfall could be heard throughout the shop. Surprisingly, however, there was a lighter set of sounds following behind. George emerged and then Angie King's small frame appeared, clutching a small brown paper parcel as if her life depended on its contents. She shuffled past Carol, gave a mouse-like squeak in response to her and Harry's greeting, and exited the shop as quickly as she could. Harry watched her go and then turned back to the twins. Both were extremely tall and thin, with ashen complexions and seemed to be in their mid-thirties. As well as being mirror images of each other, they wore exactly the same brown, corduroy trousers, dark blue shirts and a green chemist's apron. Indeed, it was almost as if neither wanted to be distinguishable from the other.

'Is this the best place for us to talk? I wouldn't want to be disturbed for the next few minutes.'

'Sorry! We have to stay open for the public,' both Arthur and George answered in unison.

'Very well. Let's hope that the shop remains quiet. 'Could you tell us about an argument you seem to have had with Charles Drinkwater a few days ago? In his office.'

The twins looked at each other, both now seemingly restrained over who should go first.

'You were overheard by someone who said it was rather heated,' Harry continued.

It was George who decided to answer, 'It was something and nothing, that's all. We felt that we'd been typecast in the play.'

'And not for the first time,' Arthur continued. 'Who had to play the ugly sisters a year or two ago, when we did "Cinderella" as our panto? We did!'

'Then there was Tweedledum and Tweedledee in the carnival pageant' George stated, with real animosity in his voice. 'We were fed up with it. We're not even the right size to play them!'

Then, with no sign that they recognised any irony in the statement, whatsoever, both said in unison, 'We're individuals!'

'I see,' said Harry, aware that behind him, Carol was attempting to stifle a similar laugh to himself.

'Well, you may both find it amusing, but it was important for us to have it out with Mr. Blackwater,' George said.

Harry regained his composure, 'And you're sure there were no other issues between you? We wouldn't want to find, at a later date, that you might have had a motive to want to see him dead.'

Both men looked undeniably shocked at the very notion that they might have had anything to do with the producer's death and vehemently argued their innocence in the matter at some length, continuing to finish each other's thoughts and sentences with alarming rapidity.

'Okay,' said Harry at last, when he managed to get a word in, 'do either of you know of any reason why anyone else might want to have seen Mr. Blackwater out of the way?'

Arthur was first to reply, 'We've been talking about that these last couple of days. Have you talked to Reverend Brown yet?'

Harry nodded.

George continued, 'Did he tell you about him swapping roles with Derek King?'

Harry nodded again.

'We think that might have something to do with it!'

Harry looked a little confused and it was Carol who spoke first, 'That doesn't seem to make a lot of sense, does it? If I was in "Hamlet", I'd be happier playing Claudius than Polonius, so the only person that would be unhappy would be Mr. King, surely?'

'Exactly', the twins replied in unison.

Harry began to get more frustrated. 'So, you're suggesting that the person who would have most wanted to get revenge on Charles Blackwater is Derek King?'

'Yes'

'The one person who couldn't possibly have killed him because he was already dead.'

'But was he?' countered George.

'Yes, of course he was,' said Carol, starting to become as frustrated as Harry, 'We saw him dead, didn't we?'

George and Arthur looked at each other before the latter continued. 'But perhaps his spirit still walked abroad!'

'His spirit?' Harry asked, incredulously.

'Like Old Hamlet's ghost in the play. Derek King was seeking revenge for his own death because Charlie had made him play the part that got himself killed,' George said, as if it made all the sense in the world.

'So, you're suggesting that Derek King's spirit visited Charles Blackwater's home, had a drink of wine with him and then stabbed him?' Harry asked, attempting to hold back the frustration that he was feeling about the wasting of his time.

'Absolutely,' the two chemists replied.

'And who do you think might have murdered King, in this scenario?' Carol asked.

'Well,' said Arthur, 'this may seem a little more far-fetched.'

Harry looked over at Carol with raised eyebrows. She, in turn, furrowed her brow to show that he should hold back his obvious irritation and let them continue.

'Yes,' continued George, 'we think that it was probably Will.'

'I don't think we've come across anyone involved with the play called Will. Was he in the cast, or a member of the crew?' Harry asked, trying to search his memory for anyone called Will, Bill or William.

Both twins had a somewhat perplexed look on their faces, that seemed to imply that they thought Harry rather stupid.
'Will Shakespeare, of course,' they again said in unison.
'William Shakespeare?' Carol said slowly. 'The playwright? From Stratford? Who died over four hundred years ago?'
It was George who was first to try and substantiate what both, obviously thought, was quite the clearest candidate for the murder. 'Who else? Don't you see? His spirit was angered by the way Derek was playing the part of Polonius. He really wasn't a very good actor at all. Will would have been appalled at the way he was destroying one his finest works. So, he manifested himself behind the arras and, well, got rid of him.'
'That's quite a theory,' said Carol, mainly to fill in the silence that followed George's pronouncement. She looked across at Harry, but, for once, he seemed speechless. 'Is there anything else you can think of that might help with the case?' she continued.
'Isn't giving you both murderers enough?' replied Arthur.
Just as Harry seemed to be finding his ability to speak again, the shop bell rang and an elderly couple entered the chemists, the lady clutching her prescription.
'Sorry, business calls,' said Arthur and he went back behind the counter, as George climbed the couple of steps up to the pharmaceutical section.
'We may need to speak to you again,' called back Harry, as he and Carol made their way to the door, but both twins were already preoccupied in their duties.
'What on earth was all that about?' asked Carol, as they found themselves back out on the street.
'I'm not sure. I've been involved in a couple of cases where people who dabbled in the paranormal have tried to help with a case, often for their own ends, but I've never met anyone quite as sure of what they say as those two. Either

they are totally convinced of their own beliefs, or...'
'Or?' asked Carol.
'Or, they are consummate liars who have come up with an act to throw us off their scent. Remember, they're still up there as prime suspects according to that quote we found by King.'
'That's true. I'd forgotten about that with all the spiritual stuff.'
'Exactly! And that might be precisely what they intended!'
'Interesting that Angie looked to be more than an ordinary customer. Coming down the stairs with George like that. Looked highly suspicious clutching that package for dear life.'
'Drugs again, I'm guessing,' said Harry, as they began to make their way back towards The Green. He was about to say something else, but his phone pinged. He got it out and read the message. 'Daniel wants to catch up with me about this performance that's going to be put on. Want to tag along?'
'Not this time. I'll let you have a chance to chat with him by yourself. Wouldn't want to look too clingy! I might pop back to the hotel, grab a coffee in the room and then do a bit of retail therapy. I need to grab a couple of little presents for some of the department and I know you hate shopping.'
'Okay. See you later. I'll try and get some copies of some of those reviews and pictures off old Charlie's memory stick.'
Harry kissed her on the cheek and then strode off in the direction of Daniel's temporary situation rooms.

INTERLUDE

CHAPTER 32

Not a clue! They haven't got a clue! That's what makes murder so much fun. They didn't suspect anything when that bitch of a wife died and, now, they've got two more to get their teeth into and they're all running around like lost puppies that can't find their food. King was even killed in front of a whole audience and they still can't work out who it might be. Absolutely brilliant!

It was a shame about Charlie Drinkwater; he'd done a lot of good stuff, but he couldn't be left to live. Not with what he said. Especially once he started spouting off in his kitchen. Good job those knives were nice and handy. A good blade that one had. Sliced through the flesh very nicely!

Question is: will that be the end of it? Possibly, it might be nice to think that's it, but, somehow, I don't think so. Another little "problem" seems to have raised its ugly head and I think I'm going to have to deal with it in the usual way! After that, in the fullness of time, the police go away and everything gets back to normal. Yes, that's a "consummation devoutly to be wished", but murder sort of gets under your skin – the excitement, the blood rush. Funny phrase that, "blood rush". It's not just one's own blood that rushes at the moment of execution, but the other person's blood as well. Lots of stabbings and quite a lot of blood spilling. It might almost be a shame to leave it there!

And now the play is to be performed again. Plenty of opportunities! "Hamlet" should have bodies strewn across the stage by its end. It only seems right! Although I don't really think I can wait that long.

CHAPTER 33

'Bet you think I'm mad letting this lot put their play on again?' asked Daniel, once Harry had settled himself down and been given a fairly disgusting cup of weak tea. He'd made his way back to the Town Hall where it had all begun and to the situation room that Dan and the others had set up.
'Not really. I've seen quite a lot of madness this morning and you don't come anywhere near any of that!' Harry smiled at his friend and filled him in on the conversation at the chemists, as well as what they had gleaned at the library, which he feared was precious little. He then continued, 'Anyway, I think it's probably quite a clever move on your part.'
'Only quite?' reproved Daniel.
'Don't want you getting too cocky! Yea, it might shake up the situation a little. Turn over another couple of stones to see what's underneath! There's a lot of anger and pent-up emotions in that drama society of theirs and it'll do no harm to bring them all back together and see what emerges.'
'Thanks for the vote of confidence! I am a little worried about whether Miss King is going to be able to cope though. I did have a word with her before giving my blessing,' said Daniel.
'How did she react?'
'Unemotionally is probably the best way to describe it. She just looked past me for a few seconds and said it would be fine.'
'No other reaction?'
'Not a thing. I tried, but got nothing. Listen Harry, what do you make of her?'
'Drugged up to the eyeballs most of the time, or so it seems. Clever enough and happy to play the men in her life off

against each other when it suits.'

'Clever enough to commit patricide, do you reckon?' asked Dan.

'Listen to you with the clever words. Been on a course, have you?'

Daniel smiled.

Harry continued, 'Kill her own dad? Given the right circumstances, it's possible, but I'd say unlikely. However, I wouldn't put it past her to manipulate someone else into doing it for her.'

'Steve Grey, maybe?'

'Possibly. I'm not sure Roger Heart would be up to it. Angie found her mother after she was killed, you know.'

'Yes, we do function whilst you're out and about enjoying yourself.' Daniel again smiled and Harry held his hands up in a gesture of submission. 'I had a full report emailed over from the investigation that was undertaken at the time. Not very pleasant reading'

'Did it shed any light on the murders up here. Seems more than a coincidence that King's wife gets murdered and then he gets bumped off years later.'

'Years later is right. We're talking about something that happened pretty much a decade ago and a long way away from Pikesmere.'

'Where did it happen?'

'Small village. Smaller than this place if you can imagine that. Down in the Chilterns.' Daniel went over to his laptop and, after a moment, seemed to find the emailed report that he was looking for. 'A place called St Peters Hill. The distance and the gap in time make me think we're dealing with separate crimes, but you're absolutely right about the coincidence regarding the King family. There's something else, as well, that might link the cases.'

'Go on,' said Harry.

'King's wife was killed with a knife, a thick, serrated blade. She was stabbed three times. Forensics reckon the first one cut into the abdomen, but it would have been at least one of the other two that hit vital organs and killed her.'

'And that's what Angie found the following morning? That's awful. Poor girl. Did they find the knife?'

'Oh yes. The murderer had, it seems, casually washed it in the sink and then left it near the microwave, as if they knew it wasn't going to help catch them. This was another cold, brutal and calculated murder.'

'How did they get in?'

'Apparently, Mrs. King always left her door unlocked until she went to bed. Small village, nice and safe, or so she must have thought. Derek King's statement indicated that he'd told her on several occasions not to do this when he wasn't there, but she had obviously ignored him.'

'Where was he? Any possibility he could have done it?'

'Killed his own wife and then left her for his daughter to find? I don't think even King would be that callous! However, we both know that, in a lot of cases, these sorts of crimes are committed by people who know each other, particularly family members, so the police down there did look into King's whereabouts. It seems that he was at a developers' conference in a hotel in London. Witnesses stated he was definitely in the bar with them until 11.30. His wife's death was calculated to have taken place between 9 and midnight, so he was ruled out of their enquiries.'

'Anything else that might be of use?'

'Only one thing. King reckoned his wife might have been having an affair.'

'Really? It wouldn't be surprising if he was as obnoxious then as he seems to have been recently.'

'Quite! But, no one else seemed to know anything about it. None of her friends had any inkling of something going on and there were none of those helpful little hints that we sometimes find in diaries and so on. Nothing! In the end, reading between the lines of the investigating detective's statements, the police gave up on this as a viable line of enquiry and there seems to have been a decision taken that it was likely to just be Derek King's overactive and malicious imagination that there'd been an affair going on; so, who know?'

'It would give us some sort of motive, though,' said Harry, trying to clutch at something that might have been useful in what Dan had told him.

'For King to have done it, maybe. Knows, or thinks he knows that his wife is having an affair, so kills her. That'd work, except, as I say, there were several witnesses that place him far enough away for it to be impossible.'

'Was there nothing at the house where she died that could help with identifying the killer?' Harry asked, somewhat exasperated now.

'The report states that it had been raining that day and the ground was still wet. They thought they might have got a shoe print outside, but the murderer must have stuck to the gravel paths and there was nothing of any use to forensics. Also, there was a half-drunk glass of red wine on the kitchen table where it happened.'

'Just the one? Not like Blackwater's then?'

'No. Fingerprints and saliva tests indicated it was hers and no one else had touched it!'

'Pity! I was starting to think that we might be after a wine connoisseur. That might have narrowed the field.'

'No such luck. Oh, I've also got this for you. Now don't say I never give you anything.' He handed Harry a file and he looked inside. 'Copies of the reviews and pictures that Carol wanted to have a look at!'

'Brilliant,' said Harry, 'I was going to ask about these.'

'Well now you don't have to. Peruse them at your leisure. Anyway, I think we're both up to speed now, so I look forward to seeing you at the production.'
'I can't wait,' said Harry, as despondent as a school pupil who knew he had a three-hour Literature exam coming up. He left Daniel mulling over several more reports and made his way back towards The Green where he thought he might just manage a swift pint at The Lion before meeting back up with Carol, telling himself he'd be working because he might take a quick glance at the file he had just been given.

CHAPTER 34

Meanwhile, Carol had refreshed herself with a black coffee back in the hotel room and had then ventured back into Pikesmere to enjoy some midday sunshine and indulge in one of her favourite pastimes: shopping! There were several, small independent shops in the town that sold local gifts. There were tea towels with outline drawings of the mere and the birdlife that inhabited it; items of porcelain with similar images; and racks of postcards with views of the area. Who, wondered Carol, as she browsed some of these shops, still bought postcards in this day and age, when you can take a similar picture on your phone, include yourself, and send it, instantly, to anyone who might be nominally interested in what you might be doing? Even so, she had just managed to find a couple of small gifts to take back to school the following Monday, when she glimpsed Angie King walking slowly on the other side of the road. As nonchalantly as she could, Carol crossed and tried, as casually as she could, to walk up beside her.

'Angie,' she said, acting as surprised as she could sound, 'Fancy seeing you again.'
'Small town isn't it?' was her only reply.
'Do you mind if I walk with you? Maybe you could point me in the direction of some good shops to buy presents?'
'Free country!' she said, but did not take up the offer of sharing any local retail knowledge she might be in possession of.
'So,' began Carol after a moment, 'I see you're all going to be putting on "Hamlet" again. Hard for you in particular, I should think.'
'I guess,' the younger woman replied, 'but not as hard as losing both your parents in murders!'
'I suppose so,' agreed Carol, somewhat taken aback by the brutality of the response. 'You know, it's alright to admit you're hurting, struggling even. Sometimes, it's easier to talk to a relative stranger than it is to friends.'
'You sound like some of my teachers at college.'
'Do I come across that obviously?'
'Just a bit!' And for the first time that Carol could remember, she saw a slight smile cross Angela King's face.
'Listen, why don't I take you for a coffee? We can either sit in silence, or we can have a bit of a girly chat. What do you say?'
Angie pondered the proposition for a few seconds before deciding that it might be a good idea, despite her misgivings. 'Alright. There's a place that does really nice hot chocolate down towards the mere. When I was younger, dad used to..' She trailed off and the childish exuberance of a moment ago faded instantly.
'Come on, then. Lead the way. I'd love a hot chocolate.' And as she said it, Carol linked arms with Angie and let her take the lead and walk them towards the tea shop.
It only took them about five minutes to get there and much

of the walk was undertaken in silence, King occasionally wiping away a tear as she seemingly remembered similar times when she had visited the same establishment. Carol hadn't wanted to force her to confront her memories, but knew that, sometimes, it was better for these pent-up emotions to be released. At least Angie King wasn't in full Ophelia mode for a change!

They found the café almost deserted and sat at a twee, lace-clothed table, set in a bow window, with views across to the mere. A young waitress, possibly even younger than Angie, dressed in an old-fashioned black and white maid's uniform, complete with more lace stitched around her pinny, took their order for two hot chocolates with whipped cream and extra marshmallows. Surprisingly, it was King that spoke first.

'Has your husband worked out who killed dad and Charlie then?'

'Well, he's not my husband, but he might be one day, but let's just say, he's working hard on it. Once he's on a case, he doesn't let anything get in his way.'

'Bit of a Rottweiler, is he?' She again smiled and Carol couldn't help but think how much prettier it made her seem than her usual, angst-driven, demeanour.

'You might say that. This is supposed to be a holiday, but he still wants to get to the bottom of it all.'

'Well, I hope he's better at it than the lot who tried to find out who killed mum. They were useless!'

'I'm sure they did their best.'

'They spent most of their time, from what I can remember, questioning dad; and he wasn't even about that night.'

'It must have been horrible for you. Can you remember much about it?'

'Not really, thank goodness. I still see the blood and mum lying on the floor, in my nightmares, sometimes. When I'd woken up that morning, I'd gone into mum's bedroom like I usually did and found she wasn't there. I called her, but, of course, there was no answer. I didn't know why at the time, so I went downstairs and saw her.'

'That is so sad, Angie. I can't begin to imagine what it must have been like for you. What did you do?' Carol stared at this young, vulnerable teenager who had suffered so much tragedy in so few years.

'I phoned 999 like mum had always said I should if there was a problem and told them I needed an ambulance; then I just sat in the kitchen with her. I think I thought, or perhaps hoped, that she wasn't dead.'

It was just at that moment that their mugs of hot chocolate arrived and the mood changed almost instantly, as Carol had seen it do several times before over the last few days. Angie moved off the topic of her mother's death and talked about college and what she was hoping to do in years to come. The sorts of dreams that lots of young people had about travelling and so on, but Carol knew that, for Angela King, the money she was likely to inherit made all of it possible. As she opened up about her aspirations, it was noticeable, however, that there was no mention of Roger Heart, or Steve Grey, or, indeed, any partner that might join her in her adventures. Carol let her pour out her thoughts, realising that, with Derek King's reputation, this might be the first time the girl had been able to discuss them with anyone who might be interested and willing to listen. She sipped her hot chocolate, making sure not to get a whipped cream moustache, and waited for an opportune moment to speak.

'You've certainly got your life mapped out. I hope it all comes to fruition for you.'

'Thanks for listening to me ramble on. I think it will happen, now.'

This was the first time that Angie King had suggested that

her father's death might actually have not been as tragic as it might, at first, appear, so Carol decided to press the point a little. 'Now? Do you mean now that your father is no longer here? We know he could be a little, how should I put it, domineering.'

'Oh, he could certainly be that, but I wasn't thinking of dad. No, I've realised over the last few days, well, weeks really, that it's been Roger that's been holding me back, not dad. He talks about drama school, but I don't think he ever wants to leave Pikesmere. I think he'd be happy to just stay here and waste his talent and his life. Well, not me! I'm going to see the world and live like there's no tomorrow because, if all these tragedies in my life have taught me one thing, it's that it could all end quicker than anyone imagines.'

'You've certainly got an adult head on young shoulders,' replied Carol, impressed with what she was hearing. 'Does Steve Grey have a place in these plans, then?'

Angie almost spat out the last of her hot chocolate as she laughed at the thought. 'Not a chance. Oh, he's a bit more fun than Roge and has a bit more drive, but that's all there is to Steve. I'll let you into a little secret, I enjoy teasing him and stringing him along. Do you think I'm a wicked person for doing that?'

'We've all done it!' remarked Carol, as she thought back to her own teenage years and envied Angie's self-awareness. 'You do what's best for you, so long as you don't hurt anyone too much along the way!'

'I'll try. Is that it, then? Interrogation over?' She smiled, however, as she said it.

'One last thing, if I can sound a bit like Colombo?'

'Who?' asked Angie, straight-faced.

'Never mind. Bit before your time. Bit before mine if I'm honest. Sunday afternoon reruns whilst waiting for Harry to get in! Anyway, what I was going to ask was, do you think either Roger, or Steve, could have killed your dad for whatever reason?'

Angie thought about the question for a while before replying. 'I'm pretty sure Roger couldn't. He might have wanted to, all the hassle that dad gave him, but he's a real pacifist. I've seen him catch wasps and spiders and take them outside when I'd have just killed them. I reckon he'll turn Buddhist one day. No, he wouldn't be able to.'

'And Grey?'

'Now he could do it and he had more motive because of dad getting him put away, but I'm pretty sure he didn't. If Steve had wanted to do it, he'd have used his bare hands. That's the sort of bloke he is. Chalk and cheese, him and Roge. One wouldn't hurt a fly, the other likes to use his fists. A dagger wouldn't be his choice of weapon.'

'Thanks, Angie. That's been a great help and I hope it's been good for you too.'

'It has. Very cathartic!'

'Good choice of word. I wish some of my A-Level students were so articulate.'

'The Aristotelean purging of emotion.'

'Wow. Even more impressive. You must have a good English teacher.'

'It was Charlie who taught me all about it, actually. Charlie Blackwater, the director.'

'Really?' said Carol, surprised that he would be the source of Angie's knowledge. She started to stand, but then settled again, as the young woman obviously had more to say on the subject.

'He was such a clever man, was Charlie. Not just knowing stuff like that, but, sometimes, it was as if he could see right through you. Right into your soul, if you know what I mean. He'd know you'd had a bad day before you said anything and almost what you were thinking.'

'I think I know exactly what you mean. I've got a headteacher who's just like that. You can't get anything past her.'
'Exactly! I think that's why he got killed!'
'He knew something about the murderer, you mean?'
'Oh, he'd have known. Nothing went on in our drama group that Charlie didn't know about. That's why he was so great with his casting. People didn't grow into their parts like you usually do with a play. He'd get people who were already like that and give them the parts that suited them. He used to say that if it was good enough for Shakespeare, it was good enough for him! Arrogant bugger!' She smiled.
'It's true what you've just said. Whilst we've been involved with your play group, I've kept pointing out to Harry how clever Mr. Blackwater's casting was. How almost every person really suited their role! Steve, as Fortinbras, the man of action; Roger as Hamlet, the melancholic introspective young man; the twins as Rosencrantz and Guildenstern; even your father as the domineering father.'
'I bet you include me in that list,' giggled Angie, knowingly.
'Well, far be it from me to say anything,' replied Carol slowly, not wishing to spoil what had been a pleasant and useful interchange.
'It's alright. You don't need to worry that you'll offend me. Like I said, Charlie was a master at the art of casting. He could see Ophelia in me: lovesick at times, manic at others, dictated to by the oppressive father who wouldn't, or couldn't, give her any freedom. I just hope Charlie wasn't prophetic and that I end up drowning myself under some willow tree.'
'I'm sure you won't, Angie,' replied Carol, quickly, although not entirely as sure about that as she tried to sound. 'Thank you so much for chatting to me so honestly.'
'It's easier when there's no coppers around. I like your fella,

but he's still a policeman.'

'That he is,' replied Carol, as she got her card out to go and pay at the till.

'Let me get them,' said Angie, rising. 'I've got the money, you know.'

Carol acquiesced, as Angie went over to the till. 'That you have, my girl, that you have', she thought.

As they left the tea shop, Carol asked one last question, 'Any idea where I could find anything like a watercolour or oil painting of the mere? I like to have something to hang at home, to remind me of places I've visited. There're loads of tea towels, but I don't think they'd look very good hanging on the wall of our flat.'

Angie laughed, 'That's the easiest question you've asked me. Try Stew's place. He has an area, towards the back of the shop, where he lets local artists show their paintings. There's usually quite a nice selection and some of them are pretty good. See you tomorrow night at the play.'

With that, Angela King skipped off towards her home, whilst Carol messaged to find out where Harry was, got the reply that he was enjoying a pint in the pub, so decided to finish her shopping by visiting the Manning emporium once again.

CHAPTER 35

The glass, automatic doors opened with their usual, accompanying sound effect and Carol looked above the rows of stock, where banners hung telling shoppers where they could find pet, kitchen and bathroom items, as well as soft furnishings and tools. Nothing, however, indicated that there might be an area devoted to paintings, or local artistry. She remembered that Angie had told her that these were usually kept towards the back of the emporium, so she started to make her way down the central aisle of kitchen products, briefly stopping, on several occasions, to look at a particular set of pans, various utensils and a selection of air-fryers, one particular model she had been nagging Harry, for some time, that they should get. As she got towards the end of the aisle, she met Mandy, the same young shop assistant that they had come across last time they were there. She was on her knees this time, holding a machine that was printing out new sale price tickets that she was diligently sticking onto various oven gloves. Carol was about to ask her about where she might find the paintings, when her eye was drawn to a recess, a bit further on, which looked to have just what she was looking for. The young girl seemed relieved not to have to help anyone and continued with her prescribed job.

Carol was surprised at the wealth of talent that greeted her, as she began to make her way around the small, but well lit, back section of the shop which housed the paintings, line-drawings and sketches that she had been looking for, all beautifully hung on display boards. Some were priced too high for Carol, despite them being amateur, but others were reasonable and a couple of these took her eye more than some of the really expensive ones. There was a particularly beautiful water-colour of the mere, painted from the far side and including Roger Brown's church in the background. Another was painted in oils and featured a proud looking pair of swans in the foreground, with the blue expanse of the mere behind, making them look almost three-dimensional in their representation. Just as she began to try and narrow down her choices, a shadow was thrown across the stand upon which the swan painting was hung and a familiar, booming voice made her turn round and smile.

'I'll do you a good deal on those, if you're interested!'

'Mr Manning! Uh, Stew. Nice to see you again. Yes, I would like to buy one, but I can't make my mind up which I prefer.'
'Why not have both, then? Whenever I can't make up my mind, I try not to force myself and just get both. Makes life all the better, I reckon.'
'What sort of deal can you do? Won't the artists mind if they don't get the asking price?'
'This isn't one of those posh art galleries. That's why they let me try to sell their wares. Most are happy just to make a sale.'
'Do you get a percentage?'
Stewart Manning smiled, 'Not at all. Not at all! It all goes to the artists. Their need is greater than mine.'
'That's extremely generous of you. Giving up a part of your shop and not expecting any renumeration.'
'Just being public-spirited, that's all. It's a small town and a bit of goodwill goes a long way round here. Found that out in my first shop when I was down south and it's even more true in Pikesmere. I prefer it up here though! Anyway, most of them come in at least once a week to check whether there's been a sale and they usually end up buying stuff in the store. Good for all of us!'
Carol was about to reply, but just as she started to speak, she abruptly stopped, her eyes drawn to the signature at the bottom of the church and mere water-colour. It was clearly signed "C. Blackwater". Manning followed her stare and realised what had drawn her eye and stopped her speech.
'Yes, it's one of Charlie's,' he said. 'His talents were not just in the dramatic sphere. He was quite a proficient artist as well. There're various scenes of town life, painted by him, hung on many a Pikesmere wall. I've got one of his hung at home myself. This one was his latest.' He paused for a second or two and then continued, 'Sadly, it seems, his last.'
Carol dragged her eyes away from the painting and back to

the larger-than-life figure that stood in front of her. As he mused on what he had just said, he seemed to have shrunk slightly in stature and she thought she glimpsed a watery eye begin to form, before he obviously dragged himself back to the present and regained his usual, brash self.

'Well,' he said, 'he won't be needing the money now, so I'll tell you what I'll do for you. Buy one of the others and I'll let you have Charlie's as a keepsake. Remind you of your time in our little town.'

Carol couldn't decide quite how callous, or thoughtful, this sounded and she wasn't sure whether she wanted, in times to come, to look at her wall and be reminded of the murder of the artist. 'That's very considerate of you, Stew,' she eventually replied. 'I'll take this swan oil as well, if that's ok.'

'Good choice. Good choice. Let's get them both wrapped up for you. The weather looks as if it might be on the turn, so we wouldn't want them to get any rain on them if it does.'

He took them off the display board upon which they were hung and started to make his way to the tills near the doors, marching away with long strides, leaving Carol attempting to keep up. It was almost as if he was scared she might change her mind if he gave her half a chance.

As she searched in her purse for her debit card, Carol thought she might as well attempt to gain another insight into the proposed performance of "Hamlet" the following evening. 'I'm looking forward to catching the whole of the play, tomorrow. Will we be seeing your portrayal of Polonius as you suggested the other day?'

'Ah, you remembered that I said that, did you?' he replied. 'Better be careful how much I say to you, with a memory like that. Yes, that's why I'm rushing your sale a little bit. I was just off to the Town Hall when I spied you looking at the artworks.'

'Really? Are you rehearsing?'

'Yes, this evening, but, before that, I need to make sure the stage is all ready. The police have been messing about all over it for days – well, you'd probably know better than me.'
Carol didn't, but thought it better not to disabuse Stewart Manning of her amateur role in the whole process, or say anything about the idea that a murder investigation might be more than just a case of 'messing about' with his precious staging. Instead, she simply replied, 'I expect so.'
'Well, if I'm going to play Polonius, I won't have much chance to sort out much backstage, so I thought I'd better get in there early and make sure everything is ready for the rehearsal and then the performance. Not even sure whether they've been up any ladders and fiddled with the lighting rig. That'll take me forever to reset if they have.'
'I'm sure you'll cope. You seem to be an organised sort of chap.'
'Thanks for that. I think some of the cast just see me as a bit of a charlatan. Good for building a bit of set, or repositioning some lights. Well, perhaps if I can pull Polonius off tomorrow, I might be accepted as a thespian as well.'
'All the best for it. Break a leg.' said Carol and she made her way out, clutching her well-wrapped paintings under her arm. However, as she made her way back into the town, something had begun to nag in a small recess of her mind, but she couldn't, for the life of her, recollect what it was.

CHAPTER 36

'Did you manage to find everything you were looking for?' asked Harry, as Carol sat down next to him in the same spot of the public house where they had watched Angie King's "mad scene" the previous night.

'Pretty much. I've been surprised at how many independent shops there are in such a small town. I've got a surprise to show you as well, but you can get me a G & T please.' She looked down at the two empty pint glasses sat on the table. 'Looks like I have a bit of catching up to do. Perhaps you better make it a double.'

Once Harry had sat back down with her drink, he asked, 'What have you got to show me then?'

'All in good time.' She took a sip of her gin to create a little tension. 'Firstly, I've been having a bit of a girly chat with Angie King.' She filled Harry in about what they had talked about and then brought out the larger of the two packages that had been sat on the floor near to her seat.

'I hope that wasn't too expensive,' joked Harry.

'It was free actually.'

'Really?' Harry was never convinced when Carol said that something had been free. 'How come?'

Carol removed the brown paper covering from the bottom corner and showed Harry the signature.

'Charles Blackwater, eh? A man of many talents that one.'

'Indeed he was.'

'Where did you find it?

'Stewart Manning's shop. He's got a section set aside for local artists.'

'Very public-spirited of him.'

'That's exactly what he said about himself!'

'I bet he did.'

'Now don't be horrible. He said I could have it for free.'

'What was the catch?'

Carol took a longer sip of her drink this time, before replying. 'I had to buy a second one.'

'Bet he likes his "Buy One Get One Free" offers!'

'Anyway, they're both lovely paintings.'

'I believe you. Anyway, I'll tell you, now, what I've been

hearing off Dan.' Once he had finished with his recap, he passed the file over to Carol and stated, somewhat mendaciously, that he had spent most of his time in the pub trawling through the pages, but nothing had jumped out. Having taken a cursory glance at them, Carol said, 'I'll take a more thorough look through these once we get back to the hotel,' and she placed the folder carefully in one of her bags. It was about three-quarters of an hour later that they both emerged from the pub and set off back across The Green. Carol was about to ask what they should get up to for the rest of the afternoon when Harry's phone rang and he stood by the stocks and answered it. Although Carol couldn't hear who was on the other end, she guessed it might be Daniel and could see Harry's face go slightly pale.

'Thanks, Dan. We'll get right over.' He put the phone back in his pocket and said, rather bluntly, 'There's been another murder.'

'Where?' asked Carol.

'The church of all places. Dan wondered if we could go and have a look. But listen, you don't have to come. It might be pretty gruesome by the sounds of it.'

'I managed with Derek King, didn't I?' replied Carol, not wanting to be left out. 'Who is it?'

'Oddly, Dan didn't say. If you're up for it, then, we'd best go see.'

Whether or not Carol was going to go was really a moot point because, by that time, they had already started walking towards the church and it was only as they made their way through the police cordon tape, at the foot of the steep bank that led up, past the town cenotaph, to the old, sandstone church, that she realised that she was still carrying her pictures and bags of presents and how she really felt being laden down with frivolous shopping was probably not the ideal way to enter a murder scene. Harry, of course, was oblivious to her dilemma and focussed entirely on getting in and seeing what had actually occurred. The huge wooden doors, with their heavy iron handles, stood slightly ajar and the worn stone carvings of angels and saints, on each surrounding pillar, seemed to watch inscrutably as they entered.

The interior was vast and vaulted with huge, dark wooden beams, a witness to the fact that, at one time, the whole town could, and probably did, gather here. The pews looked to be Victorian and there were small, brass nameplates attached to the end of some of them, marking which family had either donated it, or maybe had it reserved for services. The dates, all in the 1800s, indicated this was another relic of the past. Juxtaposed with this antiquity, modern fluorescent lighting lit the main aisle and served to supplement the natural light, or lack of it, due to the overcast conditions outside, which permeated through the various, highly colourful, stained-glass windows that filled the walls. Several brightly adorned flags of the British Legion and other respected institutions hung above the whole scene. Harry was, Carol assumed, probably oblivious to everything other than the crime scene itself and began to make his way down the tiled floor of the central aisle, towards the pulpit and the altar, where Daniel, Sergeant Pearson and another, bespectacled man stood looking down at the carpeted area in front of the large brass cross and candlesticks.

Carol, surreptitiously, placed her bags and packages down on one of the back pews and hurried down to catch up with Harry. As she reached the area in front of the altar, she caught sight of Mike Brown sat in one of the pews to the right side of the church. The reverend's head was bowed in prayer, with his hands firmly clasped together in front of him. 'He's not the new corpse then!' thought Carol. As they had made their way to the church, Brown's name had come up in their speculation as to who the body might be.

The body, however, as Carol turned to view it, was female. She lay, face down, on the red carpeted steps leading up to the communion rail, her yellow dress stained by copious amounts of blood; a knife had been plunged into her back and left there. For a horrible moment, Carol thought that she might be physically sick, as a wave of nausea swept through her, but she controlled the urge and looked again at the lifeless object that had, until very recently, been a living, breathing human being. Her first instinct was to think it might be Angie King, with whom she had met only an hour or two ago and shared hot chocolate, but the woman looked to be a little larger than Angie's diminutive frame and Carol reprimanded herself for almost feeing relief that it was not "Ophelia" that lay before her. After the initial shock of what she was looking at, her brain began to tune back into the discussion that was taking place to her side. The oldish man, with glasses, seemed to be a doctor and was going through the findings from his initial examination of the corpse.

'Although the knife in the back has done a lot of damage, it is not the wound that killed her,' he said. 'When you lift up the body, you see that there is a wide gash across the throat and round to the neck which has severed the carotid; it was this that, I think, killed her. Sickening as it might seem, the knife looks to have been plunged into the back once the victim was lying dead on the ground, almost as an afterthought and just somewhere to leave it. Horrible. Truly horrible! And after poor Charles' death as well.'

Are there similarities, doctor? Anything to indicate it was the same killer?' It was Daniel that had asked the question.

'Well, seeing as we haven't had a suspicious death in Pikesmere all the years I've lived here and, now, three in the same week, and all with various types of blade, I hesitate to do your jobs for you, but I'd say the indications are pretty conclusive.'

'Thanks for coming so quickly, doctor. Our forensic team will be here soon to take over.'

'My..' The doctor seemed to be going to say 'pleasure', but thought better of it and hurried off down the aisle.

Carol found her voice at last. 'Who is it?

Daniel turned to her, as if realising for the first time that she had accompanied Harry. 'Reverend Brown tells us it's one of his parishioners. A lady called Gloria Bebb. She's on the roster for doing the flowers and polishing the brasses. It looks as if she'd come in to do the latter when the assailant struck.' He indicated a cloth and a plastic basket of cleaning equipment that lay at the bottom of the pulpit and that Carol had missed, having been fixated on the body itself.

Reverend Brown had finished praying and made his way over to them. 'She was a lovely woman. Always willing to help out. Been doing the flowers for at least two or three years now. Never complained, just got on. The only time I've ever heard her annoyed was when she told me off for not buying the right brass cleaning products. She told me she'd buy her own from now on, so that it would be right.' He smiled at the memory.

'And you found her here, did you?' asked Harry.

'Yes, I'll often pop in to say thank you to the ladies that help; for the hard work they put in to make the church look so inviting. I knew it was Gloria on today, so called out to her as I entered through the vestry. When there was no reply, I thought it was rather odd, as she always had a cheery reply, but then I came through and found her lying here.'

'Does she have anything to do with the play that you're performing?' asked Harry.

'Oh no. I don't think she even came to watch anything that we did. Not interested in that sort of thing, from what I could

gather. I tried to tempt her to come along, but I don't think she ever did.'
'Did you call 999 immediately?'
'Yes. Well, not quite. I prayed for a moment, as it was pretty clear that she had passed away. Then I called.' Brown looked a little embarrassed at this.
'That's okay, Reverend,' said Daniel, quickly. 'We'll forgive you that, considering your vocation.'
'Does she have any family?' asked Harry.
'No, she was a widow, I think,' Reverend Brown responded and thought for a moment. 'Yes, definitely a widow. I remember her telling me that she didn't like to talk about her deceased husband, as it stirred up too many sad memories. They'd never had children and she moved up here to get away from the past and start again after his death.'
'Any idea how he died? She's not that old.'
'She never said. As I've suggested, she didn't like to talk about it and I never asked her age. One doesn't, does one? I would say she was probably in her late forties, so no, not so old at all.'
'Do you have her home address?' asked Daniel.
'It'll either be in the vestry or up at the vicarage. May I go and have a look for it?'
'If you would,' replied Daniel and the vicar nodded and departed, through the side door beyond the pulpit, which obviously led to the vestry from which he had first entered. Once he had closed the door behind him, Harry sat down in one of the front pews and shook his head. 'Dan, what the hell is happening in this town?' He realised what he had said in the church and looked towards Carol to see if he was going to be in trouble later. She shook her head in disbelief, but smiled to show it was more than justified.
'Your guess is as good as mine at this stage,' replied Daniel, also shaking his head, but this time in agreement with

Harry's question. 'Just when you think you might have a handle on all this and reckon your suspects are part of that drama lot, something like this happens. Gloria, here, seems to have had nothing to do with the play or the group.'

'Which makes our friendly reverend the only link,' said Carol, only realising that her musing had found voice after she had said it.

'Very true,' said Daniel, 'but also very circumstantial. We'll obviously look into it though.

'Are you still going to let that blasted play go on after all this?'

'Not sure at this stage, if you'll pardon the pun.'

Carol was not impressed with the light-heartedness with which Daniel was talking, whilst standing next to a woman's lifeless body, but she controlled her disappointment with the man she thought she had some respect for and hoped that Harry would never act like that. Instead, she pointed out, 'Well, you'd best decide pretty quickly. I've just been up to Stewart Manning's place and he was rushing to get to the Town Hall in order to prepare for a rehearsal tonight.'

'Really,' said Harry, 'you didn't say.'

'Didn't I? Oh well, I'm telling you now. Must have forgotten.'

'Look,' said Daniel, 'I know I've already ruined most of your holiday, but can I ask another big favour?'

'You can try,' replied Harry, suspecting what might be coming.

'I'm going to be tied up here the rest of the day and probably well into the evening. Like I said to the vicar, forensics will be here soon and, well, you know what it'll be like, Harry.'

Harry nodded. He knew exactly what Daniel would have to do.

'Could you both go along to tonight's rehearsal? Be my eyes and ears as it were. If this hadn't happened, and I'd have known it was going to take place, I'd have made sure to be

there. Like we said this morning, the whole point of letting the play happen is to see if we can uncover something.'
Before Harry could answer, Carol replied, 'Of course we'll go and do some spying. It'll be our pleasure, won't it Harry?'
'Does it mean we don't have to go to tomorrow night's performance, then?' asked Harry, keen to salvage something from the train wreck of the day.
'We'll see,' said Carol and it was then that Harry knew he was doomed, because whenever she said that, it meant definitely not. Dan grinned and after saying copious amounts of thanks, the large wooden doors of the church opened and the forensic team that had, only recently, been sent back to Shrewsbury, made their way into the building. Daniel went over to talk with them and Carol and Harry made their way outside again, Carol making sure that she collected her bags and paintings on the way. Stewart Manning had been correct when he had said the weather was turning. The wind had picked up and there was moisture in the air, so Carol was pleased that he had made her have the artwork wrapped up. They made their way down the hill from the church, the path bordered on both sides by the graves of townspeople dating back several hundred years. Although neither of them spoke, both Carol and Harry were acutely aware that there were now three more bodies to be buried.

INTERLUDE

CHAPTER 37

Well, that was an easy one, wasn't it? The trick, of course, is to know people's routines. If you know that, then planning a murder is easy. Once you see the Brasso, you know it's that time of the month to get those candlesticks polished and gleaming for Sunday crowd.
She's to blame, though. Has had it coming for a while. Putting too much pressure on for anyone's liking. Then starting to make snide comments about how Derek King's murder was a bit like her husband's. Trying to make some sort of connection. Then she started on about Charlie's death. Similar M.O. she thought. Didn't think she had the brains to even put two and two together and she'd certainly not know what 'Modus Operandi' means. Probably just heard it on one of those true crime programmes she liked to watch. She should have been more careful! Being suspicious is never good for anyone!
What is it that Hamlet says? Oh yes, "Foul deeds will rise, Though all the earth o'erwhelm them, to men's eyes."
Ha! Not this time, my Danish friend!
There're no returning spirits seeking revenge around here to help fill in the missing pieces. Just clueless coppers and brainless teachers, running about, here and there, expending all their energy, while the bodies just mount up.
Talking of which: soon be back on the stage. Oh, what fun is to be had.

CHAPTER 38

"Foul deeds will rise,
Though all the earth o'erwhelm them, to men's eyes."
Roger Heart's voice seemed that little bit more plaintive as he delivered the line out to a somewhat emptier hall than the last time he'd been in his costume, on the fatal night of King's murder.
Carol and Harry had just managed to catch the end of Act I, scene 2 of the rehearsal, having left their hotel a little later than they had anticipated. Although Carol was happy to get going, despite the storm and accompanying heavy rain that had hit just after their evening meal, Harry said it would soon pass and they waited in the foyer for an abatement.
The stage looked exactly the same as before, as they entered the hall and, although a few of the cast, who were sat around watching the rehearsal in the room, turned to see who was coming in, no one seemed too surprised at their intrusion, having been chatted to, interrogated, or cajoled by the pair, over the last couple of days.
'I told you we'd miss the start,' whispered Carol, as they pulled out a couple of chairs from a nearby stack and sat at the back of the hall, close to the double doors through which they had just entered.
'I wasn't going to get drenched and, anyway, we haven't missed much have we?' replied Harry, quietly, as he took his wet coat off and hung it on the back of the chair.
'No, luckily for you. Only about ten minutes, or so.'
'That's alright then.'
'So, what exactly should we be looking for this evening?' asked Carol.
'Anything and everything,' was Harry's enigmatic reply.
'Well, that's a great help, I'm sure, Mr Know-it-all inspector!'

Harry sighed. 'I guess the main thing I want to see is the reactions to each other. We've been talking to them all individually, pretty much, but this is the first time they've all been back together since King and Blackwater's murder, so someone might give something away. It could just be a look, or a gesture, or maybe the way they talk to one another, or even deliver a particular line.'

'Shush!' interrupted Carol, they've started Scene 3. This should be interesting because Polonius is on a lot in this one. It'll give us a chance to see what Stew Manning is like on stage!'

They sat in silence and watched Andrew Cross and Angie King open the scene as Laertes and Ophelia, brother and sister, discussing how each should behave whilst apart. It was all going well, Carol thought, until Angie delivered the famous admonishment, ' "Whilst like a puffed and reckless libertine, Himself the primrose path of dalliance treads, and recks not his own"... Andy, what the hell are you doing?'

Angie King was staring at her co-performer, as he had turned his back to the audience and seemed to be stuffing his hands into his tights.

She couldn't help but burst into fits of laughter as he replied, 'It's this bloody codpiece that I've got to wear. It keeps slipping down. It's like playing with a box in cricket.'

From the wings, a booming voice announced the presence of Stewart Manning. 'Thank you both for ruining my entrance. Can we carry on, please?'

'Sounds like our friend Stew has taken over the role of director as well as Polonius,' whispered Harry.

'That wouldn't be surprising. Stage managers often take on that role once a performance is up and running. Directors move on and leave it in their hands to ensure the smooth running of a production.'

'Thank you, miss. Very informative as usual,' grinned Harry, as Carol elbowed him, non-too gently, in the ribs.

The young pair on stage had managed to control their giggles at last, and the errant codpiece, and Cross delivered the line that heralded his father, Polonius' arrival.

"I stay too long – But here my father comes."

Manning strode onto the stage, script in hand and wearing Derek King's costume from a few nights previous. It looked slightly small and tight on him, but then, thought Harry, so did Stew's own suit that he was wearing when they interviewed him at his shop. Before Laertes could deliver his following two lines, Stew began reading from his script. Cross looked at Angie King, gave an exasperated sigh and just let the scene unfold. Despite him reading his lines, Manning was extremely convincing as the manipulative, yet pompous father figure.

Carol turned to Harry and murmured, 'He's actually pretty good. He's using the iambic beat of the lines, but not so slavishly that it sounds monotonous.'

'Been watching Kenneth Branagh again,' retorted Harry, but he had to admit that, for someone who was just standing in, Stew was doing a pretty good job.

Just as they reached the end of the scene, without any further clothing malfunctions, the double doors behind Carol and Harry opened and an out-of-breath Mike Brown entered, dressed in his regal, fur-lined gown and obviously ready to take up the reins as King Claudius. Most of the cast turned to see who had entered and there were a few audible gasps from some.

Manning put his hand up to shield his eyes from the spotlights and to look at what the disturbance was out in the hall. He called out from the stage, 'Michael, my dear fellow, we didn't expect you to come tonight. We all understood that you might be, how might one put it, indisposed after what you've had to deal with today.'

'The town grapevine has obviously been doing its work,' said Carol, as Mike continued up the hall and faced Manning on the stage.

'Didn't think it was fair to expect you to read in my part as well as play Polonius. Bit of a stretch even for your inestimable talents!' said Brown, and he made his way backstage with a number of the cast patting him on the back and praising him on his commitment to "the boards".

Lorraine Davies was even heard to remark with the age-old cliché, "Well done, Mike, the show must go on and all that, eh?'

Harry turned to Carol and said, as quietly as he could, 'Did you detect a certain degree of coolness between the reverend and our new Polonius?'

'Particularly icy, I would say,' replied Carol. 'Now why might that be, I wonder? We didn't get any sense that they weren't on good terms earlier, did we?'

'Not that I can remember and, as you know, I remember everything!'

'Except my birthday!' replied Carol.

'Once! Just once I forgot it and, in my defence, I was in the middle of another murder investigation at the time. You're never going to let me forget it though, are you?'

'Not a chance!' smiled Carol and they turned to watch what was now happening on the stage.

Mike Brown had just entered as the ghost of Hamlet's dead father. Harry remembered how Carol had explained that this was a clever device, sometimes used by directors of "Hamlet", over the years, to give the impression that Claudius was very similar to his dead brother and this is possibly one of the reasons why Gertrude marries him so quickly after the death of her husband. It was also, Carol had pointed out, a good way for smaller acting companies to get away with less male actors. The reverend had not had time to change into the ghost's armour, so, instead, simply delivered his lines dressed as Claudius, which gave the scene an even more surreal quality than it had had on the night of the real performance. It was not the quality of the performances on stage, however, that had piqued Harry's interest. Angie and Steve Grey were deep in conversation at the far side of the hall and, after a minute or two, Angie went to walk away. Steve grabbed her arm, but she pulled it from him and stalked out the side door that led, Harry knew, to the kitchen area of the Town Hall. Steve left it until the count of five before following her, well aware that Mike had seen the exit of Angie from on stage, but clearly unable to do anything, as he had two big scenes to get through before the end of Act I.

Harry got up and went to make an excuse to Carol, but she had been watching the altercation as well and simply said, 'Go!' He walked across to the closed kitchen entrance, took a breath, and walked in. The sight that greeted him was not what he had expected to find.

Harry thought that, like that fateful evening a few days ago, he was going to have to intervene, in his chivalrous way, to help a damsel in distress. Instead, he found the two young people in a passionate embrace. His arrival seemed to do very little to cool their ardour and it took about ten seconds before they acknowledged his presence, during which time, Harry had debated whether or not to just slip back through the kitchen door and rejoin Carol. Just as he was about to do so, they broke their clinch and it was Steve Grey that spoke first, 'Enjoy watching that, did you?'

Grey had a way of riling Harry with almost everything he said and did, but this was intentionally inflammatory and the only thing that held Harry back was knowing that, if Carol had been there, she would have told him that it wasn't worth it. Instead, he simply said, 'Just popped in to get a glass of water, if that's alright with you two?'

'Be our guest. Glasses are in that cupboard over there. We'll even let you have it for free.' Steve Grey smirked and Angie stifled another giggle, at least the second that evening. A record, Harry thought, in his dealings with her.

'Are you sure you weren't charging in to be my knight in shining armour, again?' asked Angie.

Harry was surprised that his own imagery of whatever intervention he thought might be required, had been appropriated by the young Angela King. Her empathy and understanding were truly well beyond her years.

'Maybe a little,' admitted Harry, 'after what I witnessed out in the hall.'

'You've really got to learn to tell fact from performance,' Grey said. 'Like to keep what we get up to a bit of a secret from the rest of them. Wouldn't want anyone to come barging in and finding us smooching, would we? Makes it more exciting as well.'

'That would never do,' replied Harry, willing to go along with the banter and in answer to the question posed.

'If they think we're just having an argument, that lot'll keep well out of our way. It's only well-meaning policemen that might not take the hint!' Angie smiled as she said this, though, as she pointedly took Steve Grey's hand.

'If you're both fine then, I'll leave you to it,' Harry said and turned to leave.

'Don't forget your glass of water,' called Grey, but Harry had already exited and closed the door behind him.

'Everything alright?' asked Carol, as he sat back down.

'Absolutely great!' murmured Harry and he resolved to not be so quick to poke his nose in where it didn't belong - before realising that was exactly a major part of his job!

CHAPTER 39

Act 2 had concluded and the cast had all decamped to the kitchen for a well-earned cup of tea and a biscuit. Neither Carol nor Harry had been invited to join them, so Carol decided to ask about what had happened earlier and Harry explained finding Angie and Steve together.

'That's odd,' replied Carol, after a second or two. 'When we were chatting earlier, Angie was adamant that she wasn't really interested in either of the lads. Maybe she was just messing him about again.'

'Oh, they were definitely messing about from what I could see,' said Harry.

'That's not what I meant!'

'I know! I was just..' But before Harry could finish, angry voices were being raised in the kitchen and then, a few moments later, Mike Brown came striding out, closely followed by Stewart Manning. The fact that both were in full costume gave the whole scene a somewhat farcical mood to the audience of two still sat in the relative darkness at the back of the hall.

'I had no intentions of trying to take over your part, Michael. I was merely reading in for Claudius. None of us expected you to be here, this evening.'

No, but I gather you were lapping up the limelight.'

'Who told you that?'

'It doesn't matter. Suffice it to say, we're all aware that you've been very quick to jump into a dead man's shoes.' Manning stared at the vicar with rage and then seemed to become calm, almost as quickly as Angie King's mood swings could take place. 'Come on, Michael. You know very well I wouldn't think of doing that if it wasn't to help out the society. You've had an awful day. Let's not fall out over this.

We've got a show to put on!'
Mike Brown hesitated and almost looked as if he was unwilling to let, whatever it was that was gnawing at him, slide, but Stew, in his usual ebullient manner, opened out his arms and gave the reverend a bear hug which served to suppress any negative response the vicar was about to give. When he broke the embrace, Manning marched past Harry and Carol and out the doors at the back. Brown watched him go until Manning had left the room and then he slowly made his way back into the kitchen.
Harry turned to Carol. 'I've never seen a vicar with such a look of malevolence as that!'
'Me neither. Stew Manning's right, though. He has had one hell of a day.'
'We're coming up to the scene when King died aren't we?' asked Harry, changing the subject.
'Yes, I hope Mike isn't behind the arras with a dagger, waiting for Polonius. We don't want another one killed, like King.'
'I wouldn't put it past the reverend, the mood he seems to be in. We'd best keep our eyes open!'
'It's not me that falls asleep during Shakespeare,' laughed Carol, as the cast resumed their seats in the hall, Stewart Manning returned, marching up through the hall and opened the curtains on Mike's Claudius discussing Hamlet's state of mind with the twins from the chemist, reprising their roles as Rosencrantz and Guildenstern. Lorraine's Gertrude, this evening, to Carol's mind, was more subdued than it had been a few nights ago. This wasn't surprising, given the circumstances, but it actually made her acting seem better and less overacted. Angie's Ophelia was as good as ever and again Stew Manning's recitation of his lines was respectable. Soon, they all exited and Roger Heart entered to give the most famous soliloquy in the English language.

'To be, or not to be – that is the question', he began and Carol was forced to contemplate the resonance of that line to the cast here tonight. The question of whether it was better to be alive or dead had truly become manifest in Pikesmere this week.

Heart was continuing his speech, absolutely nailing it and showing the evidence for why he could easily get into drama school. 'The undiscovered country from whose bourn, No traveller returns', he was saying and this time it was Harry who, with a moment of understanding, of this archaic language, mused over his role as detective here tonight and every day. Three people had been sent to that "undiscovered country" of death and it was his job to seek out their murderer, or, possibly, murderers, and bring them to justice.

The soliloquy ended and Roger Heart had a scene with Angie, where both showed their skills and, despite it being a rehearsal, brought so much passion to their lines that Carol felt a tear welling in her eye. Heart, at last, exited and Angie gave her short speech that heralded the return of Mike Brown and Manning.

Just as she was saying the final line of the piece, there was an agonised shout from backstage. It was the voice of Manning, but not his expected entrance. Harry stood, ready to rush to the stage in the same way as he had done several nights before, fearing, again, for what he might find.

However, he had only managed to take a single step before Stew Manning entered stage left clutching his lower leg – a fair feat for a man his height and size. 'Sorry, everybody. Bloody nail sticking out the back of one of the flats. Wait till I get hold of the stage manager!'

Everybody laughed, even Mike Brown who had entered from stage right, and the scene continued until he delivered the closing line, 'Madness in great ones must not unwatched go.' Again, Carol couldn't help but think that this play was made for the scene of a murder because whoever had done what they had done to poor Gloria today, and the other two before, must be tinged with madness.

Scene 3 included Claudius' kneeling in prayer scene and Brown took his place centre stage with Heart standing backstage in the gloom, pondering on whether he could murder him, but, in so doing, send his soul to heaven rather than hell. Brown's soliloquy was delivered well, but Carol was annoyed that many of his important facial expressions were unclear because his face was in shadow from his positioning on his knees. The RSC would never have approved, she thought. Harry, however, was unconcerned and, at one point, she had to jab him in his side as his eyes began to slowly shut.

The act progressed until it was again time for Polonius to hide behind the arras. Harry wondered how Stewart Manning must be feeling, standing in the exact place where Derek King, his predecessor in the role, had been killed. If he had nerves, they weren't evident, as he moved behind the material. This time, however, the scene continued smoothly and Stewart Manning managed to complete his time as Polonius and return to his usual role of stage manager, completing the necessary scene changes and bringing the rehearsal to a close without any further outbursts, or parts that gave Harry, or Carol, concern, or, unfortunately, help in their search for the resolution to the crimes that had seemingly begun in this very hall.

The cast departed with hugs and farewells and all seemed to be looking forward to the following night's performance, in Charlie Blackwater's honour. Few mentioned Derek King in their discussions and none, Gloria Bebb.

ACT V

Like as the waves make towards the pebbled shore,
So do our minutes hasten to their end.

CHAPTER 40

The following morning, after breakfast, Carol and Harry decided to take a break from their investigations and have a walk down to the other water feature of Pikesmere, it's canal. Built in the eighteenth century as part of a system that carried coal and freight from Wales to the crucible of the Industrial Revolution, as it was then, in South Shropshire and to the newly growing mill towns of the north, the Pikesmere Arm of the waterway now seemed to be almost entirely part of the leisure industry, as well as providing a home for a few hardy souls who chose to live on a narrowboat.

As the two approached the canal, they could see a large, now abandoned, warehouse with advertisements painted on its walls that dated back over a century and indicated its importance as a warehouse for the Shropshire Union Canal. It's dilapidated wooden doors, facing out onto the canal, signified its trade being wholly from the waterway, as opposed to the road system. The roof, too, was in a real state of disrepair and one could only imagine what the inside was like.

'What a shame that these old, historic buildings can't be put to some good use,' Carol said, as they began to walk along the water's edge, past the barges and narrowboats that were moored there, displaying beautiful, coloured signs promoting their marina of origin and decorated by flowerpots

of all shapes and colours. Despite it being a reasonably warm day, after the storm of the previous evening, most had smoke emanating from their small, black chimneys, indicating that their stoves were lit.
'Good place for another murder, I reckon,' replied Harry, as he looked back at the disused warehouse. 'They wouldn't find the body for months in there, if not years!'
'Do you ever think of anything other than crime?' asked Carol. 'When we first started going out and friends of yours said you had a one-track mind, I thought it might be something completely different!'
Harry smiled, 'It can be arranged, if you want to give the canal a miss and get back to the hotel.'
'Let's just carry on walking,' replied Carol.
'Spoilsport!' retorted Harry. It was partly true, however, what Carol had said. Once Harry was on a case, he could become fixated until it was solved. He felt that it made him a good detective and the force had promoted him accordingly, but he sometimes, in more lucid, reflective moments, realised that it must be difficult for Carol. She had her own profession with its interminable marking and planning to be done, but he knew that he was unreliable in keeping to plans and would often come home late, roll into bed and be asleep in seconds. This holiday was supposed to be a break, for both of them to chill and spend time relaxing together. Well, they were spending time together, but Harry didn't think that "relaxing" was the right word to describe what had been going on. He was about to apologise to Carol, but, just at that moment, it was she who brought them back to the murders and her enthusiasm for delving into the case and helping, reminded him that she was, by all accounts, enjoying the week, despite the macabre turn that it had taken the night they had made their way to that fatal performance.

'Did you think Mike Brown was bumping off Stew last night when we heard him cry out backstage?'

'I'm not sure what I thought was going on,' admitted Harry. 'I wouldn't have been surprised whatever had taken place with that lot. I can't think of any other case I've been involved in, where there are so many suspects, three murders and no real clues to work with, apart from a scrappy bit of script and a shedload of motives.'

Carol nodded. 'It would certainly be a surprise to find that a seemingly well-liked vicar had perpetrated all those hideous murders, but the death of Gloria, yesterday, in his own church of all places, certainly throws the spotlight on him, doesn't it? Who else from the society would have known she was going to be there in order to kill her so quickly and get away. The vicar could have come in at any moment and caught someone else, so it might make sense that it was him that did it, don't you think? Sorry, I'm rambling aren't I?'

Harry nodded, but said, 'Yes, a bit, but it's nice to hear you so involved. I was literally just worrying that you might not be enjoying our holiday, but it's clear that you are, which means I am as well.'

With that, he hugged her and they carried on walking towards a white, wooden bridge that spanned the canal and took the towpath to its other side.

'I love puzzles, you know I do. So, what do you think of my deductions, Holmes? Anything that might be enlightening? Sherlock used to say that Watson, although "not luminous himself, was a conductor of light". Am a conducting any light for you?'

Harry knew that she was partially teasing him, but that was a small portion of what made her the woman that he loved and the fact that she could dredge up quotes, from most works of literature, made her even more adorable. 'You always bring light into my world,' he said, with rather more schmaltz and sentimentality than he had meant it to sound like, 'However, I'm not convinced that our local vicar could bring himself to commit what, in his eyes, would be such terrible sins. Remember the way he spoke to us at the vicarage, about the torments of Hell and how his faith does not allow murder.'

'He could have been lying,'

'And break another commandment? You're right, though. I'm not sure any of them have told us the whole truth yet and the reverend may be the same. Nevertheless, the assumption that only he would know where Gloria Bebb was going to be at the moment of her death is probably untrue.'

'Why?' asked Carol, as they walked up the old, Victorian cobbles that led onto the white bridge and stood looking along the length of the canal, with its boats and waterfowl.

'She was a member of a team of ladies who helped in the church with the cleaning and flower arranging. There are rotas for who does which days and weeks and these are posted on noticeboards. There was one pinned up in the porch outside the church door. I noticed it as we were leaving yesterday.'

Carol turned and looked at him with that sense of admiration she always felt whenever he did something clever. 'You noticed that as were leaving? I was too busy grabbing my present bags and pictures.'

'And that, my darling, is why you can quote Sherlock Holmes, but I wear the deerstalker! I also spoke to Daniel on the phone this morning and he said that the roster is always printed in the monthly church magazine that is posted through at least a third of the letterboxes in the town. Unfortunately, the list of suspects cannot be narrowed down to Mike Brown on that score, I fear.'

Carol looked deflated, but Harry continued in a more upbeat and positive tone. 'However, Reverend Brown does still have a motive for killing Derek King, due to his talks with Angie and, who knows, there might have been something untoward between him and Charlie Blackwater that we haven't yet uncovered, although he seemed to have been grateful to have been given the part of Claudius rather than Polonius, so we may not be onto a winner there!'

Carol decided not to be downhearted, so moved the conversation onto the next set of thoughts that had been swirling in her head throughout, what had turned out to be, yet another disturbed night's sleep. 'Okay, I'll accept that I may not be on the right track with the vicar. Let's think about what you saw in the kitchen.'

'I'd rather not,' replied Harry, not wishing to remind himself of what he had walked into.

'Sorry! I'm going there. Let's assume, for one moment, that Angie King was lying to me about her relationship with Steve Grey.'

'Not that far-fetched an idea. There's a lot more to that young woman than appears on the surface, I reckon. She was really good onstage last night, pretty much as good as Roger Heart. She can probably lie very effectively when she needs to. I'm beginning to think that the whole insane act in the pub was just that: a part of her act. Maybe even the drugtaking is just a smokescreen!'

'Accepted! As someone who deals with teenagers all the time, I don't think you're a million miles away from the truth in thinking that. So, given that we're on the same wavelength over Angie King and, given that she has had a world in which she has had to grow up without a loving mother and with an overbearing, and cold, father, how might she have responded to the passionate advances of a slightly older, extravert lad who had already served time and sacrificed himself for her? Rather than just 'playing him along' as she suggested she was doing; might it not be

more likely that she actually is in love with him?'
'Absolutely!'
Harry thought that Carol was on much firmer ground with these suppositions and he let her continue. He knew that her experience with young people was much more extensive than his and that she probably had a much better handle on Angie King than he could ever have.
'What if they colluded to get rid of her father. Grey wouldn't be happy seeing King behave the way he did to the girl he loved. He already had a reason to hate him from the recent past and he certainly wouldn't hold back in the way Roger Heart might do. We've seen him aggressive. I bet, if Angie gave him the right push, he could easily have murdered Derek King for her. I know I've suggested all this before, but I'm certain there might be something to it.'
'I wouldn't argue with any of that and you know that I've had a bit of a downer on Steve Grey ever since we first met him. However, can we find a motive for him to also kill Charlie Blackwater. Nothing seems to have come to light to indicate there was any bad blood there, neither for Grey, nor, indeed, for Angie King, who, from what you said, seemed to see her director as a sort of mentor.'
'That's true,' replied Carol, 'but maybe we just haven't found that out yet.'
'Granted,' said Harry, 'but there's also the question of Gloria Bebb. There doesn't seem to be any link between her and those two. We're not even sure that they knew her at all and I doubt Steve Grey is one of those people who gets a church magazine through his door every month!'
'You never know,' replied Carol and they continued down onto the towpath on the other side of the canal.
Their discussions carried on, back and forth, as they walked under another bridge, this time made of red brick and past Pikesmere Marina, situated in a large open field to one side

of the waterway. A sign on the towpath advertised that there was a small shop situated there selling anything a holidaymaker, renting a narrowboat, might want, or need. There must have been, thought Harry, at least seventy boats moored in the marina and he was pleasantly surprised at how popular boating on the inland waterways had become. The canals near to where Carol and he lived were not particularly appealing, with the occasional shopping trolley half submerged in their brown waters, but here, where small ducks swam between bullrushes and the odd dragonfly swooped down over the water, he could definitely see its attraction to those wishing to holiday at home, rather than soak up the sun on the Costas. As he realised his thoughts were beginning to sound like an advert for staycations, Carol decided to bring up another theory that she had been working on.

'What if Stew Manning did it? He was backstage when Derek King was murdered.'

'True,' replied Harry, but he was also up a ladder at the time and Mike Brown and Andrew Cross both verify they nearly knocked him off as they ran onto stage after King's death.'

'He's been pretty keen to take over the role of Polonius from him. Jumping into a dead man's shoes and all that!'

'I just don't see wanting to play a part in memory of someone who you've just stabbed is a motive for murder.'

There could be another reason that we've missed.'

Carol was starting to sound exasperated, but Harry only fanned the flames. 'That can be true of all of that lot. There's got to be something we're missing. Something that not only provides the motive, but links the three deaths together.'

'That's what we've been trying to do, isn't it?' asked Carol.

'I guess so. I'll tell you something, though. I had to attend a police conference once where a load of university bods lectured a room of detectives about how to do their jobs better. As you can imagine, most were not received very favourably by the audience, but there was one lady who did say something that resonated with a lot of us who were dealing with murders in the real world. She was a criminal psychologist and said that, apart from robbery, jealousy and vengeance account for the motives in nearly all killings. A few of us were sat in the bar, later, and were going back over a few of our cases and it turned out that she was spot on.'

'So, where do we find the jealousy and/or vengeance in these three murders? What about Roger Heart? He strikes me as the jealous type,' stated Carol, bluntly.

'First name that sprung to my mind as I was saying all that. He'd definitely fit the profile of the jealous lover spurned, but it wasn't Derek King that was making Angie spurn him; it was Steve Grey and he's still very much alive.'

'Maybe it was vengeance then?'

'We're back to the same problem, though,' said Harry. 'Heart might have wanted to take out his feelings of vengeance on King, but would he have been physically capable of doing it. Mike Brown might have wanted to avenge all the things that Angie had "confessed" to him about her father, but would his faith have allowed him to do so? Even Lorraine Davies would have probably liked to help Angie by getting rid of her father, but she was on stage at the time. As for the rest of them, I can't put my finger on any strong motive of vengeance, or jealousy, that would have driven them strongly enough to kill King.'

'So, your criminal psychologist hasn't been very helpful,' said Carol.

'Not at first glance, no, but it might give us the direction in which to delve. Leaving Gloria to one side, as we seem to have found very few, if any, things that link her to the drama society – in fact, little background at all at the moment -

what about Mr. Blackwater? Can we think of anyone who was jealous of him, or be wanting to take revenge?'

Carol thought for a second or two, before replying and then said, with a cheeky grin on her face that told Harry this was not going to be helpful to their enquiries, 'The twins at the chemist of course. For making them play Tweedledum and Tweedledee!' They both laughed as they turned onto a public footpath that led away from the canal and across a field back towards the mere and the Mereside restaurant where they had eaten lunch a couple of days before.

Carol continued, 'Then there's Stew Manning, who desperately wanted to play Polonius and so killed off Charlie Blackwater in revenge for being asked to be stage manager instead! Or perhaps it's..'

'Alright! Let's stop there and just enjoy the rest of our walk. We're just going round in ever decreasing circles.'

'But darling.' said Carol, as she linked her arm with his, 'the point of ever decreasing circles is that you eventually end up at the centre!'

CHAPTER 41

Having decided to have lunch back at their hotel and forego the previously delicious ploughman's by the mere, they decided to buy an ice cream from the quaint, little, black and white kiosk that was open nearby and then sit on one of the iron-wrought benches that were placed, strategically, along the mere's edge, so that holidaymakers could sit and watch the swans, geese and ducks as they dived for food on the water. Just as they sat down, Harry's phone rang and he handed Caz his "99 with a double Flake" so he could use both his hands. By the time he had finished the conversation, much of the ice cream had melted down the cone and Carol had been forced to lick the drips herself and ended up eating more of it than was actually left.

'Sorry!' she said, as she handed it back to him. 'Was it important? I assume it was Dan.'

'It was.' Harry started to lick at what was left of his cone and munch away at the chocolate sticks which, at least, were still intact, despite Caz' temptation to take a bite. 'They've been starting to piece together Gloria's last movements yesterday. Her neighbour saw her leave around midday. Apparently, she was out in the garden, the neighbour that is, and shouted over to Ms. Bebb, who went across and had a bit of a chat. It seems that there was nothing out of the ordinary. They talked about the fact that there might be a storm later, which of course there was, and how the price of cleaning stuff for the church was going up and up and that she might have to start to ask the reverend for some cash from the parish funds if it kept rising. The neighbour didn't feel that there was anything else on her mind, nothing that might have suggested that she had been threatened, or anything like that, although she had heard a raised voice through the walls of their semi-detached a couple of nights previously, but had put that down to Gloria shouting at her dog.'

'What sort of dog was it?'

Harry looked at Carol and smiled, 'Of all the questions you could have asked, that was not the one I was expecting!'

'So?'

'So, what?'

'The dog. What breed was it?'

'Funnily enough,' replied Harry, 'I didn't ask Dan that one, although he did say the neighbour was looking after it, so you needn't worry that it isn't being cared for!'

Carol told him that she hadn't been worrying about that at

all, but, in actual fact, that was exactly one of the first thoughts that had crossed her mind.

'Anyway,' continued Harry, 'Dan reckons that when she left from chatting to her neighbour, she went to the chemists for her prescription – apparently she suffered from Type2 Diabetes and was on medication to control it – went to the cashpoint and got ten pounds out, before going to buy some dog food and cleaning stuff from Stew's emporium up the road. She then went to the butchers where she bought a pork chop and finally went back home, presumably to feed the dog and put the chop in the fridge, before leaving for the church a little while before Mike Brown found her dead at the altar.'

'And do we think any of that information was worth the loss of half your ice cream?' asked Carol.

'Not a bit of it, although the part about the shouting is interesting. If it wasn't the naughty dog, then who was she shouting at and could that have led to her death the following day?'

'Did the neighbour not see anyone arrive or leave?'

'It's a pity it wasn't Mrs. Hubbard who lived next door. Then we'd really know what was what. Unfortunately, Gloria's neighbour had closed her curtains for the evening and didn't think it was worth peeping out to see any comings and goings. Nosiness just isn't what it used to be, is it? She reckons that Ms. Bebb hardly ever had visitors during the day, apart from the milkman, postie and papergirl, but that she did hear her door going at nights, occasionally.'

'Oo, now that's a bit more like it. Something more salacious to get our teeth into.'

'Salacious?' asked Harry.

'Naughty gossip! Cleans the church brasses during the day, up to no good at night.' She suddenly stopped herself and took a final bite of her cone. 'Sorry, that was terribly dark of

me. Talking ill of the dead like that. I feel dreadful.'
'Don't beat yourself up too much. Happens all the time at the station. When you're dealing with death, sometimes you've just got to lighten the mood. Otherwise, we'd all be manic depressives. You're right, though. If Gloria was seeing somebody – and there's no reason why she shouldn't have been, as far as we know she was single – why haven't they come forward to find out what's happened to her?'
'Maybe they travel around and only see her when they're back in town.'
'Quite possibly, but Dan said there was no sign of anyone else having been in Gloria's house at all. Certainly not anyone who might have stayed over, even occasionally.'
'No extra toothbrush? That would have been a nice clue. Especially if it had been blue!'
'Sexist! Anyway, there was nothing! So, if she did have a close 'friend', and if they don't travel around a lot, we might be looking at them being the murderer. And if they murdered Ms. Bebb, did they also murder King and Blackwater?'
'And what about the why?' added Carol.
'Oh yes,' replied Harry, 'that's the biggest question of the lot. What motive links four deaths?'
Carol nodded, looked out across the mere and then turned back to Harry with a jerk of her head. 'What did you just say? Four?'
Harry smiled with a malicious grin. 'I've kept the best until last. Dan told me something else.'
Carol gasped. 'Oh no, there's been another one. Another murder! Is it another member of the cast?'
'Give me a chance and I'll tell you. It's no one in Pikesmere, but it is closely related to the case. You remember Mike Brown telling us that Gloria was a widow and that she didn't like to talk about her husband's death?'

'Yes,' said Carol and then she realised. 'No!'
'So, Dan has discovered on the police database that Gloria came back one day and found her husband had been stabbed in their lounge. Same as our friend seems to have been doing up here. There's nothing to positively suggest that it's the same killer and it did happen a few years ago and in another part of the country, but circumstantially it seems likely.'
Carol thought for a moment and then audibly gasped. 'Angie King's mother died in similar circumstances, didn't she? About ten, or so, years ago. Perhaps that four is actually five! Five corpses! This is sounding more and more like a murderer who really likes the thrill of the kill!'

CHAPTER 42

After their lunch back at the hotel, as they headed back to their room, Carol raised the subject of the evening's performance of "Hamlet". Her primary concern, much to Harry's amusement, in the light of the morning's revelations about Gloria Bebb, was whether they still needed to get tickets and how that was going to work now that Charles Blackwater was dead.
'Do you think we've got to go through that whole routine of visits to Lorraine's and then back to the Town Hall. Surely not?'
'Is that really your main concern in all this?' replied Harry grinning. 'At this very moment, our killer may be planning to strike again at tonight's show and you're worried about how we get our tickets.'
'If our murderer is going to strike, I don't think his majesty's constabulary would look very efficient if they missed

catching the criminal because they hadn't got a ticket!'
'Fair enough! Dan said he wanted to be there as well, so we need three!'
'Dan's file that he gave you!' exclaimed Carol. 'With all that's been going on, I forgot all about those pictures and reviews. Give me half an hour to take a look through them.'
With that, she recovered the file from the shopping bag where she had secreted them and began to methodically trawl through each one, occasionally holding one of the pictures closer to her face as she attempted to scrutinise it more carefully before shaking her head and placing it back in the pile. There was one that she seemed to spend the most time over, picking it up twice and then putting it back down.
'Something of interest?' asked Harry, who had been watching her throughout, amazed that she was finding the whole exercise so interesting.
'I can't be certain, but I think Derek King is on one of these photographs from a while back. It looks as if Charlie Blackwater was having his picture taken at some medical seminar and King just happens to be in the background, but I'm sure I recognise the profile of another person who's also in it, but it's too blurry to quite make it out. I'm going to leave it and then come back to it later, see if distancing myself from it makes a difference.' She got up and started to put her coat on. 'Come on, then. Back to the alluring Lorraine's. She'll be thrilled to see you again.'
Harry didn't have time to make a pithy reply before his coat had been flung to him and Caz had opened the hotel room door and was off into the corridor.
They arrived at Lorraine's shop in a little over five minutes and the now familiar tinkle of the bell above the entrance ushered them into the cramped surroundings of the clothes shop. The proprietress greeted them in her usual effusive

style, paying particular attention to Harry, just as his partner had predicted only a few minutes earlier.

After a few pleasantries, Carol said, 'We're actually here to discuss tonight's performance of "Hamlet".'

'More questions? Oh dear! Fire away!'

'No, no. You misunderstand me,' replied Carol, a little taken aback by the reception she was getting. 'We just wanted to know what the protocol was for buying tickets this time.'

Lorraine seemed to visibly relax as she answered and both Carol and Harry wondered why she was a little on edge again. 'Oh, I'm terribly sorry. You must think I'm terrible for biting your head off like that. Please forgive me.'

'The tickets?' Harry tried again.

'Oh yes. Well, anyone who can prove they were present at that dreadful evening when Derek got killed can have a free ticket on account of the performance being, how should I put it, cut short!' Like Derek King's life, thought Harry, although he didn't give voice to it!

'That's great,' said Carol, 'and do you have tonight's tickets here for us?' She expected another convoluted system of getting hold of them, but Lorraine surprised the two of them.

'Oh, yes. They're just in the back, here. Two tickets for tonight's commemorative performance.'

She turned and started to walk towards the door to her office.

'Three, actually,' shouted Carol, a little more loudly than the cramped surroundings of the shop required.

'Three?' replied Lorraine, as she turned back to them. 'I seem to recall only selling you two before.'

Before, Carol could speak and mention Daniel's intention to join them, Harry said, simply, 'We've got a friend joining us.'

'And did they purchase a previous ticket?'

'No! I'm afraid not. He arrived, how should I put it, rather late and missed the actual show.' Harry grinned at his own little joke.

'Very well,' replied Lorraine, 'you'll have to pay for that one then!'

'No problem,' Harry said and he got out his wallet.

Tickets bought, Carol looked at them and realised they would be sitting in pretty much the same seats as they had been a few nights previously, whether by chance, or by design. Maybe Lorraine was trying to issue the tickets to people so that they had similar positions in the hall to those that they had paid for before! Just as Harry reached for the door handle, Lorraine spoke again.

'Are you any closer to getting 'em?'

'The killer?' asked Harry, somewhat redundantly. 'We're working on it.'

'It's still a work in progress,' admitted Carol, rather exasperatedly. 'Is there anything else you might have thought of that could help in any way? Something that has sprung to mind now that a bit of time has passed. I know that sometimes happens to me.'

'Not really. Everybody seemed pretty normal at the rehearsal, last night. Except..' Lorraine was obviously debating whether to say something and then decided to dive in. 'Except, that tiff, between Mike and Stew, was a bit out of character. For both of them, really.'

'In what way?' asked Harry.

'Well, it was something and nothing, wasn't it? I've seen Stew blow up over his precious set a time or two, but not about who plays what parts. To be honest, he is a bit of a perfectionist when it comes to making sure the stage is right! Then there was Mike's reaction, but, I suppose, he had dealt with another murder, right on his doorstep, so to speak. That'd give anyone an excuse to act out of character, wouldn't it? Poor thing!'

'Reverend Brown, or Gloria?' asked Carol.

'Both, I guess,' replied Lorraine and she looked as if she might have a tear in the corner of her eye.

'Did you know Gloria Bebb well?' pursued Carol, discerning that there might be something that could help them.

'I wouldn't say very well,' replied Lorraine, 'but we were about the same age and she'd started to come into the shop a few months ago to buy material to make some new dresses. She didn't have a lot of money, you know, so was watching the pennies, as it were. Anyway, we got chatting a bit, about getting older and losing our looks a bit and so on.' She turned to Harry, 'Not that I'm at that stage yet, of course. Nor her, really!'

Harry smiled and graciously replied, 'Absolutely not. Please carry on.'

'Well, she never said anything explicit mind you, but I got the impression, about a month ago, that she had a bloke that she was interested in. The dress patterns she was getting were just that little bit more, well, you know, sexier; more revealing!'

'Definitely a man?' asked Carol.

'I'd say so, although you can't be sure nowadays, can you?'

'You think she was trying to dress to impress, then?'

'I reckon so. About a week ago, though, she came in clutching something in her hand. It could have been a letter, or maybe a cutting from a newspaper. I never got to see it close up because she stuffed it in her handbag, but her eyes were red and she'd obviously been crying. Well, I got her a cup of tea and asked whether I could help, but she said not. It was something she had to deal with herself. She drank her tea and seemed to calm down, but before she left, she turned, just where you two are standing now, and said, 'I've made the most terrible mistake! I just never suspected anything!' and then she walked out. That was the last time I saw her alive. What do you think she meant?'

'I'm not sure, yet,' replied Harry, 'but that has been extremely useful. Do you mind if I tell the detective in charge of the case, so he can send an officer round for you to make a formal statement?'
'I suppose so if you think it will help. I don't like talking to the police though!'
Harry smiled, 'Well, you're don't seem too bothered talking to me.'
'You're not like them others, though. You've got a kind face, you have. Not like that horrible sergeant Pearson who thinks he owns the place. He told me off a bit ago for accidently dropping a bit of paper down by the mere. Pompous twit.'
'Just doing his duty, I'm sure,' smiled Carol and she looked at Harry to warn him not to pile in on insulting the sergeant. 'I'll ask Daniel to send a female police officer if it'd make you feel more comfortable giving your statement.'
'Told you he was kind,' said Lorraine, looking at Carol whilst she said it before returning to look at Harry and sidling a little closer to him. 'I wouldn't mind a kind looking, young policeman, if he's got one of those to send.'
The emphasis, thought Harry, was definitely on the words "young" and "man". 'I'll see what I can do for you,' he said.
'Do you reckon any of what I've told you might help in catching this murdering bastard?' asked Lorraine.
'It just might,' replied Harry. 'It's all these little things that add up and help.'
It was at that moment, however, that Carol had those feelings again that something in this conversation had been really important. It was like a cold shiver ran up into her brain and she made a mental note to go over it again with Harry later on.
'Well hurry up before we're all bumped off!'
And with that, Lorraine turned her back on them again and walked up the small flight of steps to her office.

'Lovely!' said Carol, once they were outside on the pavement again.
'She's right, though,' said Harry. 'This has got to stop!'

CHAPTER 43

As Daniel, Carol and Harry took their seats for that evening's performance of "Hamlet", a sense of déjà vu swept over Caz as she recognised the back of Rose Hubbard's head in front of them. Harry, this time, was extremely careful not to bump her seat as he sat down, a feat in itself considering the length of his legs and the narrowness of the space between rows. It was reminiscent of sitting on a budget airline, but without the reward of the rush of hot air when the cabin doors opened.
Despite him not knocking her seat, Ms. Hubbard turned her head and greeted Carol and Harry as if they were long lost relatives who had arrived to surprise her. The pleasantries over, she turned back in her seat and Dan whispered, 'It's like you've lived here all your life. How do you do it?'
Before Harry could reply, Ms. Hubbard turned back around and said, 'He's got a kind face and says very nice things about my cake! So, mind what you've got to say, young man!' And with that, she turned back again. Daniel raised his eyebrows at the phenomenal hearing of the elderly lady, but decided not to say anymore. Harry, however, luxuriated in the glow of twice in the same day being described as "kind", an epithet that he didn't usually associate his police activities with. Perhaps the slower, rural life of Pikesmere was having an effect on him, despite the horrors of the last week, all of which had been underscored as they arrived at

the Town Hall to find Sergeant Pearson and several other uniformed officers standing guard at the entrance.
The house lights dimmed, but, before the play began, a spotlight fell upon the centre of the curtains and Stewart Manning emerged, dressed ready to play Polonius; he addressed the somewhat fuller audience that had ventured out for this commemorative performance, than had been present on the previous night of the production.
'Ladies and Gentlemen,' he began, 'thank you so much for attending our performance of Shakespeare's famous tragedy, "Hamlet", this evening. As I'm sure you are all aware, it is in other tragic circumstances that we gather here tonight. The loss of two of our number has stunned us all and it is in their names and honour, that we perform for you now; as well as poor Gloria, who has also been taken from our little community this week. It is only to be hoped that we can do them all justice in this production. Tonight, I shall be playing Polonius, the role that dear Derek King was supposed to be playing and if I can do it even a fraction as well as he portrayed the part, then I shall be very pleased to have stepped into his shoes in his memory. Thank you, again.'
With that, he disappeared back through the curtains as the audience gave a round of respectful applause and the curtains, after a few moments, opened. The scene was as it had been the night of King's murder: the battlements of Elsinore castle with the small fire, blazing again stage right and the wooden cut-out wall standing at the back. Whether Stewart Manning had done some restorative work, or whether it was just that the cast was being less heavy-footed, the set did not shake this time, nor give the impression that it could all collapse at any moment.
'Who's there?'
'Nay, answer me. Stand, and unfold yourself.'

'Long live the king!'
As the actors delivered their opening lines one more time, Carol mused over everything that had transpired since she had last heard them performed in this hall. She considered the troubled half-child, half-woman that was Angie King. Could she have killed her own father? But if she did, who could have murdered her mother, all those years ago? Surely the young child that she had been then would have been incapable of committing such a heinous act? And then there was Gloria Bebb's husband. Angie couldn't have done that one either! All that would mean there were two murderers, though! A possibility, she admitted to herself, but not as satisfying a solution as she hoped would be the outcome of the present criminal investigations.

What, then, about Angie's suitors? The melancholic pacifist, or the thuggish mechanic: could either of them have perpetrated any of these crimes, either for their own motives; or in league with the girl they loved? Carol taught enough literature to know the violent ends that the emotion of Love could drive a man to, but that was just for a literary set of plotlines, wasn't it?

Then there was the reverend, a man obviously devout and pious enough to despair at the evil he had been plunged into, as Angie 'confessed' to him about her life with her father and the physical and emotional abuse that it had entailed. Could his Christian zeal have overtaken his subservience to his commandments? Angie would be at the centre of that motivation, as well! Harry had talked about vengeance being a prime reason for murder. Is that what had happened? What is Angie's part in all this, if any?

Carol dragged her focus back to what was happening on stage. There she was, Angie King's Ophelia, standing up to her brother and her father in the play. How much of the strong young daughter of the play was a representation of

Angie herself? Stew was still doing well, reading in Polonius' lines and even showing that he had learnt a few, allowing his eyes to leave the printed text and deliver them direct to the other actors. Impressive, thought Carol, considering how short a time he had been playing the role. Could the avuncular entrepreneur be involved in all these murders and, again, to what end? Did being overlooked for an acting role and relegation to working behind the scenes constitute a motive for murder? If Charles Blackwater got all his other casting calls so right, would he have made a mistake when asking Manning to be stage manager?

Andrew Cross was doing well as Laertes, as well. The whole cast seemed to be rising to the occasion and trying to prove Blackwater was correct in his conviction that this small-town amateur group could actually pull off a performance of "Hamlet". Could Cross have committed the crimes? Had the clown become the killer? Were the practical jokes and pranks just a means of covering up a dark secret that they hadn't yet unearthed? Time was running out if that was the case!

Scenes with Mark Prince's Horatio and then the twins' Rosencrantz and Guildenstern came and went, with similar questions going through Carol's mind, making it nearly impossible for her to concentrate on the play itself and it almost came as a relief when the interval was announced and the houselights came up.

'Better than last time,' said Harry, as he turned to her.

'Yes, I think so, too,' murmured Carol, but without much conviction.

'I thought it was much better. You alright?'

'Fine! It's just that I can't concentrate on the play because all I can think about is which one might be the murderer. How do you do it, Harry?'

'Do what?'

'Switch off. Compartmentalise the job from the rest of it.'
'Same way you do from school, I guess,' replied Harry.
'Apart from bringing home tons of marking, you don't let a bad lesson with your Year 10s stop you from enjoying your weekend, do you?'
Daniel, who had been listening to the conversation, decided to butt in. 'In the police, you have to learn to let it in while you're on the job, but then push it out when you finish for the day. If you don't do the first, you're not going to be a very good copper, but if you can't do the latter, you're going to burn out by the time you're forty!'
'Or earlier!' added Harry.
The houselights flashed to let the audience know that the second half was about to begin and Carol realised that the almost obligatory raffle had been left out this time, presumably the feeling in the drama group being that it was not a seemly part of the honouring of the dead to be handing out unwanted toiletries and out of date chocolates. The Act where King had died in the previous performance began with a scene where Lorraine, as Queen Gertrude, discusses Hamlet's madness with various other cast members. Carol did her best to concentrate, but, yet again, her mind would not allow it and she pondered on the fact that she and Harry had always disregarded the clothes shop owner as a suspect, due to the fact that she was on stage the whole time that King had been murdered. However, thought Carol, had they missed something? Was there a way in which she could have done it to help Angie? After all, this was the world of theatre where illusion and misdirection is the norm. And up cropped Angie's name again: what is it about that girl that makes everyone want to help her?
The play continued with Carol really forcing herself to get involved with the plot and attempt, at one point, to stop Harry from interrupting the action with a snore. He swore

that he had not fallen asleep, but Daniel insisted, in a whisper, that the plea would not stand up in a court of law, to which Rose Hubbard turned round and gave him a long stare that chastised his interrupting of her concentration and reminded them all again of her remarkable powers of hearing.

Carol returned her attention to the stage, at the point where Mike Brown's Claudius is attempting to pray and Heart's Hamlet was standing behind him deciding whether to kill him, rapier drawn, just as Carol had told Harry about days earlier when they'd been told by Roger, as an excuse for his tardy entrance later, that he had been looking for the very sword that he was now holding.

"O, my offence is rank, it smells to heaven;
It hath the primal, eldest curse upon't
A brother's murder!"

Brown's intonement of the lines was almost as if he was giving one of his Sunday morning sermons and the word "murder" was allowed to ring around the hall before he continued. The soliloquy was delivered extremely powerfully and the whole hall, including even Carol now, was fully engrossed, as he reached the final lines and knelt in prayer, as his parishioners must have seen the actor do many times in his church, at the very spot where they had found Gloria Bebb lying with her throat slashed open, forty-eight hours ago.

"Bow, stubborn knees; and, heart with strings of steel,
Be soft as sinews of the new-born babe!
All may be well."

As Hamlet delivered his follow-on lines, unheard by the praying monarch, Mike Brown gave a stunning, angst-ridden performance, his face a portrait of anguish and pain, as he presumably drew upon the events of the last few days to portray the raw emotions that the character was supposedly

feeling. Despite Heart's powerful rendition, Carol felt that the audience's eyes kept being drawn back to Brown's facial features as he knelt before them.
At last, he rose and delivered the rhyming couplet that concluded the scene and prepared to usher in the now infamous closet scene where King had died previously.
"My words fly up, my thoughts remain below;
Words without thoughts never to heaven go."
As he stood and began to exit, Carol turned to Harry and Daniel with a sudden outburst that she knew would annoy Miss Hubbard, but, at that moment, she didn't care. She had had an epiphany so important that it couldn't wait.
'I need to see both of you outside. Now!'

CHAPTER 44

The play was over! The rapturous applause of the audience, perhaps an indication of their enjoyment, perhaps a mark of respect for the dead, was also over. They filed out past Sergeant Pearson and one of the other officers, the rest of the police contingent having been sent to guard the various other exits around the exterior of the Town Hall. Rose Hubbard was one of the last to leave. She saw Harry and Carol standing to the side waiting for them all to depart and sidled over to them. 'You know, don't you? I can see it in your eyes!' she said.
'I couldn't possibly comment, Miss. Hubbard,' replied Harry, but the slight smile that crossed Carol's lips indicated that the elderly lady with the incredible hearing was right. Or at least, they all hoped that they were. Daniel had sent for one or two final bits of information, but everything that Carol had explained to them had made sense. Now, they just had to

get a confession. As Miss. Hubbard made her farewells and left, the front doors were locked and Pearson took up a stance similar, Carol thought, to that which she might imagine a legionnaire on Hadrian's Wall, awaiting an attack from the North, might look like.

Just then, Steve Grey's loud, angry voice came from the main hall, where quite a few of the cast, now changed back into their normal clothes, were standing around waiting to find out what was happening, their leaving having been obstructed by the police officers outside.

'You can't do this,' said Grey. 'After a show like that, I need a pint and if I don't get to the pub now, they're not going to be serving!'

Daniel, followed by Carol and Harry, entered the hall.

'Sorry, Mr. Grey, but nobody's leaving just yet. We need to have a few more words with you all,' said Daniel, in an authoritative tone that seemed to do the trick. He made his way over to the kitchen and called a few of the rest of the cast, who'd been sat around grumbling at their incarceration, into the main hall. Eventually, the whole cast and crew were sat in the audience's seats, the curtains had been opened and Daniel was now stood, rather surrealistically, Carol thought, in the throne room of Elsinore Castle; or so it seemed, to those looking up at him from the rows of seating below. Harry stood to one side, leaning against the stage on the floor of the hall, choosing not to share the limelight with his friend. Carol sat in one of the seats midway down the hall, hoping that what had come to her during the production was both correct and the key to its solution.

'This,' said Dan, beginning to outline their thoughts, 'has been one of the trickiest cases I and my colleagues have had to deal with. Because you have all been suspects this past week, we thought it only fair to share our ideas with you, in this rather Agatha Christiesque way.'

Not a real word, Carol thought, but she forgave him seeing as it was she, herself, who had suggested it might be of benefit to do it this way rather than in private, down at the station, where denials could not be verified, or otherwise, by witnesses.

Harry took up the baton. 'We were faced with what eventually looks to be five murders.'

'Five?' asked Andrew Cross. 'I only count three.'

'Three here in Pikesmere,' continued Harry, 'and two in differing parts of the country and a decade apart.

'Is one of them my mother's death?' asked Angie as she stared at the floor rather than at either of the two detectives.

'I'm afraid it is,' replied Daniel, from the stage. 'We were unsure as to whether the murders were linked, but it now seems clear that they were.'

'And what about the fifth?' This time it was Lorraine Davies who spoke.

'Actually, Lorraine, it was something you were chatting about to us the other day that led us to dig a little deeper and discover that Gloria Bebb's husband had been the victim of another murder, seemingly with the same method of killing being employed.'

'Five brutal deaths, all perpetrated with a blade of some description; all planned and carried out with precision and no sense of compassion, or even normal humanity,' stated Dan, 'and one of you, in this room, looking at me now, is that sadistic and malicious killer.'

The cast slowly turned their heads, one way and then another, looking almost unbelievingly at their fellow thespians, unwilling to truly accept what Daniel was saying. It was Stewart Manning who spoke first. He was sat towards the back of the cast, near to where Carol had positioned herself and he stood up in the aisle, his booming voice filling the hall, just as it had done at the start of the evening when he had introduced the play to the audience.

'Inspector. Inspectors.' He emphasised the plurality for dramatic effect, 'I for one am unwilling to believe that anyone in our little drama society could be capable of what you are suggesting. We all know each other, both from putting on our shows, to outside where we live, hand in glove, with one another. Do you not think that such a callous killer would have given themselves away at some point?'

'It seems not!,' said Daniel, 'now please sit yourself down again, Mr. Manning, and let us continue with what we now know.'

'Or what we think we know,' thought Carol, still unsure as to whether her suppositions were correct. So often over the past week, she had thought that she might be onto something, only for her ideas to be analysed and found wanting by those who did this sort of thing for a living. It was only this evening that certain ideas seemed to fall into place and both Harry and Dan had not been able to find a flaw in her propositions. Hence why they were sat here now. It was, however, quite possible, Carol knew, that the whole thing would fall apart and that they, and particularly her, would look extremely foolish, especially laying it all out in such a public forum.

'So,' said Daniel, 'shall we begin?'

CHAPTER 45

'I'm sorry, Miss King,' said Daniel, as he came down from the stage to stand on the floor at the opposite side of the stage to Harry, 'but we need to start with your father's death, here in this very hall nearly a week ago.'

'That's alright,' replied Angie, almost in a whisper, 'I'm ready.'

'Harry, do you want to take the lead on all this, seeing as how it was you and Carol that have done a lot of the heavy lifting?' Daniel asked and he stood back, leaning on the kitchen door frame with his arms crossed.

'If you like,' Harry said and turned to Carol. 'Feel free to butt in if I get anything wrong, or miss something out, won't you?'

'You can bet on it,' replied Carol, her hidden fingers firmly crossed that this was all going to go to plan.

'Again, apologies Angie, but your father was not a liked man, was he?' asked Harry.

She gave a slight nod of the head, as an indication of her assent to this statement.

'And this meant that suspects and motives were numerous. Almost all of you in this hall had reasons to either dislike him for what he had said or done to you in the past, or the way in which he treated Angie here. So, let's consider some of these motives. Angie, you yourself seem to have almost hated your father. Although he did not in any way break the rules of the confessional, it was clear from what Reverend Brown told us, as well as the testimony of others, that your father was both emotionally and physically abusive towards you. That alone might have been enough for you to wish him dead.'

'That's true, but I didn't kill him. I swear,' Angie cried out from her seat on the front row.

Harry continued, 'And you had the opportunity. You were, by your own admission, backstage at the time when the murder took place.'

'I was in the loo,' she said.

'That's what you say, but it would have been only a few short seconds that would have been needed to get behind the carpet..'

'Arras,' shouted Carol from her seat down the hall.

'Sorry, "arras", commit the crime and then return to the toilet before the body was discovered.

'But that's not what I did,' repeated Angie.

'I believe you,' responded Harry, 'I don't think you killed your own father. For several reasons.'

'Thank you,' whispered Angie, but she seemed to sink further into the plush velvet of the chair she was sat in.

'However,' Harry paused for moment, for effect, 'that is not to say that you weren't a part of a scheme to get rid of him. There is no doubt that there are several people in front of me who might have done almost anything for you. For a start, isn't that right Mr. Grey?'

Steve Grey, who was sat next to Angie King, stood up at the mention of his name and eyeballed Harry for a few seconds before speaking, 'Yeah, that's right. Of course I would do anything for her. Anything but murder, that is. Where's your proof for any of this?'

'You're handy with your fists, you're hot tempered and, most importantly, you've taken the blame for Angie before, leading to your incarceration. I reckon that, given the right motivation, you could have murdered Mr. King quite easily.'

'Well, how wrong you are,' spat out Steve Grey, 'if you think I would do something that would get me put back inside again. They were the worst months of my life and I don't want to experience that for another instant. So, unless you've got something a bit more like real evidence, I

suggest you withdraw the accusation.'
He sat down and took Angie's hand, but it was noticeable from Harry's vantage point, that she almost immediately withdrew it and placed it back in her own lap.
'A strong response, Mr. Grey, and I would expect no less from you.' Harry turned to look across the aisle of seats. 'What about you, Mr. Heart? Would you do almost anything for your Ophelia?'
Roger looked up and Dan could see that there were tears in his eyes as he spoke. 'I wish I could say yes. I wish I could have murdered him, for Angie's sake. None of you in here have seen what I've seen. Seen the monster that he was. I wanted to kill him a hundred times, but I couldn't. Even for Angie, I couldn't.' Roger Heart began to sob and, for once, it didn't seem that his acting skills were required.
'Well,' said Harry, after a moment, 'you'll both be glad to know that we don't consider either of you the perpetrators of Derek King's murder.'
'Even though I bet you wish you could pin something on Steve Grey,' thought Carol, as she watched the action unfold.
'So, who else might have come to Miss King's aid in her time of need?' Harry scanned the cast before letting his gaze rest on the vicar, who was now back in his dog collar and meeting Harry's stare with a steely gaze of his own.
'Reverend Brown. You have known about Miss King's pain for quite a while now.'
'I have,' Mike Brown replied, in a monotonal voice, very different to his performance as Claudius only an hour or two ago.
'Do you prefer your bible readings from the Old or the New Testament?' Harry asked.
'It depends on what the occasion requires,' Brown replied slowly, well aware of where the detective was leading him.

' "An Eye for an Eye" etcetera,' suggested Harry.
' "Love they neighbour",' retorted the vicar. 'I'm sure we can exchange biblical references all evening, inspector, but I'm not sure it will get us anywhere.'
Carol wasn't sure that Harry actually could quote much more of the bible, so she was pleased when he took a different tack.
'You were separated from Mr. Cross in the dressing room for just long enough to get on stage and murder Mr King. We've checked and it is quite feasible.'
'I'm sure it is,' said Brown, 'but it isn't what happened. Andrew could just have easily done it whilst we were apart backstage.'
'Now hang on a minute, Mike,' said Andrew Cross, 'throw me under the bus, why don't you? I didn't kill anybody. I'm just your friendly, neighbourhood window cleaner. What possible reason might I have for doing old King in?'
'Funny you should ask,' replied Daniel, intervening for the first time in a while and giving Harry a bit of a break. 'Our records show that Mr. King and you have had arguments on several occasions, one fairly recently, to do with him contacting both the county council about health and safety issues regarding your job, as well as reporting you to HMRC regarding cash in hand payments for your services. Is that not the case?'
'I was disputing both of those allegations,' replied Cross, now living up to his name and being quite cross indeed.
'But you won't have to do that, now that King's dead,' suggested Harry.
Cross went to speak, but Harry continued. 'You're a bit of a joker, aren't you Mr. Cross? The society's resident clown. Enjoy making people, uh..' He looked across to Carol for help.
'Corpse,' she said.

'That's right, corpse,' Harry continued. 'A particular speciality, we gather, is messing with the props table.' Harry was pleased that he had at least remembered the word "prop".

'I might have done a bit of fooling around in my time,' agreed Cross. 'What of it? Doesn't lead to murdering anyone. Just a bit of fun.'

'Good cover, though, for you to be handling a real dagger before you plunged it into Derek King...'

Carol was concerned how Angie might react to such a brutal description of her father's death, but she hadn't reacted, as far as she could tell, and Harry was continuing full throttle.

'No one would think anything of you carrying the real blade round. If you got caught, people would just think that you were playing another prank. Isn't that correct, Mr. Cross?'

'But nobody did see me carrying a "real dagger" around because it didn't happen. I never went near the props table that night, or go behind the arras with a dagger.'

'Let's move on then,' said Harry. 'Who else might wish to help out Angie King? What about you, Lorraine? You two are very close aren't you?'

'I'd like to think so,' Lorraine replied and she smiled across to Angie, who had, at last looked up and turned to face Lorraine.

'Almost a surrogate mother you might say.'

'I'd prefer to think of myself as a big sister.'

'I bet you would,' murmured Carol. She hoped nobody had heard, but she noticed Stew Manning give a little laugh in front of her.

'Regardless of whether it's mother or sister, might you have been willing to get rid of Angie's father in order to spare her any more pain?' continued Harry.

'Like others in this room have said, I would have done almost anything to help the poor child, but, as you well know, seeing as you were sat out here watching, I was on stage, in full view of the entire audience.'

She made it sound like she was performing in front of thousands at the London Palladium, thought Carol, but Lorraine was now in full flow.

'I really would have assumed that, as a detective, you would have thought your accusations through a little better than that. How could I possibly have been both on stage and behind the arras at the same time? I had literally just spoken to Derek, as Polonius, in that scene, before he went and hid himself. The whole thing is absurd.'

'Again,' said Harry, 'just as Angie may not have committed the crime herself, but colluded with someone else to do the actual physical act, you may well have masterminded King's downfall, mightn't you?'

'I fear, dear inspector, that you have been reading too many works of fiction..' Lorraine stated.

'Now I know for a fact that isn't true,' thought Carol, but this time she kept it to herself and did not give Stew Manning any further food for amusement.

'I am no criminal mastermind,' continued Lorraine, 'I'm just a simple shop owner who likes a bit of drama on the side.'

Harry remembered the semi-pornographic DVDs that he'd found on the shelf in Lorraine's flat, but decided that this was not the gathering in which to expose her past. Instead, he said, 'You may be right.'

Before he could continue, Daniel's phone beeped and he opened up the message that he had been sent. All were silent whilst he read the message and then gave a nod to Harry who immediately looked across to Carol and smiled. She instantly knew that this was the last bits of the puzzle falling into place. The information Daniel had received was the evidence they needed to support the theories that she had put forward earlier. Her suspicions, she hoped were about to be vindicated. She might have just help solve her first murder case!

INTERLUDE

CHAPTER 46

They really don't have a clue. When the hall was sealed, it looked like the time had come. Maybe all those spilled litres of blood had finally brought a reckoning and meant the time had come to face the music. Doesn't look like it though. These policemen really are floundering about like some child's toy floating in the waves, being thrown this way and that by the tide.
The best detective novels always have the gathering of the suspects and the laying out of how and why the crimes have been committed, but this just seems like a fishing exercise. Let's try everyone in turn and see if they crack. Well, that's not going to work, is it? No way!
Three women dead and two men. Don't really like imbalance. Perhaps it would be best to find another man who needs to visit "the undiscovered country from whose bourn, No traveller returns". Just to balance up the scales! Yes, when this fiasco is over and they're no closer to finding out the truth, maybe there'll be one more death. After all, it would be a shame to end it with Gloria. She was such a pathetic specimen of a human being. So needy! It would be better to end on a bigger character than that!
This should be fun!

CHAPTER 47

It was Stewart Manning that broke the silence, rather than the detectives that were on their feet. 'Any chance we could get some refreshments if this is going to take much longer? We've all had a long evening on stage and I, for one, am absolutely parched. The hot water urn is on in the kitchen. It won't take long to get some tea on the go.'
'Good idea,' said Daniel.
'I'll go,' said Mike Brown and he got up to make his way into the kitchen. Lorraine and Mark Prince followed and, soon, the cups of tea were being brought out, for those who wanted them. Daniel took the proffered drink, but Harry refused, eager to get on with the evening's business that was quickly becoming tomorrow morning's, as the clock on the wall ticked towards midnight. He and Daniel had taken time during the hiatus in proceedings to confer over the messages that the latter had received and, although Carol was desperate to know the details, he had not shared anything with her. She had noted, however, that Sergeant Pearson and the other police officer had now taken up positions inside the hall, guarding the double doors at the back. She was not sure whether this was an indication of the fact that things were becoming more serious, or whether it had just become too cold outside!
Once everyone was sat back down, Harry brought the room to order and began with a shift in focus. 'Perhaps it would be a good idea, at this stage, to discuss your producer, Charles Blackwater's death and see whether it can throw some light on any of the other murders.' He turned towards the twins who had been whispering to each other whilst sipping their beverages.
'Sorry to interrupt your conversation, gentlemen, but could

you tell us all a bit about your relationship with Mr. Blackwater?'

George looked at Arthur and both looked like naughty schoolboys that had just been caught talking on the back row of the classroom. Both had turned red and seemed reticent to be the first to answer.

In the end, it was George Mansfield who spoke first. 'Like we told you before, we had a few grievances over casting, but it certainly wasn't something that we would turn to violence over, let alone murder.'

'We both thought he was a great producer,' continued Arthur seamlessly, 'we just wanted to expand our repertoire of roles a little bit.'

'And same question to you, Mr. Manning. What was your relationship with Charles Blackwater like?' Harry asked, turning and directing the question down the hall, to the man who had just played Polonius.

'We had our fair share of arguments over whether some of his wilder ideas could be put on in here, with our makeshift stage and so on, but, again, nothing to warrant killing him. Really, inspector, I don't see that this is getting any of us much further.'

'What about your role in the drama group?' continued Harry, choosing to ignore Manning's final statement.

'What on earth do you mean by that?'

'Tonight, you seemed very pleased to be performing on stage, at last. Did you blame Charles Blackwater for never casting you under the spotlights, rather than merely setting those same lights for others?'

Before Stewart Manning could answer, Lorraine came to his defence. 'I'm not sure whether you have ever had much to do with the theatre, inspector, but that is simply not the way it is! The stage manager is a very important part of the whole performance, second only to the producer in some respects. Charlie was putting a lot of faith in Stew by trusting him to make the play go smoothly, isn't that right?'

'Indeed it is,' replied Stew Manning. 'Thank you for that vote of confidence, Lorraine. As you must have picked up last night at our rehearsal, Harry, when I had my little "chat" with Mike, I had no desire to play Polonius. I was happy with my backstage role. I took it on, only to pay tribute to both Derek and Charlie. Nothing more!'

This got a small round of applause from the rest of the cast, but Harry continued, ignoring the use of his first name, 'It was the smooth running of the show and, in particular, the lighting, that I was moving onto, actually.'

For the first time that evening, Manning's face took on a slight frown. It seemed as if he didn't like his role, or professionalism, to be questioned in any way.

Harry walked to the centre of the hall floor in front of the stage, so as to be able to make better eye contact with Stewart Manning. 'Let's go back to the first night of the play, shall we? Where did you say you were when Derek King met his death?'

'Up the ladder, fixing the spotlight, for the umpteenth time. Mike and Andrew both collided with it as they came up onto the stage and nearly knocked me off. I've told you all this.'

Mike interrupted, 'That's correct. It was a good job he wasn't at the top, or there could have been two deaths that night.'

'You were coming down,' continued Harry, 'from putting in the new bulb to illuminate Claudius' face during the time he gives the speech when he's on his knees?'

'That's right!' said Stew.

And this was what had led to Carol's epiphany that had taken place that evening. Harry glanced at her and she nodded, almost imperceptibly. 'That's very interesting, Mr. Manning, because when we came to see the rehearsal last night, the king's face was still in semi-darkness. I wouldn't have thought anything of it, but my partner, Carol, is much more observant and well-versed in stagecraft. When, this evening, Mike's speech was so well lit that his agonised self-questioning about the murder of his brother was evident for the first time to her, it reminded her about the night before. Nothing has happened on this stage from the moment of Derek King's death until last night. If you had changed the bulb in the spotlight, as you said that you had, on the night of his death, Mike Brown's face would have been illuminated last night. But it wasn't, meaning that you hadn't been changing the bulb at all on that fatal evening. Instead, you murdered King behind the arras then went to the ladders you had strategically positioned nearby, climbed up a couple of steps and waited for someone to witness you on them. You then pretended that you were actually coming down and joined the rest in discovering the body. Isn't that so?'

Harry had held Stewart Manning's stare throughout his exposition of how Carol and he had worked out what had taken place. He wasn't sure what he expected, but it wasn't what took place.

Manning began a slow handclap. 'That is a tremendous attempt at trying to incriminate me, but I'm sorry to spoil what is obviously your big moment! You might have noticed how makeshift this stage is and that includes the lighting, which we have to put up ourselves, before we start any shows. I had been up the ladder changing the bulb, on the night of poor Derek's murder, but I hadn't checked the wiring that had blown it in the first place. That spot is only used in the prayer scene, so I didn't realise it had blown again until last night's rehearsal. I popped up again this evening, before the performance, changed it again, checked the connections and, Hey Presto, tonight we saw Mike in all his glory! It was a good try, Inspector, but maybe it's time to move on to your next victim'

CHAPTER 48

Carol was feeling a little more unsure of her convictions now, but Harry broke Manning's gaze, just for a second, and met her worried look. He gave her a smile in reassurance and then returned to the man who he wanted and needed to break.

'No, I don't think I want to move on to anyone else just yet, Mr. Manning.'

'Have it your own way,' said Manning and he lounged back in his seat with a confidence that worried Carol, only two rows behind him.

'I think we might take a few minutes, now, to consider the death of Gloria Bebb in the church a day or two ago. Did you know her, Mr. Manning?'

'Of course. We all know each other in Pikesmere. She'd pop into the shop every so often. Buy some dog food and cleaning stuff for the church, that sort of thing. What of it?'

'I think you might have known her a little better than that,' Harry replied.

'I don't think so!'

Harry, at last, turned away from Manning and looked across to Lorraine. 'Ms. Davies. Could you tell us all what Gloria told you last time she was in your shop?'

'About the fact that she had been upset?' said Lorraine.

'If you don't mind,' replied Harry.

'I'm not sure I can remember what I told you exactly.'

'We've got your statement if that'll help?' said Daniel, helpfully.

Lorraine thought for a moment and then continued, 'I think it was something along the lines of the fact that she felt she had made a really bad mistake because she'd just found out something that she hadn't suspected before.'

'Thank you,' said Harry, 'that's exactly the bit that we're interested in. You also thought she might have been seeing someone romantically for the last couple of weeks. Is that right?'

'Yes, it was the sort of dresses she was making.'

A couple of the cast members laughed, but Lorraine continued. 'You can tell a lot from what people are wearing and the sort of material they are making them out of. I'm pretty sure that she had a new man.'

'Jealous eh, Lorraine,' said Andrew Cross, but Lorraine turned and gave him a withering look and he quickly apologised. 'Pick your timing', Harry thought, as he turned back to catch Stewart Manning's stare.

'Mr. Manning. Might you have been Gloria's new "friend" for whom she was making the effort to look more appealing?'

'Absolutely not!' Stew replied.

It was at this point that Daniel decided to step in. 'That's very odd because when we showed a picture of Gloria Bebb to your shop assistant, Mandy Gibbs, she recognised her as a lady that she would often see you taking through to the back office whenever she had visited over the last few weeks and that she seemed to have stopped paying for her stuff. Is that right, Mr. Manning?'

'Look, I didn't want to speak ill of the dead, but Gloria Bebb was having money problems. She asked me, in confidence, whether she could have some dog food and brass cleaner on tick, as it were, and I took her through to the back to sort it all out so that there'd be no gossip from anyone eavesdropping. You know what it's like in a small town. That's all. Nothing untoward. Just trying to help out, like a do!'

'You did a deal with her,' stated Harry.

'Yes!'
'And did that include sexual favours?'
'Of course not. What sort of person do you think I am?' asked Manning.
'I think that's what we are seeking to find out!' replied Harry.
Stewart Manning stood up. 'I think this has gone on far enough. I don't like having my reputation tarnished in front of friends, thank you very much. I'm a respected businessman in Pikesmere and I think, if you want to continue with this charade, we'd best do it with my solicitor present. He turned and made a step towards the back doors, but stopped, near to Carol, as Harry continued.
'For 'tis the sport to have the engineer, Hoist with his own petard.'
Manning slowly turned to look again at the detective. 'Are you auditioning for a part now, Harry? It's a little late, I think.' A few of the cast members smiled at this and Steve Grey laughed out loud, but others had now turned and were staring at Manning as well, aware of the growing evidence that the detectives were laying out.
Harry, too, smiled before continuing. 'That was the quote we found near to where Derek King had been murdered. On a page torn from his own playscript, done in his dying seconds. We got bogged down with the second part, debating about who might have been caught by their own schemes, but it was the beginning that he was trying to tell us something with. Who, Mr. Manning, in all the drama group, would be best described as "the engineer"? Who fits that description better than the stage manager; the person who engineers the scenery, the lights, everything?'
Manning took another step backwards before answering. 'So far, all I've heard are wild guesses, hearsay and circumstantial bits of supposed evidence. If that's it, I'll see you in court.'

Harry looked for a moment at Angie. 'I'm sorry for what I'm about to say, Angie.' He turned back to Stewart Manning. 'How long had you been having an affair with Derek King's wife, Stew?'

There were audible gasps of shock and now all eyes were turned on the stage manager. 'It might have escaped your notice, Harry, but Derek was a widower. It's one thing to accuse me of something with Ms. Bebb, but even I would have difficulty having an affair with a non-existent woman. He's been single ever since he came to Pikesmere, as far as I know.'

It was Daniel that now intervened. 'In Pikesmere, yes, but we've just had the confirmation that we'd requested that, at the time of Mrs. King's death, ten years ago, you were the proprietor of a small garden centre, just off the M25. About ten miles from the Kings' residence. Is that correct, or not?'

'And before you answer,' said Harry, 'let me remind you that when you chatted with Carol at your shop, you were very clear that you much preferred living in Pikesmere than "down south" and that you'd "moved around", quite a lot.'

'No crime in moving businesses,' replied Manning, but his demeanour indicated that he was, now, far less sure of himself.'

'No,' continued Daniel, 'but it's also interesting to have discovered that you also had a small shop only a few miles away from where Gloria Bebb and her husband lived. Not as far south as Mrs. King, but it's a strange coincidence, is it not? Especially when we have learnt that her husband was murdered there at the time you were living close by. A murder perpetrated in the same way as Angie's poor mother and the deaths in Pikesmere!'

Manning looked down at the floor and then slowly raised his head again, to look, first at Daniel, and then at Harry. He put his hands into his coat pockets and stood up straight, almost defying them to arrest him. Carol looked up at him from her seat and he almost reminded her of some of Shakespeare's tragic heroes, who, moments before their inevitable demise, fated to die, gained a few seconds of a stature that they had lost through the course of the play. She berated herself for thinking of Stewart Manning as anything but a callous and brutal killer, but her musings were short-lived as his right hand emerged from his pocket with a short, but deadly looking, knife and, the next instant, he had pulled Carol from her chair and was holding the blade to her throat.

CHAPTER 49

Harry went to step forward, but was stopped by Manning who almost whispered in a voice that no one in the room had ever heard him use before, husky and guttural. 'Don't move an inch if you want to keep her alive.' He turned a little, 'Nor you Pearson, or sonny boy next to you. Now, if we all keep calm, no one else is going to die. I'd decided earlier I wanted a further male death, so I'd prefer not to have to kill another woman. I do so hate imbalance!'
It was evident to everyone in the hall that this was not the jovial shop proprietor and stage manager that they all thought they knew. It was almost as if there was another human being, or more rightly some savage, bestial creature, inhabiting Stewart Manning's body. A maniacal killer had been ensconced in their group and no one had suspected him.
Despite being desperate to save Carol, Harry knew that he could do nothing, at that moment, to help her and that any attempt might be both fruitless and tragic. He and Daniel, as

well as the two policemen at the back doors, stood transfixed, as Manning's blade made the smallest of indentations into Carol's neck. Her eyes were wide and her breathing somewhat laboured.

'So,' continued the knife-wielding murderer, 'this is what's going to happen now. The lovely lady here and I, are going to walk out, very slowly and no one here, or outside, is going to stop us, so you better get a message to your buddies outside to warn them about not interfering. The slightest sign that anybody is attempting to get in our way and my hand might just slip and who knows what damage that might cause to this charming little neck?'

Manning started to slowly edge backwards towards the double doors at the back of the hall. The policemen opened the doors in anticipation, not wishing to precipitate anything that might lead to him hurting Carol. Daniel and Harry stood immobile, also fearful that anything they might attempt could cause further bloodshed.

Stewart Manning, however, was not going to take a further victim that night. With a swift movement, Carol lifted her right arm, whilst simultaneously grabbing his right wrist, the one holding the knife, with her left and pulling it down towards her chest as far as she could. She pinned his arm to her torso so that he could get no angle on the knife and her raised right arm and shoulder, despite his extra height and stature, stopped him from moving it still further. She knew that he was too big for her to pivot out from under him, so, instead, she pushed her head forward and bit down, as hard as she could, into the forearm that was now lodged around her neck.

Manning's scream was visceral, as if it began deep in his soul and rose to the surface like some howling banshee. Harry knew that this was his moment to help. He leapt forward and, within an instant, or so it seemed, he was next to the grappling pair. Blood was streaming from the stage manager's arm, but he managed to be keeping hold of the knife and it was still ominously close to Carol's neck. Harry took hold of Manning's wrist as Carol released it and the detective twisted it hard so that the blade dropped to the floor. As soon as its clatter was heard on the wood below their feet, Sergeant Pearson, with a speed Harry thought he was incapable of, had moved to behind Manning and was pulling both his arms behind his back allowing the other police officer to put handcuffs on him and the two of them wrestled him to the ground whilst Harry took the shaking Carol into his arms and hugged her.

For a moment, he was unclear as to what the sound was that seemed to be filling the hall, but then he realised that it was applause coming from the cast members that had been watching the whole routine dumbstruck and were now showing their appreciation in the best way a drama group knew how. It was Lorraine who got to the couple before Daniel could, slowly extricating the still quivering Carol from Harry's arms and calling on Mike Brown to get a very sweet tea from the kitchen. 'How very English,' thought Daniel as he walked to Harry and shook his hand before congratulating Carol on an incredible performance.

'Worthy of Kenneth Branagh,' he joked, in an attempt to begin to lighten the mood.

Lorraine, meanwhile, had turned to the prone figure of Stewart Manning and, in a very unladylike manner, bent down and spat in his face.

'That's for Gloria,' she said. 'She didn't deserve what you did to her and neither did any of the others. I hope you rot in Hell!'

'I have faith that he most certainly will,' said Reverend Brown, as he came over with the sweet tea for Carol.

'However did you manage to do all that?' asked Daniel, as

Harry sat down next to Carol and took her free hand in his whilst she sipped her drink.
'Self-defence classes at school,' Carol said, quietly. 'I covered a couple of the Year Ten girls' classes in PSHE. Just happened that one of them was on how to deal with an assailant with a knife, although the outside instructor that we'd brought in did recommend to usually just go along with someone wielding a knife, rather than try and be a hero!'
'That's my trick,' said Harry, 'I never used to listen to my teacher, either.' He smiled at her and she began to smile back.

CHAPTER 50

Daniel, Sergeant Pearson and the other police officers that had been covering the exterior of the Town Hall had taken Stewart Manning away for further questioning after the detective had read him his rights and promised that he would be going down for a very long time. Carol seemed to have recovered from her ordeal incredibly quickly and was now sat near Angie and Steve Grey, on the front row, chatting to both of them animatedly, whilst Harry looked on from the far corner near the kitchen door, where he was stood making sure that the garage mechanic was not flirting too much with Carol.
The rest of the drama society seemed loathe to depart and several had asked Harry whether it would be allowed for him to outline, further, how and, more importantly, why, Stewart Manning had done what he did. With Dan gone, Harry walked over to Carol and asked whether she felt up to doing a double act with him, in order to explain what they had discovered and worked out. She said she was only too

willing to do so and, after a couple of seconds, they were both stood at the front of the stage waiting for the gathering to take their seats again and become silent. It almost felt like they were going to start a performance of their own little play, watched, from the stage above, by the throne room of Elsinore Castle. Perhaps the ghost of Hamlet's father would make an appearance and show his satisfaction that "the foul crimes done" had indeed been "burnt and purged away" that evening.

Harry began, 'I'd like to start by thanking you all for your patience, not just this evening, when we felt we needed to go through all this to make sure that we were correct in our theories and to force Stewart Manning's hand..'

'Although we hadn't counted on it being quite so violent,' added Carol with a small grin. This received another smattering of applause from the gathered thespians.

'Indeed!' continued Harry over the claps, 'Not only for this evening, but also for all your help with the case over the past week. Like so many investigations, all the little threads of information that you gave us in our chats all helped to create the picture that led finally to our recognition of the killer and helped to solve the crimes.'

'As you're all aware,' said Carol, 'I'm not a detective, but it's been fascinating to be involved and get to know you all so well. I've felt over the week that, at the risk of mixing metaphors, it's all a bit like a jigsaw puzzle: finding individual pieces that fit together and then, finally, as the last bit is slotted in place, the whole picture becomes clear.'

It was Angie King who was first to say something. 'Why did Manning kill my mother? Do you know?'

'We think that he might have been rather a serial philanderer,' answered Harry. 'He's never married, but seems to have a knack for befriending lonely wives. At the time of your mother's death, your father was away a lot on business and she had, perhaps, become lonely. Indeed, the night she died, she was alone, with you, again, in your house in the country, while Mr. King was in a hotel in the city, drinking with business colleagues and enjoying life. I'm pretty sure that Manning will make a statement outlining the fact that he had tried to seduce your mother, unsuccessfully it seems, so had decided to take his revenge on her after she'd spurned his advances.'

'It became clear,' Carol said, 'that Mr. Manning is, to a large extent, a misogynist, a woman hater, when he finds himself rebutted by them.'

'And is that why Gloria died, as well?' asked Mike Brown.

'Partly, yes.' replied Harry, 'We'll come to Ms. Bebb in a moment. We think that having initially been friendly to Mr. Manning, Mrs. King realised that, for the sake of her marriage - and you, Angie - she couldn't indulge in an affair with him and that was what, tragically, led to her violent end.'

Angie began to sob a little, but Carol said, 'Angie, you have a personality that seems to encourage people to love and support you. Roger Heart and Steve Grey are evidence of that, as well as Reverend Brown and Lorraine, but it began with your mother. Her love for you was what made her decide to say no to Stewart Manning in the end. Her love for you was stronger than her detestation of your father.'

'So, I'm to blame for her death,' stated Angie King.

'Not at all,' intervened Harry, quickly. 'Never think that. He is the one with whom all the blame lies. It was him that pursued your mother and it was his psychological inability to be turned down, which led to his act of revenge. He is the guilty party, not you.'

Through her sobs, Angie managed a slight smile at Harry and a muffled, 'Thank you.'

'It seems that Gloria's husband died a few years later for, in a way, similar reasons,' said Carol. 'Investigations have now shown that he had been suspicious that his wife, Mrs. Bebb as she was then, was seeing someone else. He'd spoken to two of his colleagues at work about it. We think that, this time, Stewart Manning had actually started seeing Gloria, but that when her husband came home early one day and found him in their house, alone, an argument ensued and ended with Manning killing him. Gloria was quite a weak-willed person and it looks as if, when she returned, she accepted Manning's word that it hadn't been him that was responsible, or that maybe it was simply an accident.'

'Lorraine, it was you that helped us decipher some of what might have then happened. Gloria and Manning must have grown apart after her husband's murder, but when they found themselves living, again, in the same town, he probably began to try and seduce her again until, a few months ago, she started to succumb to his supposed charms. They took up a relationship once more, but, a day or two ago, she seems to have discovered some evidence to suggest that Manning had not only murdered her husband, but had done so in a premeditated manner. He'd lied to her and attempted to pull the wool over her eyes. She probably accused him of this when she visited him at his shop the day she was killed and that led to her death on the steps of the church altar. When cornered, Stewart Manning could act quickly, ruthlessly and with incredible viciousness.'

'Poor Gloria,' said Lorraine. 'She was rather gullible, from what I knew of her, especially where men were concerned. I think she thought that she had found some degree of happiness again in her life. Who could have imagined that it would lead to her being killed in such a horrible way?'

'Indeed,' said Harry, 'and so we come to the murder that we thought started all this; the death of Derek King, behind the arras, during your first night of the play. You've heard, already, about how Carol came up with her theory about Manning, driven by noticing the spotlight and so on, but we now need to look at the motivation for his death.'

'Before you do that,' said Andrew Cross, 'could you explain how the two of them, Stew and Derek King, ended up in the same town? Who followed who? As far as I can remember, they both joined the society at about the same time.'

There were murmurings, from others in the cast, that this had seemed to be the case.

'That's something that we're unsure of at the moment,' answered Harry, 'although I think we'll find that it was not a coincidence that they found themselves together again!'

'If I was to put money on it,' added Carol, 'I would say that it was probably Stewart Manning that followed King to Pikesmere, for some perverse reason that only he is aware of. It probably fulfilled some morbid pleasure on his part to be close to King and to be a figure of continuing torment, knowing that it was him that had killed his wife. In the end, however, it would lead to him eventually being caught. You've all been performing "Hamlet", so you'll know all about the way in which hubris, or pride, leads to a person's downfall. That looks to be what happened to Manning. He was so sure of himself and his abilities to dupe everybody, that he was willing to live dangerously and shadow King in this way.'

'As Carol says, it seems that following King here was Manning's big mistake because it led the latter to start to piece the past together. Although we can assume that he knew nothing of Manning's relationship, or otherwise, with his wife, it is very likely that, as both were businessmen, they would have met at social gatherings whilst they were living down south. King was not one to keep his thoughts to himself and so started to suspect that Manning may have known his wife.'

'His overt questioning and prodding,' continued Carol, 'must have led Manning to start to worry that his previous crime might be unearthed, so, what started out as a malicious plan to follow King, torment and rile him further for his wife's unwillingness to let Manning have his way, eventually meant the husband had to follow the wife and die at his hands.'

'Before he got too close to the truth,' added Harry.

'Which leads to the final death that needs explaining. That of Charles Blackwater. Throughout this past week, it has become so evidently clear that your producer was a remarkable man, said carol. 'Apart from being an aspirational director for your group, and a mentor to the younger members, like Angie, he was an astute reader of human nature. His casting of "Hamlet" was amazing. I hope I don't offend anyone by saying that almost all of you plays a character that is representative of your own personalities. That is a remarkable talent and one that obviously worried Stewart Manning.'

'Because anyone that aware and intelligent was a real threat to his security. In his own statement, the night of King's death, Charlie Blackwater stated that he had overheard King accuse Stewart Manning of, and I quote, "something or other". It was probably this that led him, rather foolishly perhaps, to delve into his stage manager's past and then, even more dangerously, invite him round to present his suspicions.'

'They drank wine together,' continued Carol, 'in the victim's kitchen, before going through to his study where, presumably, he showed Manning the evidence that he thought he had uncovered. It took me a while to remember it, but I'd been looking through some old pictures that Charlie had stored on a memory stick. They seemed fairly innocuous to begin with and that was probably why Manning had thought nothing of it, but one showed Derek King in the background of a newspaper photo that had been taken at a medical conference where Blackwater had also been present.'

'Why was that important?' asked Mark Prince, who always seemed reticent to speak, but couldn't help himself this one time.

'It wasn't so much that King was in the background, but someone else, who's image was rather blurry: the profile was of a large, solidly built man who could only be Stewart Manning once all the other evidence is in place.'

'And why was that important?' asked Mike Brown.

'Because,' replied Carol, 'it was further proof that he lived close to where King had previously worked and where Mrs. King resided. We assume that there was more evidence than this, but Manning destroyed it after the murder. This one photo was left because it was in with lots of other personal stuff and he presumably didn't have time to go through everything that might be incriminating. How strangely coincidental it seems that all three of them were in that one picture, taken randomly for a newspaper.'

'Unfortunately for Mr. Blackwater, Stewart Manning had, fairly recently, sold him the magnetic kitchen knife set, that hung on the wall and it was one of his own knives that he used to murder him for getting too close to the truth. He'd sat in that kitchen many times, discussing this very set of "Hamlet", so was well aware, even before he arrived that evening, that if his crimes were to be uncovered, a weapon would be available to silence poor Charlie.'

'And that's exactly what happened,' said Carol.

The evening came to an end and although a few of the cast still seemed not to wish to depart, despite it being the early hours of the morning, eventually the hall cleared and just Lorraine was left, collecting up the teacups and washing up. Eventually, she returned from the kitchen and started to put her coat on.

'Well done my dear,' she said, as she came across and shook hands with Carol. 'You did a bloody good job, the pair of you.' She kissed Harry on the cheek, turned, and walked off down the rows of seats before exiting.

Carol turned to Harry and grinned. 'Come on then Loverboy, let's make the most of our last night in Pikesmere!'

EPILOGUE

Isobel was again behind the reception desk at The Golden Pheasant, just as she had been on that day of their arrival, as Harry and Carol made their way over, after another pair of delicious 'Full English' breakfasts. After a few pleasantries about hoping that they had enjoyed their stay at the hotel and asking whether they were happy to get a copy of their final bill emailed to the address on file, rather than a hard paper copy, Isobel also thanked both of them for solving what she described as 'the horrible, horrible murders" that had taken place that week. She sought to assure them that Pikesmere was definitely not, usually, a dangerous place to visit and that she hoped they would return one day, perhaps for a more relaxing and pleasant stay. Carol was unwilling to admit just how much she had enjoyed the sleuthing, despite almost having her throat cut the previous evening, and simply said that she very much hoped to come back again.

As they entered their room for the last time, Harry turned to Carol and said, 'Have you really enjoyed your week?'

She smiled back. 'For the umpteenth time, it's been a great

week. Admittedly, it hasn't been that relaxing, but it's definitely been a real eye-opener into the world you inhabit every day. Now, come on, let's finish packing or we're going to miss our lovely bus ride back to Shrewsbury station and, if we do, we're stuck here for another three days and I don't think my headteacher would be very impressed by that!'
Suitcases packed, they wheeled them through the lobby and out onto the pavement, turning right towards the bus stop. As they did, however, they heard a voice calling to them from a little way behind. They turned and saw Angie King running towards them, followed, a little distance further back, due to the heels she was wearing, by Lorraine Davies. Somewhat out of breath, Angie caught up with them and said, 'I'm so glad that I caught you before you left. I just wanted to say a huge thank you for what you did last night and, I guess, throughout the week. You not only found my dad's killer, but also my mum's as well and it's laid a lot of ghosts to rest.'
'It was our pleasure and honour,' replied Carol and she gave Angie a hug, just as Lorraine finally caught up.
More breathless, the older woman said, 'We hope this won't be the last time we see you in Pikesmere. You've made a lot of friends here and we'd love to see you again.' She turned to Angie and asked, 'Have you told them your news?'
'Give me a chance,' replied Angie and she turned back to Carol and Harry. 'I've decided to see a bit of the big, wide world that people tell me exists outside of Shropshire. I'm going travelling, probably the Far East, Bali and maybe Australia. Who know what's out there?'
'Well, we both hope you'll have a wonderful time,' said Carol and then she added, mischievously, 'Anyone going with you?'
'I don't think so,' said Angie, smiling conspiratorially, 'Who knows *who* is out there as well?'

They made their farewells, accompanied by further hugs and then departed, leaving Harry and Carol only three minutes to get to the bus stop, knowing, however, that it would almost inevitably be late.

They had just reached the stop when a large, sleek, black car pulled up next to them and a familiar voice rang out from the interior.

'Fancy a lift into Shrewsbury? We're heading in that direction,' said Daniel Price, a beaming smile across his face.

'It would be rather rude to refuse such a kind offer,' said Harry and he opened the boot and put their bags inside. Once they were in the somewhat more comfortable means of transport than they had been expecting, Dan said, 'I'm glad I caught you. Thought you'd like to know that Stewart Manning has made a pretty full confession and that almost all our theories were correct about how and why.'

'All Carol's theories,' corrected Harry as she gripped his hand and squeezed it.

'Absolutely,' agreed Dan, 'I doubt we would have got there without your help and insight.'

Carol blushed.

'I reckon she might be a keeper, this one Harry,' the detective continued.

'I reckon you might be right,' said Harry.

'Only might?' asked Carol and they all laughed.

Carol turned and gazed at the meadows that were flying past them. 'I could get used to living round here,' she thought, 'even if there is the occasional murder to tackle.' As was often the case with Carol, quotes flooded her head and some of the last lines of "Hamlet" came to her mind; she smiled to herself.

"Take up the bodies – such a sight as this,
Becomes the field, but here shows much amiss."